DEATH ON THE ROCKS

DEATH ON THE ROCKS

A John Rawlings Mystery

Deryn Lake

This first world edition published 2013
in Great Britain and 2014 in the USA by
SEVERN HOUSE PUBLISHERS LTD of
19 Cedar Road, Sutton, Surrey, England, SM2 5DA.

British Library Cataloguing in Publication Data

Lake, Deryn author.
  Death on the rocks. – (A John Rawlings mystery; 15)
  1. Rawlings, John (Fictitious character)–Fiction.
  2. Pharmacists–England–Fiction. 3. Bristol (England)–
  Social life and customs–18th century–Fiction.
  4. Inheritance and succession–Fiction. 5. Impostors and
  imposture–Fiction. 6. Detective and mystery stories.
  I. Title II. Series
  823.9'2-dc23

ISBN-13: 978-0-7278-8354-4 (cased)

All Severn House titles are printed on acid-free paper.

Severn House Publishers support The Forest Stewardship Council™ [FSC™],
the leading international forest certification organisation. All our titles that
are printed on FSC certified paper carry the FSC logo.

Typeset by Palimpsest Book Production Ltd.,
Falkirk, Stirlingshire, Scotland.
Printed and bound in Great Britain by
TJ International, Padstow, Cornwall.

For my two handsome grandsons, Henry and Elliot Lampitt, who, with great effort and patience beyond the call of duty, taught me how to master my autocratic computer and my self-willed printer – but only just!

Acknowledgements

Without the help and guidance of my great friend Mark Dunton, supremo of the National Archives in Kew, who journeyed with me to Bristol where we attended the Bristol Archive Office and also many pubs along the way, this book could not have been written.

One

It was a very strange letter. Very strange indeed. It had been brought to John Rawlings, Apothecary, by Fred, the general factotum of the shop in Shug Lane, Piccadilly, who hung round nosily while John broke the wax that sealed it. He looked up.

'When did this arrive?'

'Just now, Sir. The post boy brought it. I took it from his hand directly.'

'I see.'

Fred still stood, staring beadily.

'Haven't you got any work to do?'

'No, Sir. I've swept the floor and the shop is all clean and tidy.'

'Well sweep through again. There is no such thing as too clean.'

Fred reluctantly went off to fetch his broom and John looked at the letter.

Honourable Sir. I beg you though you do not know the Signatory to peruse these words. I can claim only the slightest Connection with your Goodself and that is through a cousin of Your Friend Samuel Swann Esq. I believe that you have helped to solve Problems with the Esteemed Magistrate Sir John Fielding and I now wonder if you can help me Solve One of a personal Nature with which I am confronted.

My Wife sadly Passed From this Life some Six Years ago. She had Been Married before and I met her Son, who lived with us until he ran away from home aged Fourteen Years. Despite our best Endeavours, he refused to return Home. My Wife, under the terms of Her Will, had left her Son – her only Child – a considerable fortune in Diamond jewellery and of this he was advised by My Lawyer, Who put an Advertisement in Several Newspapers. Accordingly, He arrived in this Country some Months Ago to take Receipt of His Inheritance.

I come to the Point. I did not recognise Him at all. It was

as if a Stranger had Walked into My House. He had Changed out of all Recognition. When he knocked upon My door I first refused Him Entry but he called out Jovially, "Do you not Know Me?" and I was forced to let him in. Sir, I Beg of You a Favour. Please could You Come to the small village of Clifton, outside Bristol, and help me Somehow to Identify this Man.

I shall, my dear and Honoured Sir, Be Most Grateful if this could be done at some time in the Not Too distant Future.

John read the signature – 'Horatio Huxtable, Merchant' – then put the letter into the pocket of his long apron.

'Anyfing interesting?' asked Fred, peering over his broom.

'You haven't swept the corners,' answered John with a grin, and walked into his compounding room.

He was greeted immediately by the sweet smell of drying herbs, bunches of which hung from a beam running the length of the chamber. Looking round him, he felt in seventh heaven. Everything that constituted his art was around him: alembics, crucibles, retorts and matrasses stood on a bench near the back, while on the centre table were small oil stoves with bubbling pewter pans upon them, and several pestles and mortars, in the largest of which Robin Hazell was pounding away at a mixture of simples. John sighed. He might be a lonely widower, but in this place he could put his troubles behind him and feel at peace with the world.

Robin was now eighteen years old and had grown into the most attractive young man. Delicately built and not terribly tall, his autumnal colouring and sherry eyes had lost the naivety of youth and now appeared to make him look like an elegant faun. His hands were graceful and in them something as ordinary as a pestle contrived to become a thing of beauty. John felt protective of him, realising that the boy could well be the prey of depraved creatures of either sex.

Robin looked up as the Apothecary came into the room.

'All well, Master?'

'Yes indeed. How is that mixture coming along?'

'It's almost done.'

'Good. Let it stand overnight and we will boil it for the decoction in the morning.'

'Very well, Sir.'

John looked around him and despite the harmony he had with his surroundings, felt the first shiver of cold. It was a September evening and the nights were getting sharp. He looked at his fob watch which told him that there was another quarter of an hour until closing. Going back into the shop and seeing that it was empty – Fred having disappeared upstairs to tidy the rooms of the law students who lived above – the Apothecary opened the letter once more. The address was given as '24, Sion Row, the village of Clifton, near Bristol', the date a week previously.

The Apothecary pondered. He could ask Gideon Purle, his former apprentice, now an apothecary in his own right and a Yeoman of the Worshipful Society of Apothecaries, if he could run the shop while he went away, and he knew that Gideon would agree. But the snag about this was that young Purle devoted all his time to running John's sparkling water business in company with Jacquetta Fortune, the wretchedly thin widow whom John had asked to manage the project, and who had surprisingly blossomed into an elfin beauty with frosty lights in her golden hair.

Whether the two were in love the Apothecary had never been able to work out. Their heads were always bent close together as they leaned over sales figures and the like. Yet though he was sure his former apprentice had strong yearnings in that direction, Mrs Fortune always remained intriguingly unreadable.

How like a woman, John thought, and smiled cynically.

Once more he looked at his watch, somewhat battered nowadays after its many years of service. It had been given to him by Sir Gabriel Kent, his beloved adopted father, on his twenty-first birthday – all those years ago, the Apothecary thought, and laughed a little at the very idea.

It was nearly time to close the shop and Fred came in for his final instructions.

'Anything more to do, Sir?'

'All swept and clean for the morning?'

'Yessir.'

'Then you can pull the cover over the counter and leave the rest to Robin and me.'

'Very good, Mr Rawlings,' and Fred's hand came up into a salute.

As usual the gesture tugged at the Apothecary's heartstrings. As a baby, Fred had been dumped in a box outside the gates of Thomas Coram's Foundling Hospital and had been taken on by John out of the goodness of his heart. One day, or so he hoped, Fred would make a fine servant to someone of position, but meanwhile the little lad was acting as a general cleaner and dogsbody for the Apothecary's shop and the law students in the dwelling above. He watched as the boy pulled at the linen cover and called Robin out to help.

'Is it time to go, Master?'

'Yes. It's a cold night and I doubt we'll get any more custom.'

While the boys struggled with the cloth, John went into the compounding room and blew out the candles and oil lamps, then went into the shop and did the same. Then, having seen Fred scuttle up the stairs, he locked the door and stepped out into the night.

There was little joy left in his home, he thought as he walked along, Robin hurrying beside him. Number 2, Nassau Street, that had once been so full of love and laughter, was a quiet house now, only the ghosts of the past left to whisper down the corridors at night.

Sir Gabriel Kent, once the greatest beau in London, had long since moved to the village of Kensington, while Rose, John's beloved daughter, was at boarding school in Kensington Gore. Gideon, too, had rented a small apartment over a shop in Thrift Street now that he was no longer an apprentice. Young Robin, as custom decreed, slept in the servants' quarters in John's house. So the only other person in the Apothecary's silent home was the discreet Mrs Fortune, who worked long hours and whom he often did not see even at mealtimes. It was all rather depressing.

John patted the letter in his waistcoat pocket, deciding that he would give it his full attention after his return from having supper with his very dear friends Louis and Serafina de Vignolles. Thinking about this raised his spirits and he speeded up his progress along Princes Street, Robin hurrying along to keep in step.

An hour later, the Apothecary descended from the house and waited while a servant ran to fetch a chair. Tonight he was dressed very finely with a pair of striped stockings and buckled breeches worn beneath a fashionably short waistcoat and a narrow-shouldered coat with tight-fitting sleeves and decorated buttons at the wrist. Over this he had quite the latest thing – a broad-brimmed hat of felt and a long overcoat. Feeling tremendously smart, he waited on the corner of Gerard Street until a chair pulled up and he got inside, leaving the curtain open and gazing out at the passing parade.

The chairmen trotted along, keeping well away from the dark narrow alleys which were used by various members of the public for all kinds of nefarious purposes, sticking instead to the broader streets, the gutters of which stank with the detritus dumped in them daily. Having left Gerard Street they hurried up Princes Street, then turned down Knaves Acre and Brewers Street, then up into Warwick Street, along Beak Street, and then thankfully into Great Swallow Street, where the lights from the houses of Hanover Square lit the cobbles. John got out and paid the perspiring men generously and then sauntered along the square to number 12.

As usual a footman answered the door and John gazed around him, thinking of the time – many years ago now – when he had first stood there. It must be nearly twenty years, the Apothecary thought, and rejoiced that he had been able to make and keep such friends as the Comte and Comtesse de Vignolles.

'My dear,' called a voice from the staircase, and looking up John saw that Serafina was descending to meet him.

She was as elegant as ever, though now the sides of her hair gleamed pewter in the light of the many candles that lit their gracious home. But she still had that slight racehorse delicacy about her, the full mouth that curved so easily into a smile, the lovely bones of her cheeks reflected in the blaze of the chandelier which illuminated the steps.

'Serafina,' he said, and ran up the stairs to bow before her and kiss her hand.

In response, she took him into her arms, holding him away from her slightly so that she could look into his face.

'You have an extra line or two,' she said in the husky tones that he had always thought thrilling.

'My dear, I shall be forty next year,' he answered, giving her a crooked grin.

She threw her hands in the air. 'Don't speak to me of it. I try to remember your father's words that age is merely a number.'

The Apothecary smiled wryly. 'I say them to myself daily.'

His eye was caught by further movement on the stairs and he looked up to see a young lady approaching. A young lady so like her mother that the Apothecary drew a breath before giving a formal bow.

'Italia?' he asked.

The girl curtseyed. 'Indeed, Sir.'

'You have grown up,' he said. And it was true. John had not seen Serafina's daughter for at least two years and the miracle had taken place. She was now fourteen years old and had turned into a young woman in the intervening months.

'Do you think we are alike?' asked Serafina with a smile.

'As two pod peas, my dear.'

'Would you like to be her age again, John?'

The Apothecary smiled. 'Sometimes yes, but mostly no. Like a good wine, I am maturing in the cask.'

Serafina smiled back and looked up the stairs. 'I believe that men improve with age. Do you not think that Louis is a prime example?'

And the Comte de Vignolles certainly looked at his best, with his leonine head rapidly sporting a deal of white among the dark hair and his tall figure carrying itself with all the assurance of an older man.

'My dear John, how good to see you again.'

'And you, Sir.'

'Here is your godson, Jacques. Grown somewhat since last you met.'

Louis stepped to one side to reveal a handsome lad of about eleven with a mass of dark curling hair tied back with a scarlet bow. Jacques put his hand on his heart and gave a deep bow.

'Godfather, I am so pleased to see you again.'

'And I you, Jacques,' John answered, and gave a formal bow in return.

He had delivered the child, brought him into the world, when during a social call on Serafina she had gone into premature labour. But all had been well. Thanks to the services of John and a quick-witted maid, the tiny little boy had lived and thrived. And now here he was, grown into a regular fine fellow.

Serafina looked at him and winked an elegant eye. 'You approve of my brood?'

John winked back. 'Not nearly as much as I approve of you, Madam.'

Later that evening, when the supper had been taken and the candles burned low and the young people had yawned their way to their bedrooms, the three friends sat at the table while the port bottle was passed round. Serafina did not participate in the tradition of ladies leaving the men alone – except when in elegant company – and sat while John and Louis lit pipes and watched the blue smoke curl towards the beautiful ceiling.

'Are you happy, my dear?' she asked John, looking at him over the rim of her glass.

He sighed. 'I am content,' he answered, 'if that is what you mean.'

'No, it is not what I meant. I repeat, are you happy?'

The Apothecary glanced at her and saw that she knew the answer even before he had spoken.

'To be honest with you, I crave adventure and I miss my sons. And I still miss Elizabeth, though the pain of that has vanished with the passing of the years.'

'But you genuinely loved her?' asked Louis.

'With all my heart. And I still do. But I am not one of those people who go on pining for something that I can no longer have. I have too practical a nature.'

'You are a wise man,' said Louis. 'A lot of valuable time is wasted by those who hunger for what is lost.'

Serafina suddenly sparkled with mischief. 'We must find an adventure for you, my friend.'

John's eyes lit up. 'As a matter of fact I had a mysterious letter today.'

'From whom?'

'From a stranger. A man in Bristol – well, just outside actually, a village called Clifton.'

'And?'

'Apparently someone has turned up claiming to be his stepson, but he maintains he's never seen the fellow in his life before.'

Serafina and Louis exchanged a glance.

'How odd,' Louis said.

'And what does he want you to do about it?' asked the Comtesse.

'He has apparently heard that I have in the past worked with Sir John Fielding and he wants me to visit him. At least I think that is what he wants.'

'You must write to him this very night, John. Tell him that you will be delighted to accept the commission.'

'Where did you say he lived?' asked Louis.

'In Clifton. It's a village outside Bristol. Up on the edge of the Avon Gorge.'

'I've seen it,' Louis answered. 'It's quite small. I believe the rich of Bristol are building up there to get away from the stink of the town.'

'You must go, John,' said Serafina, her eyes suddenly glinting. 'I have a feeling it might relieve your low spirits.'

'Not exactly low, more unsettled.'

'Whatever you say,' she answered, 'but promise me you will attend upon this mysterious gentleman.'

'Yes,' the Apothecary said, 'I give you my promise.'

'Then I'll drink to that,' replied Serafina, and with that she raised her glass.

Two

Much later that night, when the Apothecary had climbed into his bed and snuggled down beneath the blankets, he looked once again at the letter. With a stomach full of wine and good food, let alone his promise to Serafina, he made the decision to visit Bristol soon.

He had been there once before as a boy of fourteen, taken by Sir Gabriel, visiting an old friend who dwelled in Queens Square. He had stared overawed at the mighty Avon Gorge, at the ferry boat crossing it, back and forth, at the young boy rowing it, scarcely older than himself. But most of all his eye had been drawn to the mighty ships riding at anchor, rowed up the narrow waterway of the channel by barges, it being too narrow and the wind too flighty to allow them to sail. Then his eyes had widened in horror as he had watched one ship unload its cargo. A hatchway had opened in the hold and out had come a string of strange people with black skins, naked but for a few tattered rags which they clutched about them. There had been men, women and children of all ages, staggering out of the blackness below and almost blinded by the light of day. There had been infants, some no older than two years. One, a terrified little girl, lost control of her bladder and stood, helpless, while urine cascaded down her legs and tears down her tragic black face.

John had turned to Sir Gabriel. 'What are they, Sir? Are they people?'

His father had made a strange sound, almost a hollow laugh. 'They are called negroes, John. And yes, they are people like ourselves.'

'But why have they been brought here?'

'To act as slaves – unpaid servants – to those who will buy them off the slave trader.'

'Even the children?'

'Yes, even them. The boys will go to some rich woman to be her little black servant. The girls will train to become maids-of-all-work. Poor little piccaninnies.'

'You don't approve of slaving, Father?'

'"If they prick us do we not bleed?"' quoted Sir Gabriel, and John understood completely.

But the horror was not over. The sailors produced a chain and passed it through the neck collars that each man, woman and child wore. Then in a line that shouted of despair and misery and enormous suffering, they shuffled off the ship and away to some unknown destination.

John stared after them, his mouth agape. Sir Gabriel put a hand on his shoulder.

'Do not upset yourself, my boy. I promise you that I shall never have a black slave running after me.'

'But, Sir, that won't stop the horrible trade.'

'One day there will be a movement against it, mark my words. But meanwhile, let the ignorant and thoughtless people continue to buy them. But be very careful to whom you say these things. Such words could get you into trouble.'

And with that Sir Gabriel Kent had turned away from the port and had started to walk inland.

John put the letter down on the chest which stood beside the bed, containing behind its closed door the ever-useful chamber pot. A few minutes later he fell asleep, dreaming of his late wife Emilia and reaching out for her in the hours after midnight.

He woke early the next morning, and passing Mrs Fortune's door on the way downstairs heard little gasps as she was laced into her corset by her maid. John smiled and continued downwards where he sat alone at the table, ate heartily and read the newspaper. He found himself peering at the small print, and the horrid thought shot through his mind that he might soon need spectacles. Indeed he was still looking intensely at the newsprint when Jacquetta rustled into the room. John rose from his chair, gave a small polite bow and waited till she was seated before sitting down again.

'Good morning, Mr Rawlings. I trust the day finds you well?'

'Yes thank you. And how are you, Madam?'

'Wonderful,' she answered, and she looked it.

Today she was attired in a somewhat old-fashioned sack back gown with a square neckline, made in a lilac shade that became her enormously. John found her very attractive and wondered why he had not proposed to her long ago. But in his heart he already knew the answer. Though Jacquetta Fortune had turned into a beautiful woman, from the skinny, half-starved creature she had been when he first met her, she did not possess that inner fire which he found irresistibly tempting.

Thoughts of Elizabeth came unbidden. She was the woman he had always wanted, full of fire and ice, dark as a gypsy and with the same wonderful impetuousness that could always delight whoever was in her company, yet with the capability to freeze a man into the Arctic wastes if she so chose. He had risked loving her, she had become the mother of his twin sons, yet despite all this he had had the temerity to walk out on her in a quite unjustified fit of pique.

'Anything interesting in the paper?' asked Jacquetta, cutting herself a slice of ham.

John looked up. 'Sir John and Lady Fielding have gone to the country to stay with the Duke of Kingston at Thoresby Hall. Apparently they left by coach last evening.'

'I take it that the Duke's wife will also be present?'

John smiled. 'You refer to the former Miss Chudleigh? You can count upon it that having achieved her objective the lady will be clinging like a veritable crab.'

Mrs Fortune pursed her lips. 'One hears strange rumours about that woman.'

But the Apothecary was no longer listening to her, his attention riveted by another item in the paper. 'Good God,' he said, then before Jacquetta could answer went on, 'Listen to this. "Finest Hotwell Water available at the cost of six shillings per dozen bottles which will be sold to the discerning customer. This fine medicinal water is perfectly without smell, pleasing and grateful to the stomach, cooling and quenches thirst. It is quite beyond parallel for disorders of the digestive and urinary tracts and has miraculously cured cases of those with a diarrhoea and gravelish complaints, particularly those who void great quantities of fabulous matter. For purchase apply to Mister Callow Hill at the Hotwell upon the Avon Gorge near Bristol."' He put the paper down and gave Jacquetta a crooked smile. 'What do you make of that?'

She made a wry face. 'Well, it is nothing new. I believe that the Hotwell Water is exported all over the world.'

'Good gracious! Why was I not aware of it?'

'Because you are an apothecary, Mr Rawlings, who just happens to have the ability to carbonate water. It is not your task to seek out would-be competitors.'

The words were sharp, but they were accompanied by such a sweet smile that John could only respond with a sheepish grin and a return to the pages of the *London Advertiser*. For after all, every word Jacquetta had said was true. He had been vaguely aware of Hotwell Water but had never turned his mind on to what it actually was. But now his curiosity was piqued. The combination of the strange letter which had been delivered to the shop yesterday and this picturesquely worded advertisement had made up his mind for him. He would go to visit Bristol as soon as his other commitments permitted.

Three

The trouble about leaving London even for a few days was the rather worrying age of Sir Gabriel Kent, John's dearly loved adopted father. The grand old man had now reached the enormous sum of eighty-eight years, a fact he put down to his daily stroll past the palace of Kensington and back. But the reality of his continuing good health could not outplay the tricks of time. Nowadays Sir Gabriel moved slowly and often sat down with obvious relief, while his hearing had grown very poor. He had a sliding silver ear trumpet which, when collapsed, fitted into the pocket of his coat. This he was somewhat shy of using in the presence of ladies, but now, with his own son standing before him, he produced the thing from his pocket, extended it to its full length, and plugged it into his right ear.

'Father, dear soul,' John said in a raised voice. 'How are you?'

'There's no need to shout, my boy. I am utterly fine and this wretched trumpet is in perfect working order.'

'Then why, if I may be so bold, don't you use it all the time?'

'Vanity, dear child. None of us likes to be reminded of the passing years, particularly in the presence of the fair sex.'

John grinned. 'Yes, I had noticed.'

Sir Gabriel laughed and said, 'I thought that my weakness of spirit would have passed unobserved.'

'It usually does, but it was when you started talking about Roman remains when the lady had remarked on the aroma remaining that it became a little obvious.'

'But only to you, I trust?'

'Of course,' John lied gallantly, 'only to me.'

He bent over and kissed Sir Gabriel on his fine old cheek, then sat down in a chair opposite his.

'A little sherry, my dear?'

'Thank you, that would be very nice.'

Sir Gabriel took a delicate sip and smiled at John over the rim of the glass. 'Well, what news?'

John sampled his sherry carefully, weighing up his promise to Seraphina, his overwhelming curiosity about Hotwell Water, and the strange letter he had received, against the thought of his father being taken ill on his own. Meanwhile Sir Gabriel regarded him, his topaz eyes twinkling away.

'You seem lost in thought, dear child.'

'Oh, sorry . . .'

'I have some news for you,' Sir Gabriel interrupted. 'I am thinking of going away to benefit my health.'

'Really, Sir? To Bath?'

'I should say not. The season is quite closed. It would be highly unfashionable to visit at this time of year. No, I intend to go to the Hotwell, which is situated at the foot of the Avon Gorge in Bristol. I believe their season runs till the end of October and there is a great deal of amusement to be had even this late in the calendar. I wondered whether you would care to accompany me?'

John took such a violent sip of his sherry that it went up his nose and ran down inside his nostrils, burning as it flowed. He reached for his handkerchief and blew the offending item hard.

Sir Gabriel looked sympathetic. 'You are surprised, my dear?'

John looked at him suspiciously. 'May I ask, Sir, how you knew?'

Sir Gabriel played the innocent. 'Knew what, my son?'

'That I was thinking of going there myself?'

'Good gracious! Were you indeed? Then I shall have a fine travelling companion.'

His father refused to reveal any further information, and John was torn between suspecting Mrs Fortune of writing and inviting Sir Gabriel to stay in Nassau Street while he was away, or believing that it was the most outrageous coincidence. So he merely looked at Sir Gabriel straight-faced and said, 'So on what day shall we depart, Papa?'

'Would three days' time suit you?'

'That will be ideal.'

The public stage had recently set a record by running a coach from Bristol via Bath to London in seventeen hours flat. In fact transport of every kind was speeding up. One could change horses at various conveniently placed inns along the six Great Roads,

Deryn Lake

where one could find good stabling and smart horsekeepers to speed up the changes. The charge was moderate: 3d or 4d per mile.

Had John been travelling alone he would have asked his coachman, Irish Tom, to try to drive faster, but in view of Sir Gabriel's great age he decided to stop for the night at the Old Chequers in Thatcham, near Newbury. There they slept well and departed at about eight in the morning, having eaten a breakfast of varying degrees of quantity, John's being large, Sir Gabriel's minimal. Thus they arrived in Bristol some eight hours later and drove through the town towards the splendour of the Avon Gorge.

It was only the Apothecary's second visit to the town, but as they approached its outskirts he noticed Sir Gabriel's fine nose wrinkle at the strange smell which pervaded the carriage.

'The tide is out,' his father said drily.

John sniffed. He could smell mud and garbage and something even worse.

'I fear you're right,' he answered.

The River Avon was tidal and though the boats on which the town relied for its trade could be towed up and moored at the bustling quays, alongside which were crammed the many houses, when the tide went out the water level dropped by some thirty feet and left the ships stranded like netted fish on the mud banks below. So the packed and jostling town of Bristol was never without its own individual stink. A fact of which John was vividly reminded when Sir Gabriel produced a lace trimmed handkerchief and put it delicately to his nostrils.

The carriage jolted and shuddered as it crossed over a waterway and then, at last, came into Frog Lane and then Limekiln Lane, heading towards Hotwell. John drew breath as the majesty of the Avon Gorge reared above him. A great rock protruded almost to the brink of the river, and craning his neck he saw sheep grazing on the grassy slopes, hanging on by sheer tenacity to the steep drop. High overhead, on the tallest hill of all, stood a solitary mill, a lonely and somehow desolate building. On the bank opposite there were signs of commercial activity, but it was to the Hotwell buildings that the Apothecary felt his eyes drawn.

As the tide was low he could make out the place where the spring bubbled forth, only to be taken to the Pump Room above by a series of valves and pumps, which was as well, he thought, as at high tide the river would be flooded with every cat and dog in the neighbourhood, to say nothing of raw sewage.

Sir Gabriel spoke to Irish Tom.

'We are staying at the Gloucester Hotel, my good fellow. I have written to them in advance. And I have booked a room for you at The Bear, which provides adequate stabling for the horses.'

'Very good, Sir Gabriel.'

The coachman picked his way over the cobbled streets, while John looked about him, admiring the riverside walk of young trees, planted so that their overhead branches met and people could promenade quite happily even when it began to rain. An attractive colonnade of shops, curving in a half circle, lined with white pillars and covered with a roof, was on his right, while ahead of him lay the Hotwell Pump Room.

'Just a little further on,' Sir Gabriel called, and his son had a sudden thrill of excitement, which he always associated with danger. As usual he made no attempt to analyse this sensation, but merely accepted it as a forerunner to coming events – though he had to admit that the tale of the Bristol merchant's unknown stepson both intrigued and puzzled him.

The next morning he and Sir Gabriel stepped forth with lively gait to the delights of the Hotwell spa, making immediately for the Pump Room, which buzzed with activity. A small orchestra was playing – à la Bath – over which the visitors shouted cheerfully at one another. There was the usual gathering of the chronically sick, some looking fit to die, mixed with the bright young set who had come to be seen in the right places. Besides these were the couples who walked stoically up and down the length of the room, looking coldly at the new arrivals and parading their finery for all the world to see. John smiled and thought that it could be a Pump Room situated in any spa in any part of the world. The characters were always the same.

As ever, despite his enormous age, the entrance of Sir Gabriel Kent caused quite a stir. Attired in his usual garments of black and white, his vast three-storey wig – hopelessly out of fashion but arresting for all that – together with his beribboned great stick, caught the eye of all present. There was a rustle amongst the people promenading and all eyes turned in his direction. Sir Gabriel swept his tricorne hat from his head and made a low bow.

'Good morning,' he pronounced in ringing tones, and made his way through the throng to the fountain at the end of the room. John followed behind as the waves of people parted like the Dead Sea to allow his father a thoroughfare.

The water bubbled up into a spout beside which stood a corpulent woman with somewhat flushed features doling out glasses to the passing parade. 'How much do you charge, Madam?' Sir Gabriel enquired.

'Sixpence a glass, Sir. Very good for the diarrhoea, the stone, the gout, the spleen and disorders of the urine.'

'My, my,' murmured John's father. 'I'll take two glasses if you please.'

John held his glass up to the light before drinking it. The water had a natural sparkle and was slightly cloudy. He swallowed it and thought to himself as he did so that it had rather a base, mineral-laden taste. But he supposed that was inevitable with a medicinal draught. It was also warm and in no way competed with his sparkling brew – not that they were in the same line of business.

At the end of the Pump Room, beyond the fountain, were windows which swept down to the river, giving a fine view of the Rownham Woods opposite. Looking to his left John could see a jolly ferryman, attired in vivid colours, taking passengers across the river. He decided then and there that he must explore the surrounding area, and that he also must call on the gentleman who had written him that extraordinary letter.

Sir Gabriel muttered at his elbow, 'Good lord, I do believe that Samuel Foote has just come in.'

John turned and looked, seeing a small, limping figure dressed in a suit of bright vermillion making its way towards the fountain. A series of rather amusing features which included a tilted nose, a pair of lively eyes and a definitely humorous mouth were crowned by a short grey wig with tight curls on either side. John's mind flashed back ten years to when he had seen the great actor appear as a woman called Mrs Cole, a Covent Garden madam who had been converted to Methodism by a preacher, namely one Dr Squintum, also played by Foote. At the end of the show John had been asked to attend a delicate young woman who had fainted through laughing so much. He himself had felt a tremendous aching of the ribs, which had lasted all the following day. That Dr Squintum was based on the famous squinting Methodist, George Whitefield, and Mrs Cole on Jenny Douglas, the most infamous of all the madams in Covent Garden, had only added to the hilarity. John had thought him one of the funniest men he had ever seen in his life and now felt an overwhelming urge to speak to him.

The small figure was approaching the fountain and a ripple of applause rang out from the cognoscenti in the Pump Room. John bowed and Sir Gabriel acknowledged the actor's arrival with a slow nod of his head.

'I suppose I'd better have a slurp of the revolting stuff,' Samuel Foote announced to the world in general. He proceeded to gulp from the glass and then said 'Urrgh,' which endeared him to John immediately.

The serving woman looked displeased. 'It's very good for the spleen and—'

'I know, I know,' interrupted the actor. 'Makes your urine less sour and cures both warts and the pox.'

Sir Gabriel looked grave and said, 'My good Sir, is that a fact?', his voice solemn but his lips atwitch.

Samuel Foote looked up at the man's great height and suddenly, by bending his body over and reassembling his facial features, became Mrs Cole.

'Oh yes, Sir. I tell that to all the gentlemen who come to see my girls. It's a right cure-all, this magic water.'

John's father gave a boom of laughter and said, 'Oh come now, Mrs Cole, I can hardly believe that.'

In his role, the actor bobbed a curtsey. 'You must think what you will, Sir.' Then a second later he had straightened and said solemnly, 'Excuse my levity, Sir. I merely jest. Allow me to introduce myself. Samuel Foote, at your service.'

Sir Gabriel bowed a little lower. 'Mr Foote, I know who you are and can assure you that I have adored your performances ever since I first saw you in *Tom Thumb* and *The Historical Register*. If I may be allowed to comment, Sir, it is your rollicking sense of humour coupled with a pair of roguish eyes that makes you such a splendid comedian.'

Samuel Foote bowed in return. 'I cannot receive enough praise, Sir. A poor actor fellow draws the breath of life from a constant stream of it.'

His face was impish as he spoke, but John felt that there was a certain element of truth in what the brilliant Mr Foote had just said.

He spoke up. 'Allow me to present to you my father, Sir Gabriel Kent, a great patron of the arts. While I, too, have loved each performance you have given. I think you are the finest comedian alive today.'

The little man visibly blossomed. 'Well, gentlemen, I take this as a great compliment. I presume you have come to the Hotwell for the social side as well as for your health?'

'Indeed,' answered Sir Gabriel with enthusiasm. 'And what of your good self?'

'I am appearing at the Playhouse over by Jacob's Well. It is a robust little place. Do you know it?'

'I believe I do. Is it by Brandon Hill?'

'In that direction, yes. Its actual address is Limekilns.'

'And what play are you performing?' asked John.

'An old piece, I fear, but very funny. It was written by my associate John Hippisley and is entitled *A Journey to Bristol*.'

'We shall come and see it this very night,' Sir Gabriel announced with conviction, and John nodded in agreement.

Having perambulated in the Pump Room and listened to the music for a while, John and his father sallied forth along Dowry Parade. Here were the pretty shops that John had spied earlier, including an apothecary's business, which was packed with people, mostly invalids, judging by their grim-looking faces. John raised his expressive eyebrows and moved on to the hat shop, where he bought one that would delight the heart of his daughter, Rose. Fashioned in straw, its emerald ribbons and tiny flowers were clearly the work of a remarkable milliner, and the Apothecary wondered how many such tradespeople currently worked at the Hotwell, providing for the needs of the thriving crowd of visitors who came to drink the water and to be seen there.

Irish Tom had not been called upon that day and had also

spent his time wandering through the streets and gazing at the sights of the Hotwell. But by half past five he had the coach round at the hotel's front gates, watching as Sir Gabriel, very grand in a swirling black cape with diamond clasps and an old-fashioned but very fine three-cornered hat, made an exit. He was followed by John, far more up-to-date in his new long, light overcoat and soft-brimmed felt hat. Not too sure of the direction, the coachman turned to his right and picked his way through the fading light of early evening.

The progress was perilous, journeying through muddy tracks and narrow lanes until eventually they came to the Rope Walk and a linkboy appeared, brandishing his torch of pitch and tow. Sir Gabriel promptly hired him and the rest of the journey was uneventful until they approached the theatre itself. Here was a scene which could have come from the jaws of hell. Drunken revellers stood outside The Malt Shovel, an ale house directly beside the Playhouse, exchanging banter with several actors, already costumed and made-up. Meanwhile, patrons were making their way inside, including several footmen who had come to reserve boxes for their masters. Ladies, raising their skirts a little to escape the mire of the street, were subjected to catcalls and whistles from the lowlife crowding outside the place.

When Sir Gabriel and John had parted company with Samuel Foote at the Pump House they had enquired as to the possibility of hiring a box and the jolly little man had told them with enthusiasm that he would see to it. So now as they made their way within, Sir Gabriel whispered to an attendant and they were shown into a reasonable box that could have housed four persons.

Looking around, John saw that the theatre had at some time been enlarged and now formed the shape of an amphitheatre, with boxes on the stage as well as in the circle. A hole had been knocked in the wall close to the seats in the pit through which a human arm holding a tray of drinks appeared at regular intervals, serving both the audience and the actors. John presumed that The Malt Shovel was doing a roaring trade. The stage itself was minute, and it now became obvious that actors exiting on prompt side would have to run round the back of the theatre to enter opposite prompt. The Apothecary was highly amused as he watched the audience take its seats.

A footman, who appeared to be sleeping in a lower stage box, suddenly shambled to his feet as the box's occupant appeared. John gaped as a heap of human blubber wobbled into the space, knocking the footman out of the way with his walking cane as he did so. The creature lowered itself onto an agonised chair and allowed his stomach to fall forward as he did so, while the footman, bowing, made his way out. The colossus ignored him completely.

He was quite the fattest man that John had ever seen in his life – and in his profession he had seen a few. It was hideously terrifying and at the same time horribly fascinating. The man's chins, of which there were several, protruded not only downwards but outwards, giving him the look of an abundant harvest moon. On his head he wore a small greyish wig curled up on either side, which only served to enhance his general enormity. He was clean shaven but his eyebrows were of a vivid saffron shade, thick and curling and doing little or nothing to enhance his looks. John gazed in total entrancement.

Feeling someone staring at him, the man looked round and scowled, then stretched his arm over the front of the box and took a frothing tankard of two quarts of ale which he proceeded to drink with obvious satisfaction. Then he belched deep, the vapour rising from the depths of his gaseous stomach. After that he wiped his mouth with the back of his hand, then rose a little in his protesting chair before settling himself back on to it, stretching out his short, stocky legs. John guessed that the man had let loose a fart, for the woman in the box next to his raised her handkerchief to her nostrils with a little shrill of alarm.

Sir Gabriel said, amused, 'I see someone has caught your eye, my dear.'

'Yes, that gross creature sitting in the stage box left. Have you ever seen the like of it?'

His father raised his quizzer and peered, then said shortly, 'No, never.'

'I wonder who he can be?'

'We must ask a discreet question at the hotel. There can surely be only one such answering his description.'

'I agree.'

Now the footmen were leaving the other boxes as the last of the patrons arrived. The candles were snuffed in the auditorium and lit by the snuffers before the stage, the musicians entered and struck up a foot-tapping air. The performance had begun.

Four

The comedy was banal but hilarious and John, looking at his father, thought that he had never seen him laugh so heartily before. In fact Sir Gabriel's cheeks were wet with tears and he applied his handkerchief several times. From the gallery above, the Apothecary could hear the sound of Irish Tom's loud guffaws, while he himself added uncontrollable giggling to the general cacophony.

The story was simple. A pleasure-seeking young woman asks her husband for permission to visit the Hotwell and the theatre. She will be accompanied by her mother, played by Samuel Foote, complete with slyly false bosom, highly rouged cheeks and a great many lascivious glances at the audience. Her husband, played by the great Irish actor Spranger Barry, taking a rest from his usual Shakespearean roles but still enunciating the words as if he were speaking as Othello, exclaims, 'Oh horrid! The Long Room is a school of Wickedness and the Playhouse a Nursery to the Devil!' This brought the house to its feet and there was deafening cheering for a few minutes. John took the opportunity of looking at the mammoth in the stage box and saw that the creature was imbibing yet another quart of ale and growing very red in the face as a result.

The play continued with much joviality, Sam Foote even doing a parodied country dance with Mr Barry, which was made all the funnier by the fact that Foote had only one leg so that the violent dips and curtseys he made beneath the hooped skirts were amusingly accentuated. The evening ended with a pantomime in which the mother-in-law is pursued by the Devil himself, who finally vanishes beneath her voluminous petticoats. The spectators, who loved a bit of rudery, clapped and whooped noisily, and while Sir Gabriel gathered himself together, his son looked once more at the occupant of the stage box.

The man's stick was handed to him by a kindly snuffer and then he drew his immense frame to a standing position and slowly waddled out. The Apothecary wondered where the man was staying and if he had possibly come to the Hotwell to try and cure his obesity. But there his curiosity had to end, for Irish Tom had sprinted down the stairs from the gallery and was bringing round the coach. Helping Sir Gabriel aboard, John thought that their first day at the Hotwell had been highly successful, but as the carriage turned back in the direction from which they had come, his eye was caught by the sight of the colossus being heaved into a coach by a team of three sweating footmen. He knew a moment of pure curiosity. Before he left he would make it his business to find out exactly who the fat fellow was.

At breakfast the next morning – which John ate like a trencher-man and at which Sir Gabriel merely picked – he produced the letter from his dressing gown pocket.

'What do you make of this, Papa?'

Sir Gabriel produced a pair of spectacles and put them on his powerful nose. Then he proceeded to read the paper twice before lowering it and asking John, 'You have no knowledge of this person?'

'You refer to the writer?'

'Of course.'

'No, I know nothing of him or his stepson.'

'My instinct is that you should go and see the man as soon as possible. Find out all that you can. And as quickly as you can. If this stepson is an imposter then the poor fellow might be in danger.'

'You think so?'

'My dear John, it is not like you to miss a whiff of trouble. I should certainly make it my business to go if I were in your shoes.'

'You have made up my mind for me. I will call on him this morning. If I can find the wretched place.'

It was even more difficult than the Apothecary had realised. Whereas Hotwell was a bustling and thriving community, Clifton was a small and remote village with only a church, a few farms and a scattering of thirty or so upper-class houses scattered between Clifton Hill and the Green. The reason for this was that it was almost impossible to get to. There were four possible routes: along the toll road which went over Clifton Downs, up a winding footpath which pre-dated the Roman invasion, by a flight of steps which led directly from the Colonnade and climbed steeply upwards, and up Granby Hill. John chose the last and had never been more terrified in his life.

His horses screamed in fear as they gallantly climbed, hooves slipping and eyes rolling – Irish Tom cursing the way robustly – up a steep and precipitous track hacked out of the rock itself. John closed his eyes and clung to the seat as he was forced into an upright position as they neared the top of the terrible ascent. Then they stopped, horses panting for breath, Irish Tom white in the face and John feeling slightly sick as they reached the end of that terrible road. Not far away lay an inn and they made for it rapidly to collect themselves before their next destination.

So it was with a whiff of brandy on his breath that John, peering out of the window, found his way to Sion Row, a small street of terraced houses built not far from the mighty Gorge itself. With some trepidation the Apothecary knocked on the front door, to be answered by a somewhat downcast footman who said in a depressed voice, 'Yes, Sir?'

With a flourish John produced his card, which the man stared at as if he had never in his life seen the like of it before.

'Do you want me to show this to the Master, Sir?'

John decided to be kind. 'Yes, if you would be so good.'

'If you will wait there, Sir, I'll see if he is in.'

'Just a moment before you do. Is his name Mr Huxtable?'

'That's the old master, Sir. The new master is Mr Bagot.'

'Then I seek Mr Huxtable, if you please.'

'Just a moment, Sir.'

Feeling somewhat isolated – Irish Tom having vanished with the coach to find a suitable place to water the horses – the Apothecary tried to imagine what Sir Gabriel would have made of the journey he had just undertaken. But his thoughts were interrupted by the arrival of a small, bustling man of some sixty years who bowed effusively and held out his hand.

'Mr Rawlings. It is Mr Rawlings, isn't it?' John nodded. 'I am so very grateful to you, Sir, for coming to see me. Yes indeed. And all the way from London, too. Thank you, Sir, sincerely. Please step inside. Can I get you some refreshment?'

The Apothecary smiled. 'First of all, let me assure you that I am staying near the Hotwell and travelled down with my father, who is here to take the waters. So please do not concern yourself on that score. And secondly, I would like to have a cup of coffee, provided you join me.'

'Oh yes, indeed I will. Gregory, fetch a tray please. Commodore is out running an errand.'

The miserable servant bowed and plodded out of the room.

Mr Huxtable sighed loudly. 'You must forgive him, Mr Rawlings. He is a farmer's son and not born to serve. Alas, this is a very small community and we must take what we can in the way of servants.'

The Apothecary nodded sympathetically.

Mr Huxtable went on, 'I feel certain that you remarked the poor quality of his livery but, alas, I am running desperately short of funds to renew it. My stepson – if so he be – spends money as if it were his birthright. And, oh Mr Rawlings, I am not so sure it is.'

The coffee came in at this juncture and there was silence while the poor servant, hands shaking violently with nervousness, poured it out, a great deal of the liquid ending up in the saucers. Mr Huxtable merely sighed again and looked at John covertly from beneath half-closed lids.

He was like a thrush, John decided, Short and slightly rotund with a waistcoat of some speckled material that generally added to the illusion. His eyes were as bright and as round as a bird's and equally as brilliant. Furthermore he had rather a jerky way of moving, hopping about on skinny little legs, which he was now doing as he advanced towards the Apothecary, handing him a cup.

'Why don't you tell me the entire story,' John said encouragingly, taking a sip of coffee and wishing that he hadn't.

'Where shall I start?'

'How about from your marriage.'

'Very well. I have been married twice, you know. My first wife was a pale little thing, a slip of womanhood, but one whom

I loved tremendously. But she was too frail to live and she died in my arms when we had only been wed a twelve-month. After that I knew I could never really love again, but then about a year or so later I met a young widow, a Mrs Bagot, and we married a few months later. She had a young son – a nice little boy called Augustus – and he lived with us quite happily at home in Bristol. But at the age of fourteen he fell in with rough company and, to cut to the bone, left home and refused to return. My wife took it very hard, I can tell you.'

'And this is the boy who has now come back and is squandering your money?'

Mr Huxtable put down his coffee cup and turned on John a face of pure wretchedness. He nodded silently.

'I see.' The Apothecary also put down his cup, the liquid untouched. 'And what is wrong with the man? Other than the fact he is a spendthrift.'

Mr Huxtable let out an involuntary groan. 'The trouble is, Mr Rawlings, that I do not recognise him at all.'

'What do you mean exactly?'

'Well, he left home a slim, ginger-haired, freckle-faced lad of fourteen and he comes back a hideous mountain of flesh, a face so contorted by double chins that it appears barely human, and a stink about him of old rotting cabbages.'

John sat rigid, a picture coming into his mind of the ogre he had seen in the theatre on the previous evening.

'Does he have difficulty in walking?'

'My dear fellow, his obesity makes it almost impossible for him to place one leg before the other. He gets along by the use of a stick, but very slowly let me add.'

The Apothecary cleared his throat. 'Tell me, was he at the theatre last night?'

'I believe so, though I am not privy to his movements. He lumbers from here in the mornings, usually about twelve o'clock. Takes my coach – the floor of which has had to be mended twice . . .'

John smiled grimly.

'. . . and arrives home in the early hours of the morning. Whereupon he falls into his reinforced bed and the whole dreary process begins again on the morrow.'

'And why did he come back exactly?'

'His poor grieving mother never forgot him. She had a portrait painted of him when he was an angelic-looking child and she kept fresh flowers in front of it until her final illness.'

'Which was?'

'Six years ago, alas. However, in her will she left him some valuable diamonds and though, of course, I could claim them as my own, she particularly begged me to give them to him should Augustus ever return.'

'And now he has,' John said quietly.

'I do not believe it,' said Mr Huxtable, with force. 'I believe this man to be an imposter — and there is one way I can prove it.'

'Then why have you not done so?'

'Because, my dear Mr Rawlings, I have never had the opportunity so to do. You see, my stepson — the real one — had a mole on his arse which was quite distinct. A round, brown birthmark on his left cheek. But this vagabond who claims to be him has never undressed before me. I have no way of knowing whether it is there or not.'

John gave his misshapen smile. 'I take your point. Frankly it is not a sight I would care to investigate.'

Mr Huxtable stood up and made a sprightly move to the door. 'Come with me,' he said.

Interested, the Apothecary rose also and followed the man into the hall.

'He has commandeered my sitting room for a bedroom after falling through the floor of his own.'

'I beg your pardon?'

'It's true. His weight was so great that the rafters collapsed and his feet and legs appeared through the ceiling. And I was entertaining Lady Tavener to tea at the time. It was a true humiliation.'

'So now he sleeps downstairs?'

'Yes, if truth be told he had such difficulty on the stairs that it is an easier arrangement all round. But, oh I do miss my sitting room.'

John followed him through a door on the left and into what had once been a large salon. It was filled with a vast bed and various items of clothing strewn about, which a servant was gallantly attempting to hang up or put away. Even though the curtains had been drawn back and the windows thrown open, a faint odour lingered on the air. John sniffed and Mr Huxtable gave him a knowing look.

'The essence of Augustus,' he said.

The cleaning boy had just picked up an enormous pair of drawers, which he was bundling up with other garments for the laundry woman. John cast his eye on the clothes and thought he recognised a high-necked shirt with a bow at the front, these both heavily stained with spilled wine. He turned to Mr Huxtable.

'So somehow you want me to get a look at this man's posterior?'

Mr Huxtable blenched. 'I would not ask that of anyone. No, Mr Rawlings. If I give you my old address in Bristol, would you make a few enquiries regarding the boy who went to sea all those years ago? Find out if anyone can remember him. Better still, if anybody sailed with him and has any further information. If you could perhaps ask a few questions in the dockside taverns it might be rewarding.'

John smiled. 'My father is only down here for a week, Sir.'

Mr Huxtable's eyes suddenly and incongruously filled with tears. 'Oh my dear chap. How thoughtless I am. Of course, of course, you have a business to run, a life to live. How dare I think you should devote your precious time to me and my little problem.'

The Apothecary was about to say something suitable when a voice spoke behind them.

'Forgive me for interrupting, Master. Just to let you know I have returned from Bristol.'

They both turned, John half expecting to see the stepson standing there, but instead he saw a magnificent human being: tall, strongly muscled, gleaming black with a crop of thick, curling dark hair.

'This is my slave – and I must admit my closest friend – Commodore.'

The slave bowed deeply. 'A great pleasure, Sir,' he answered in a rich chocolate voice.

'Commodore has been with me since he was a child,' Mr Huxtable explained. 'When I courted my second wife she already had a little black boy, given to her by her father for a birthday gift. She adored Commodore and he her. When we married he carried the train of the bridal gown; she wore blue satin and he had a little coat made to match.' He sighed and John could see tears welling up once more in the poor man's eyes. 'But when he reached puberty she would not let me send him to the plantations. We kept him as a servant instead.'

John interrupted. 'So did he know your stepson before he ran away to sea?'

'They were almost the same age. They often played together.'

The Apothecary turned to Commodore. 'How glad you must be that he has returned, my friend.'

A small smile played across the negro's features. 'If only that were the case, Sir. You see, I roundly state that this new arrival is a fraud.'

'A fraud?' John repeated.

'A fraud and an imposter, Sir,' said Commodore, and shook his head very sadly.

Nerves somewhat shattered by his earlier experiences, John asked Irish Tom to take the coach back through Bristol and out again to Hotwell, a far longer way round and through which one had to pass a toll – twice – but far better for the equilibrium. Seeking Sir Gabriel, he found him in the Long Room, engaged in a dignified minuet with a bright young woman of pleasing appearance. John could not help but smile, his father never ceasing to amaze him. He hoped fervently that when he got to eighty-odd years he would still be dancing with an attractive woman. He watched as dearly-loved Sir Gabriel reached the end, gave a deep bow, his hand momentarily flying to the small of his back as he did so, but changing the gesture into one of flourishing fingers. John applauded and gave a huge grin.

'Father, I did not expect to find you in such whirlwind pursuits.'

'Did you not, my dear? I can tell you that something has revitalised me. Whether it be the water, or the air, or the beauty of this little gem of a place, I cannot tell. But something has elevated my spirits quite wondrously. After dinner I intend to try my hand at whist. I have already met some likeable fellows with whom to play.'

'And any members of the fair sex?' John asked, making a small bow at Sir Gabriel's departing dancing partner.

'Ah, I see you mean the Honourable Titania Groves. Yes, a charming young girl. An offspring of Viscount Dartington. She is here taking the waters with her mother, the Viscountess.'

'So you are quite booked up as regards company?'

'Indeed I am. Why do you ask?'

Sir Gabriel's golden eyes were glittering with amusement and John stared at him, then gave a wry, twisted grin.

'You've guessed, haven't you?'

'I assume that your visit to Clifton this morning contained some kind of mystery and that you are on the trail of a blackguard.'

'You are right again, Father. Will I never be able to deceive you?'

Sir Gabriel looked quizzical. 'Who knows, my son? I am quite sure you have succeeded from time to time.'

'But never on purpose, Papa, I assure you.'

'And now to other matters. I presume that the man you called on has a problem?'

'Rather a large one, I fear,' and the Apothecary proceeded to tell Sir Gabriel everything that had transpired during that morning's meeting.

His father listened attentively, then said, 'And you have your suspicions it was that man mountain that we saw at the theatre last night?'

'Indeed. Surely there can't be two men wandering about like that?'

'If there are I publicly express my fear for the Hotwell.'

John chuckled joyfully and gave his father a kiss on the cheek. 'Come along, Sir. We must change for dinner. Have you been to bathe as yet?'

'No, my dear, that pleasure awaits me.'

'Let it be hoped that the large man does not attempt to dive in.'

'If he does I fear the river might rise to high tide,' answered Sir Gabriel, and they left the Long Room, arm in arm and laughing all the while.

Five

A game of whist was to be held in the Upper Long Room, owned by a cheerful and effusive man named John Barton. This room, built shortly after the Pump Room, had very fine windows overlooking on one side the River Avon and, on the other, the roofed Colonnade, which protected the shoppers from inclement weather. Breakfast was served on a Monday and Thursday at the price of 1s 6p, which was accompanied by country dances and cotillions. On Tuesday nights balls were held at the cost of one guinea for a subscription. But tonight was Wednesday and the evening was given over to play at cards and study of the daily newspapers.

Sir Gabriel made a fine entrance and John, walking a step or two behind him, made one of equal stature and far more colourful. This year the Apothecary had chosen a deep shade of old rose for his coat, cut well back to reveal an embroidered black waistcoat, tight black breeches and a pair of pink striped stockings. Sir Gabriel wore stark black from head to toe, relieved by the presence of four diamonds: one at his throat, two on his black satin evening shoes, and the fourth cut into a ring which he wore on his little finger.

Lady Dartington gazed frankly at both men, holding her quizzer to her eyes, and then nodded with silent approval. Sir Gabriel kissed her hand with an elegant gesture.

'My dear Lady Dartington, may I introduce my son, John Rawlings?'

'You may,' she said, and nodded her head graciously.

Meanwhile, the pretty slip of a thing with whom Sir Gabriel had danced earlier, raised her fan and peeped eloquently over the frill. John could not help but give a very slight bow and a naughty grin in her direction.

'Mr Rawlings, this is my daughter, Titania. My dear, may I present to you Mr John Rawlings?'

'How dee do, Sir?' answered the comely creature, rising to

her feet then dropping one of the demurest curtseys he had ever seen.

John responded with a deep bow and another cheeky grin and Miss Groves dropped her glance to the floor, then, looking up, gave him the full blaze of a pair of brilliant blue eyes.

As luck would have it the draw for partners put John with Lady Dartington, and thus he sat opposite her with Titania tucked neatly beside him. The rules of the game forbade any comment upon one's cards or luck – or lack of it in John's case. Thus they sat in tremendous silence, Sir Gabriel brooding over them like a black-clad hawk. Without moving a muscle, Miss Groves managed to generate a pleasant warmth, enveloping John in a delicious aura so that he was barely able to concentrate. He received a curious glance from his father who raised his eyebrow, then smiled and turned his attention back to the game. With great relief it was finally over, Titania and Sir Gabriel winning triumphantly, and the Apothecary, feeling somewhat shaken, pushed back his chair and went to stand by the window.

The moon was just coming up over the Avon Gorge and the beautiful sight tore at his heart. Through the glass he could hear the rapture of birds singing their praise of the beautiful day and, as he watched, the great channel of the river turned silver in the pallid light. A boat was coming upstream, a boat with three sails, white as daisies, billowing gently in the evening air. John felt totally at peace and at the same time utterly exhilarated.

He thought about staying in this place for the rest of his days, then his mind turned to the winter, the mighty gales and ravages of snow and ice whipping up the steep embankments, and knew that he was best off remaining in London with its own stinks and overcrowding.

There was a sudden commotion in the doorway and, turning round, the Apothecary saw a waiter hurriedly pull open the double doors to permit the entrance of a large man, sweating and swearing and mopping his face with a red spotted handkerchief. Shuffling forward and leaning heavily on a stick, the fellow made his way to a large armchair and into this he collapsed his entire weight, shouting for attention as he did so. John swore that he heard the chair groan, and laughed to himself for such whimsy.

Then, looking at the fat chap again, he felt a sudden lurch as he realised that this was the man he had seen in the theatre last night and was probably, if all be known, Augustus Bagot himself. Without any definite plan, the Apothecary approached and made a bow.

'May I join you, Sir?' he enquired.

The other stared at him from little mud-coloured eyes surrounded by layers of fat.

'Do I know you?' he asked.

'Not exactly, Sir, but I think I may have met your stepfather.'

The fat man made a sound which could have been anything from approval to disgust and said, 'You mean Horatio Huxtable?'

'Yes, Sir, I had the pleasure of his company this morning.'

'What did he want?'

John was immediately on his guard. 'Oh, I was driving in Clifton and he was kind enough to give my coachman directions. We fell into a brief conversation afterwards.'

'Well, how did my name come into it?'

John was floundering wildly and was rescued by Miss Groves, who appeared with a sweet smile and bobbed a curtsey to Augustus Bagot, who immediately attempted to rise from his seat but couldn't quite manage it and flopped back with a groan.

'Ah, Miss Groves,' said the Apothecary with truly heartfelt gratitude, 'I must say you played a very deft hand at cards.'

A glint had appeared in Bagot's eye. 'Allow me to introduce myself, Madam. Augustus Bagot, at your service.'

He pronounced it Bag-got, so that it sounded rather like beget.

Titania bobbed again and said, 'My mama does not like me speaking to people to whom I have not been presented, Sir.'

'Then I'll introduce myself to your mama,' Bagot answered jovially, then went silent as he saw Lady Dartington leaning on the arm of Sir Gabriel Kent and walking slowly but purposefully towards him. He hastily picked up a newspaper and lost himself in it. Titania meanwhile drooped an eyelid at John, which left him wondering whether it was accidental or not. He collected himself in time to greet Lady Dartington.

'I'm sorry I was so useless at cards, my Lady. Please forgive me.'

She raised her quizzer and gave him a long look. 'Nothing to forgive, my dear child.' Then she turned its glare onto Augustus

Bagot, who had, with enormous difficulty, crossed one leg over the other and was reading the paper nonchalantly. 'May I ask who you are, Sir?' she enquired coldly.

Augustus attempted to rise to his feet and did what he could in the way of a bow.

'Bagot's the name, Milady. I am the stepson of Horatio Huxtable of Clifton, don't you know. Been travelling abroad for some years and have just returned home. At your service, Ma'am.'

She inclined her head. 'I thank you.' She looked round at Sir Gabriel. 'Do you know this fellow?' she asked in an audible undertone.

'Never seen him before in my life,' he answered, after giving Augustus a quick glance.

'Very good.' She turned to Titania. 'Come, my dear. Sir Gabriel and I are going to have a cold collation. You of course are coming, Mr Rawlings.' She turned in Augustus's direction. 'Good night.' And with that she swept on.

'I take it your mama did not care for Mr Bagot,' he said in a whisper as he and Titania walked behind the formidable pair into the dining area.

'Well, he was a trifle on the large side,' she answered.

'You refer, of course, to his choice in newspapers.'

'Oh, Mr Rawlings, he looked like a figgety dumpling and you know it.'

And with that merry quip Titania laughed aloud and quite definitely winked her eye.

John lay awake for a long time that night, wishing he had a different nature. He had been married, had had a wonderful mistress, and yet his old feelings were rearing their head once more. The Honourable Titania Groves made him laugh, that was the best of it, and she was most definitely an outrageous flirt. The Apothecary could not help but admit that he liked her enormously.

And yet, despite all these naughty sensations, he knew that deep down he was a family man. How he loved his daughter, Rose, and how desperately he missed his twin sons, Jasper and James. They must be two years old by now, walking and talking a little, and yet he had no idea what they even looked like. It was pride that had kept him away from Elizabeth, and it was her fierce nature that had precluded her from contacting him. When he thought of her he knew that no-one could replace her, with her black hair being tossed by the Devon winds and her long, lithe body sitting on a horse with total confidence. A powerful woman – perhaps a shade too much so – and one who would attract only the brave-hearted. Yet Titania had the most engaging smile he had seen in a long time.

Eventually the Apothecary fell into a deep sleep and had a vague dream of Augustus Bagot swelling up and floating to the sky like a hot air balloon.

Still, he woke refreshed the next morning and, having break-fasted with his father, who today was declaring his intention of plunging into a bath of Hotwell water, called for Irish Tom and made his way to the city of Bristol.

The thing that struck him again about the place on this visit was the smell, which emanated partly from the docks at low tide, and partly from the streets and middens of the tenements. He was used to London and its various odours, but these raw stinks were strange to him.

Irish Tom shouted from the driving box, 'Aw, there's a terrible aroma around, Sorrh. It's making me eyes sweat.'

John opened the window a crack and shouted back, 'Tie your handkerchief over your nose.'

'No, Sorrh. 'Twould make me look like a high-lawyer, so it would.'

The smell was also of manufacturing: the brass works at Baptist Mills, lying north-east of the city and situated on the River Frome, combining with the iron foundries, the soap manufac-turers, the glass works, to say nothing of the sugar houses, the turpentine and vitriol houses, and the china manufacturer. Industry was in the air and pervaded the atmosphere of this restless, active port. Looking towards the harbour, John could see it bristling with the masts of ships like trees in a forest and thought of what havoc must be wreaked when the tide withdrew and left them lying totally encased in mud.

He had arranged to meet Horatio's black slave at The Hatchet Inn in Frogmore Street and had travelled to Bristol by way of the slippery track running along by the river. At some point

Tom had turned inland and found his way along a fashionable road, still under construction. This was called Park Street and leading off it was a curved back alley in which stood The Hatchet. John entered the inn with some trepidation, wondering what sort of lowlife frequented it and prepared to defend himself if necessary. But the place was strangely quiet and peering through the gloom he could see little custom was present. Ordering himself a pint of porter he went to sit at one of the small tables. From the back of the inn, deep down and far away, there came the mighty roar of voices and beneath his feet the floor shook. Slightly puzzled, the Apothecary cocked his head on one side, but at that second the door opened and the black man stood framed against the light.

'Good day to you, Sir,' he said in his deep, rich voice.

John smiled and said, 'Greetings, Commodore. Come and sit down.'

Thus invited, the slave sat opposite the Apothecary, giving him a remarkable opportunity to study his features. He had a good face with large, lustrous eyes and an unusually thin nose for a man from the West Indies. When he gleamed a smile he showed a perfect set of white teeth, which set John wondering how a man of his age could have maintained such a healthy mouth. Yet how old was Commodore? Forty, perhaps?

John was opening his lips to ask him when there once more came that distant roar and the floor shook beneath them like a minor earthquake.

Commodore smiled. 'There's a Rat Pitt beneath, Sir.'

'Good God!'

'Do you want to go and have a look?'

'No thanks. I'm a bit squeamish.'

Unlike ninety per cent of the male population, John hated sports that involved cruelty to animals, even the lowly rat. He had never been in a Rat Pitt but had a mental picture of the hordes of drunken men hanging out of the balconies or over the sides, while in the arena below one dog killed rats at a rate of knots, bets being taken on how many he could destroy in a given time. He knew that there were champion dogs – knew of one in particular who had lost an eye and had half his ear bitten off, being proudly exhibited by his owner. But John was sickened by the very idea. Along with bear and bull baiting, the very thought turned his stomach. He realised that some of his friends might consider him a Miss Molly for having such an opinion, but he clung to it nonetheless.

'He used to love it down there,' Commodore said softly.

John knew at once who he was speaking of. 'You mean Augustus?'

'You see, the trouble was when he found the dog.'

'I'm sorry, I don't quite follow you.'

'When he was out one day Augustus saw a dog wandering in the streets. It wasn't a handsome creature, in fact it was a down-right cur. It was squat, though heavily built, and was black with a white chest. It had a great mouth on it with nasty looking teeth and small eyes. But despite its ugly appearance, Augustus fell in love with it and took it home.'

'And?'

'Mrs Huxtable – as she was by then – let out an anguished shriek and forbade the boy ever to bring such a creature into the house again.'

'Did he obey?'

'Not he. He kept it in a kennel down on the wasteland and made it his own cherished pet. He called it Sam and it wasn't long before he discovered it killed everything in sight: rats, cats, squirrels, rabbits. It had a truly vicious bite.'

'Sounds horrible.'

'It was a monster. However, young Augustus – aged fourteen – started to frequent the Rat Pitt, here in this very inn, and began to win money with the savage brute. And that was the start of all the trouble.'

John took a sip of porter. 'What do you mean?'

'It was when he had enough money in his pocket that Augustus began to fall out with his mother and left home, complete with dog, and took a room in a nasty little dwelling house down on the docks.'

'I thought Mr Huxtable said he ran away to sea?'

Commodore sighed and shook his handsome head. 'He did, eventually. But not before he had caused a lot of problems not only in the Rat Pitt but also among the dockland fraternity; they even say he got several girls into trouble and ran away to avoid his responsibilities, though I must admit that I know little about that.'

'So how old was he when he eventually left?'

'About twenty-five and a good-looking chap. Slim, with hair the colour of marigolds and twinkling eyes. That was how I will always remember Augustus.'

Unexpectedly, tears appeared in Commodore's eyes and one ran down his cheek. 'Forgive me, Mr Rawlings, but as you can tell I was fond of the fellow. I even saw him off on his boat headed for New Zealand where he hoped to trade with the natives.'

'Did he take the dog with him?'

'Yes, decrepit though it had become. It was minus an eye and its ears were covered with rat bites. Still he took it. He was a strange fellow, with many misplaced loyalties. But I was devoted to him.'

'And you believe this newcomer is a fraud?'

'Sir, I would stake my life on it.'

'Is that because he doesn't resemble the old Augustus?'

'Not only that. His character is utterly changed. When I ask him questions about the past he says he cannot remember. When I ask him about Sam he just says that the creature died but without giving me any details. I tell you that this chap probably met Augustus and now is masquerading as him in order to get his mother's diamonds and his stepfather's money.'

The Apothecary would have answered, but at that moment a side door opened and a positive army of men walked in, all shouting and yelling at the tops of their voices. The session at the Rat Pitt had obviously ended for the day. A particularly obnoxious-looking dog bounced up to John and began to bark unnervingly.

'Go away,' he said between gritted teeth.

The owner, a fine-looking buck wearing the tightest pair of breeches that John had ever seen, came up and drawled, 'You don't like my dog, eh?'

'I don't like any dog until we have been properly introduced,' John replied evenly.

The youth grinned. 'Well, damme, I'll introduce you then. Sir, this is Tray. Tray, say how d'ye do to the nice man.'

Tray growled discouragingly and the Apothecary said, 'I really don't think he likes me. Excuse me but I'll pass on this proposal if you've no objection.'

The young man bowed, somewhat drunkenly, and said, 'Then I'll introduce myself. I'm Henry Tavener, well-known figure round Bristol. And you, Sir, are . . .?'

John rose and returned the greeting. 'John Rawlings of Nassau Street, London.'

'Ah, the big, bad city, eh? Do you have spectator sports there?'

As the reference was clearly to Rat Pitts, John decided to treat the remark seriously.

'We have thousands, Sir. Arenas in which the human race can leer and shout and show its ugly face at the cruelty meted out to defenceless animals. I personally long for the day when a young man, such as yourself, should be pitted against a team of bulls or bears for the delectation of the audience.'

Henry pulled a face, then said, 'I see that you are not my sort, Sir. I'll bid you good day.'

And with that he rejoined his bellowing crowd of friends, who were banging on the bar and demanding service.

Commodore let out a sigh and said, 'Don't be too hard on him, Mr Rawlings. He is just one of the many young men who hang round Bristol trying to find something to relieve their boredom.'

John felt terribly old as he replied, 'Has he thought of working?'

Commodore gave him a sideways grin and said, 'He couldn't possibly do that, Sir. You see, he is the adopted son of Lady Tavener, widow of Sir Charles Tavener.'

'And what did Sir Charles do?'

The black man gave him a sideways grin. 'He was Mayor of Bristol, Sir. Have I said enough?'

'Quite enough.' John smiled crookedly. 'Shall we get out of here? I think the place is getting a little overcrowded.'

Six

As they left the inn they were joined by Irish Tom, who had parked the coach at a nearby livery stables and gone into The Hatchet for a swift pint of porter.

'Oh, Sorrh, but there were a lively crowd in there.'

'Yes indeed. Now, Commodore, how are we going to get you home without traversing that terrible road again?'

'Don't you worry about me, Mr Rawlings. I came in a trap and left it in the care of a chap I know down on the docks.'

'Well, I could do with a little exercise. May we escort you?'

'Yes, indeed.'

The crowd on the quayside was immense. John felt as though he was in London's trading quarter as he thrust his way past hawkers selling everything that one could possibly imagine, even a skinny woman surrounded by children offering a baby for adoption to any kindly soul. Sailors were everywhere, paid off and heading towards the taverns, or working on the ships, hoisting or lowering the sails for inspection. Sledges, covered with goods for repair, swished past at speed, their use necessitated by the fact that carts were not allowed into the city. Everywhere was that great stink, of industry, of sewage, and of the population of this lively and bustling town.

Commodore marched through unperturbed, but Irish Tom, swearing a hearty oath, put his fists up at a sailor with a greasy little plait who trod on his foot.

'Leave it, Tom,' John ordered, and the coachman reluctantly obeyed.

A man with a red and green parrot on his shoulder was spinning a yarn for a small crowd which had gathered round him. John stopped to listen.

'. . . and there was waves, huge green monsters, aroaring down on our little ship which clung bravely on. Then the Cap'n spied an island through his telescope and shouted out, "That be it, boys. That be the place we're seeking" . . .'

There was a murmur of anticipation from the audience and John, moving on, threw a sixpence into the tin can which the ruffian had placed before him.

'You shouldn't pay rogues like that, Sorrh. He's probably never left Bristol in his life.'

'Oh come on, Tom. He's a good raconteur and that is enough.'

Further along the quay a monkey was doing tricks for the crowd. It had a small, sad face and was dressed in a red jacket and matching fez. John watched as it stood on its tiny hands and waved its little legs in the air. He wondered what it was thinking, or if it thought at all, beyond food and shelter, that is. Again he gave a coin, but this time the monkey itself brought a tin and held it out. The Apothecary only wished that Rose were with him because he knew that she and the small creature could have communicated in some strange way. And not only could she communicate with animals; he suddenly recalled the extraordinary bond that had existed between his daughter and the twins, even when they had been tiny babies.

When he thought of Rose's love for her brothers it brought the sudden sting of tears to his eyes and he had to look out at the water and pretend that the sun's dancing rays, which caused it to reflect a million brilliant lights, were the reason for the purposeful application of his handkerchief.

'Are you all right, Sorrh?' asked Tom.

'Yes, I was just thinking, that's all.'

'About the boys, I shouldn't wonder.'

John glanced at Commodore, but he had drawn a few paces in front of them and was talking to the man who had been watching the pony and trap for him.

'Yes, you're right. I miss them, you know.'

''Tis a wicked woman who will keep a father away from his sons.'

'But I walked out on her, Tom. She has every right to keep them from me.'

'If I was you, Sorrh – which I'm not saying I am, mind – I would go and see her and sort things out.'

'Even after all this time?'

'Yes, Sorrh. It's never too late on these types of occasions.'

But there their conversation had to end because Commodore was climbing into the trap and bidding them farewell.

'Thank you, my friend, for all the help you've given me about Augustus.'

'I don't know what else to say, Sir. I told you of his early life and how close we were. There really is nothing further I can add.'

'I suppose you have informed Mr Huxtable of your conclusions?'

'I have repeated them over and over again. But still he has that lingering doubt.'

'I wonder why that should be?'

'Perhaps,' Commdore said, somewhat sadly, 'it is out of a misplaced respect for his late wife's wishes.'

The Apothecary nodded. There was no answer to be made to a remark like that and he and Irish Tom watched as the slave drove off along the quayside, then turned as they heard a cheerful voice calling John by name. It was Samuel Foote, sauntering along, sprightly as you please, in a suit of striped strawberry corded silk with spangled buttons. He was accompanied by a fellow thespian dressed in a less spectacular fashion.

John swept off his hat and bowed and Irish Tom took a respectful step backwards. Mr Foote made a spectacular bow and said, 'Damme, but if it isn't young Rawlings. Just left your father, who allowed himself to be dipped in the healing waters. Allow me to introduce to you Sir John Hill, he's down here to take the waters and has obliged us with an appearance at the theatre.'

This time John bowed to the ground. Sir John was the kind of man that he admired more than any. Botanist, playwright, actor, novelist, journalist and, above all, apothecary, with his own line in herbal cures. Furthermore, he had been granted a medical degree at Edinburgh. All this and it was rumoured that he had had an affair with Peg Woffington. John's hat was literally and metaphorically off.

'Good day to you, Sir,' he said. 'I am delighted to make your acquaintance. I can truly say that I am an admirer of all your works.'

Hill smiled at him with bright eyes, their colour somewhat dimmed by the passing of the years and the amount of work they had had to endure.

'How d'you do?' he said.

'Mr Rawlings is a fellow apothecary,' said Foote, and laughed as if he had made some great joke.

'Well,' Hill replied, 'that makes two of us, does it not?'

They both laughed and John felt that he was surely missing something funny.

'Excuse me, gentlemen, but I fail to see the humour of the situation.'

Hill regarded him in a scholarly fashion. 'It was the mention of two of us, d'you see? Mr Foote and I once exchanged some acrimonious correspondence, but we made it up with a visit to the King's Arms in Covent Garden – just the two of us.'

John laughed dutifully, though in fact he failed to see anything amusing at all.

'Well, now, we are off to take a little liquid refreshment at The Rummer. Would you care to join us? You may bring your friend along, should you so wish.'

Irish Tom spoke up. 'Begging your pardon, gents, but I'll make meself scarce if you don't mind. I'm only a coachman and I doubt I could keep up with your conversation.'

Samuel Foote said with dignity, 'Your station in life means little to me, my friend. In my profession I mix with gamblers, whores and even Irishmen. I would be pleased to spend some time in your company and listen to your melodious voice, which I will then proceed to imitate.'

And he did just that, taking off Tom's way of speaking to within an inch. The four men burst out laughing and John felt how marvellous it was to be alive, to have made friends with a man like Foote, to have met someone as celebrated as Sir John Hill, and to have a servant as rich in life and experience as Irish Tom.

'Well, now, I doubt me mother would have known the difference,' said the coachman, applying a red spotted handkerchief to his watering eyes.

'Oh, sure and she would not,' said Foote, and his art of mimicry was so accurate that John laughed all over again and let out a great whoop of joy. At which Foote burst into an impromptu jig, somewhat hampered by the fact he only had one leg.

Later, when the three men were seated in The Rummer – Irish Tom having excused himself to go and check on the coach – they fell to talking. The first thing they discussed was the fact that the inn was packed with the dockside riff raff and intelligentsia. Sailors, dockers, great mountainous fellows with hands like hams and arms like bellows thronged the bar, and dotted among them were earnest-looking men in sombre suits, heads together, talking about the price of rum, or sugar, or slaves. Some looked despondent because their ships were late into port; others rubbed their hands with relish that their vessels, complete with suffering human cargoes, had arrived.

Foote ran his canny little eyes over the merchants and said in a broad Bristolian drawl, 'I am so upset that half my blacks died on the way here. We had to chuck overboard all the corpses – and the near corpses as well.'

Hill gave him an amused look and said, 'Keep your voice down. You'll get us thrown out.'

Foote put on a mincing air and said, 'Gadso, but you are a rude, rough fellow. Don't you lean on me, Sir, or I'll call the Constable.'

Sir John Hill rolled his eyes. 'Damme, but you can't take the man anywhere. He never knows when to stop.'

John leaned forward. 'Might I be serious for a moment, Mr Foote?'

'Certainly, dear boy,' the actor answered, suddenly avuncular. 'What is it you wish to say?'

'I would like to know a little more about your false leg. Is it true that you were injured in a riding accident and had to have the real leg amputated?'

'Yes. All quite true,' Foote answered, suddenly solemn, his features changing and an expression like that of a whipped dog appearing. 'It was meant to be a joke, d'you see? Prince Edward was there and laid wagers among his friends as to how long I could stay on the back of his mettlesome horse. Anyway, I mounted the beast which immediately reared and threw me out of the saddle and onto the granite cobbles below.'

'God's life! What did you do?'

'Scream,' Foote answered promptly. 'Very loudly.'

'Who attended you?'

'William Bromfield, the Prince's own surgeon and a devotee of the methods of the great Hunter brothers.'

'William Hunter delivered my twin sons,' said John reflectively.

''Sblud. I did not know you were a married man, Sir.'

'I am a widower,' John answered, and left it at that, elaborating no further. Instead he asked another question.

'If I may make so bold, who designed your false leg, Mr Foote?'

'A puppeteer, would you believe? But he did me a great service in that it was articulated at the knee. The first of its kind.'

John gazed in amazement. 'And may I know the name of this genius?'

'Mr Addison of Hanover Street, Long Acre. You should look him up, Sir, if the same thing happens to you.'

Sir John spoke. 'It is the custom of Samuel to make light of everything. But I can assure you he went through great pain and stress at the time. It was a royal joke that failed miserably in my view.'

'But it bought me a theatre,' Foote answered wryly. 'The Theatre Royal in the Haymarket. A good exchange for a leg, eh, what?'

John Hill pulled a wry mouth and John Rawlings asked, 'Is that how they repaid you, Sir?'

'Yes, it is.'

Before he could say more, Sir John came in with, 'And did he not make the best of it! His character Sir Luke Limp reduced the audience to veritable howls of laughter. I admit chortling so much I split my waistcoat at the sides. You are a great fellow, Samuel Foote.'

Just for a moment, John saw all the months of pain that the actor had gone through in order to regain his mobility, before his face took on its usual expression of puckish good humour.

Sir John Hill turned to Rawlings.

'Tell me, Sir, am I mistaken that I have seen you several times in the public gallery at Sir John Fielding's courthouse?'

'Yes, indeed you have, Sir John.'

'And why would that be?'

For once John Rawlings was indiscreet and said, 'I occasionally work with him.'

Quick as a flying bird, Sam Foote asked, 'In what regard? Surely you are not a Runner? I'd swear your father said you were an apothecary.'

'So I am, Sir. I assist Sir John Fielding in other matters.'

Foote gave an enormous wink. 'I knew it the moment I saw you. I do believe, Sir, that you are a spy.'

For once John was totally confused. 'I . . . no, you are quite wrong. I merely discuss things with him . . . sometimes.'

'Enough said,' announced Sam Foote, tapping the side of his nose and rolling his eyes in a thoroughly suggestive manner. 'I wonder exactly what kind of things you have been discussing lately.'

It was useless. Lowering his voice, the Apothecary briefly outlined his real reason for visiting the Hotwell. Sir John Hill looked astonished; Sam looked wise.

'I think I know who you mean, Sir. That great fat oaf who frequents the theatre. He occupies a whole box on his own.'

'That's him,' John answered triumphantly. 'But is he who he says he is?'

'"'I love you my Gussie, but cannot say why, 'Tis not for your beauty or wit, What can it be for, Sir?' He made his reply, 'I've come here for what I can git,'" 'quoted Samuel with a wicked gleam.

'That just about sums it up,' John answered.

'Well, my friend, Sir John and I will keep our ears open and will report back to you any suspicious goings on.'

'I thank you both, gentlemen.' John stood up. 'And now, alas, I must leave you. It has truly been a pleasure to spend this time with you and to have the honour of meeting you, Sir John.'

Everyone bowed to everyone else and then John was out on the quay once more, not quite certain of his next move. What he wanted above all was to find people who had known Augustus in the old days, before he went to sea. During his conversation with Commodore, the name of The Seven Stars had come up as a place where Augustus had hung out in his early twenties, and now John made his way towards the great tower of St Mary Redclift. Near it, so he had been told, was the small hostelry where further information might – just might – be available. John entered the lowly lane with a sinking heart.

It was a stinking place, with medieval houses blocking out the sunlight and the smell of general filth hanging in the air like a malodorous vapour. Figures appeared in the gloom, scuttling about like rats. From a doorway a female voice called out, 'Two pennies a go, Mister.' John glanced and saw a shapeless hag with her skirts hoisted above her waist, exposing a dark triangle of coarse black hair which she was thrusting in his direction. With a shudder the Apothecary hurried on.

A stream of garbage ran down the centre of the lane, thick with every kind of imaginable stuff. John wondered if he were going to come out of this experience alive or at least with his health intact. He trod in something unspeakable and was forced to scrape his silver buckled shoes on the oily cobbles. And then at last he saw the ale house, small and dimly lit with candles. Beneath the sign reading The Seven Stars, John made his way inside.

It was a dingy place but relatively clean, which was more than could be said of the landlord, who had a cloth strapped round his middle which could have done with a thorough laundering.

'Yerse,' was his word of welcome.

'Do you have any wine?' John asked, thinking that any more ale would sink him.

The fellow let out a grunt resembling a laugh. 'What you think this place is? It ain't bleedin' Hotwell.'

'So I gather,' John answered. 'I'll have a pint of porter, please.'

'Bess,' the landlord called, and an elderly woman swaddled in clothes shuffled in from the depths of the place and regarded the Apothecary with a beady eye.

'Give this genl'man a drink, will yer.'

Trying to look as unobtrusive as possible, John accepted a tankard from Bess's grimy hands and went to sit in a dark corner. A figure reared out of the blackness opposite him.

'Who are you?' it growled gruffly.

God's blood, thought John, but aloud said, 'I am John Rawlings, an apothecary of Shug Lane, Piccadilly, London. Whom do I have the pleasure of addressing?'

'Never you mind,' answered the voice. 'What you doin' in this part of Bristol?'

John decided to take the plunge. 'I'm looking for a man called Augustus Bagot.'

'Why?'

John lied desperately. 'Because I have some information that might be of interest to him.'

'What would that be?'

'I am afraid that is personal. I could not reveal the secret to you.'

A staring black eye appeared from the gloom. 'Well, you've come to the right person. Gus used to lodge with me.'

'Really? When was that?'

A hand so ingrained with filth that John could barely look at it thrust itself forward. 'A bloke like you could afford to pay for such low down.'

'How do I know that you will tell me the truth?'

There was a rasping laugh. 'You'll just have to trust me, woncher.'

John produced two shillings from his pocket and placed them in the upturned palm. The man moved further forward on his bench and John could smell a body that had never been washed, together with evil breath and above all the stink of rot and decay. He involuntarily moved back.

'I'll want more than two shullin' for what I'm about to tell yer.'

John, somewhat reluctantly, produced another three and said, 'You had better make this good.'

There came the deep rumble of a chuckle. John's eyes, which had now adapted to the darkness, saw that the man was wearing a hole-ridden and no doubt flea-infested striped jersey and that his greasy hair was tied back in a pigtail. He was talking to someone who had once been a sailor.

'Ben's the name, your worship. Ben Bull, pressed into the Navy from this very establishment. That is till I got too old to be of service to them and they slung me out.'

'But surely there is a hospital to which you could have retired?'

Ben spat a yellow glob onto the floor. 'That old place in King Street? Why, I'd rather die of drink than set me foot in such a hell hole.'

John thought to himself that it wouldn't be long, judging by the smell of the man.

'Anway, I knew Gussie when he were just a lad. He had this dog, see, and his mother didn't care for the brute. Gus used to take it to the Rat Pitt and old Sam became a champion.'

'I know this already,' John answered. 'Tell me the next part of the story.'

The other man spat again. 'Gus was a bit of a rebel and eventually he ran away from home. I knew him from the Rat Pitt and I offered that he could come and live with me. Well, he moved in, in secret 'cos he didn't want his ma to find out, then I was pressed into the Navy and was at sea for three years.'

'I hope this is going to be worth five shillings.'

'When I comes 'ome again the lad was in bad trouble.'

Despite the rank bodily smells, John leant forward. 'What sort?'

A laugh full of spittle ran out. 'Chasin' the girls, he was.'

'Did he catch any of them?'

Another laugh, this one wheezy. 'Too many. In fact two of them gave him the Scarborough warning.'

'Two?'

'Aye, truth to tell he filled two cradles before he went to sea.'

'Did he take responsibility for either of these little bastards?'

Ben laughed for a third time. 'No, not our Gussie. A likeable enough fellow in his way but a precious ass for all that. He loved life and women and gambling but little else beside. In the end he went to trade with the settlers in New Zealand.'

'And that was the last you heard of him?'

'Yes, he just upped sticks and went, dog and all.'

John was tempted to ask whether Ben had heard any rumours of Gus's return, but thought better of it. Ben coughed disgustingly, then wiped his hand across his mouth and said, 'Was that worth the five shullin', governor?'

John tossed him another coin and said, 'What happened to the two children? What sex were they? Or don't you know?'

'I never found that out. About that time a ship sailed for the West Indies and I went on it. Then sailed back and then out again. It was six years before I saw Bristol once more.'

John got up. 'You have been very helpful. Thank you.'

Ben receded before his eyes, merging into the darkness, a bundle of rags that someone had thrown into a corner and forgotten all about. For all John knew, the old sailor could well stay there until the day he rotted away.

Seven

On returning to the Hotwell, John proceeded to the Long Room and there found his father, reading a newspaper, occasionally lowering it to reveal a pair of golden eyes hidden behind a pair of wire-framed spectacles, regarding with interest the woman sitting opposite him.

She was like a haystack blowing in a strong wind, constantly listing from side to side, her hair falling down from her cap and untidily moving round her shoulders, her arms flailing about in a series of apparently meaningless gestures as she talked incessantly to her companion, an elderly gentleman slumped in a Bath chair, lids falling down over desperately weary eyes.

'And then I said to Mrs Phoebe Lightpill, "Rahlly that was not a nice thing to do, my good man." What do you think of that, Sir Geoffrey?'

'Eh? What?' said the old fellow, struggling up from sleep.

'I said . . . Oh, never mind. I do wish you would listen sometimes.' She sighed loudly and dropped one of the many unfashionable scarves with which she adorned her person.

John stooped and picked it up for her, handing it back with a slight bow. 'I believe this is yours, Madam.'

She fluttered like a small gale. 'How clumsy of me. Thank you, Sir. Thank you indeed. I am the clumsiest woman on earth, you know. Oh why am I so clumsy?'

John bowed again and would have joined Sir Gabriel but the woman continued without check.

'But there now, I'm in a right how-do-you-do. I should have introduced myself. Miss Abigail Thorney, companion to Sir Geoffrey Lucas. I was a companion to his dear wife, Lady Effie, before she passed to the realm beyond. I know it is not considered the done thing for those of the gentle sex to be attendant upon gentlemen, but I am more of a nurse, if you follow my meaning.'

John was somewhat at a loss, but was just about to introduce himself when Sir Gabriel rose from his chair and spoke.

'Madam, allow me to present myself and my son to you. I am Gabriel Kent of Kensington and this is John Rawlings of Nassau Street, Soho. We hope to have the honour of your acquaintance.'

She rose and made a complicated movement which resembled a bell tent descending to the floor, from which position she had some difficulty rising. Sir Gabriel graciously extended a hand which she clutched with desperate fingers, giggling coyly all the while. The old gentleman finally woke up and called out, 'Damme, what's going on?'

John shouted into the old man's ear horn, 'We are introducing ourselves, Sir Geoffrey.'

'Producing what?'

'No, I said introducing.'

'Oh, leave it to me,' said Miss Abigail with resignation, and bellowed at Sir Geoffrey, 'These fine gentlemen come from London.'

'Oh good. I used to live there. In St James's Square. Do you know it?'

Sir Gabriel raised his ear trumpet in a gesture of companionship and the two elderly men sat shouting at one another, leaving John to converse with Abigail. Desperately seeking for something to say, he gratefully noticed Titania Groves from the corner of his eye.

'Ah ha, there is someone I recognise. Will you excuse me if I go and speak to her?'

Miss Thorney looked thoroughly put out and said grumpily, 'Ah yes, Miss Groves. I know her, of course. But then, who doesn't? She is quite the little flirt of the Hotwell, you know. But then I suppose we all were once upon a year.'

She sighed drearily and John, relieved in more ways than one to see the attractive Miss Groves, bowed and crossed the Long Room to greet the new arrival.

Much later that evening, when his father had retired for the night and the buzz surrounding the community visiting the Hotwell had died down to a mellow murmur, John and a few others strolled along the riverside walk. He was silent, locked in his thoughts. It seemed unlikely to him that the great oaf passing himself off as Augustus Bagot could be the same person that both Commodore and the old sailor remembered with a certain fondness – a wild, naughty young man who had owned a dirty dog called Sam and who had got at least two girls into trouble before running away to sea. Yet how to prove it? Admittedly the juvenile Augustus had had a birthmark on his buttocks. But short of demanding that the present Augustus bare all – a thought that made the Apothecary feel definitely nauseous – John could think of no other answer.

It was a silver night, the moon drenching the river and the fisherboats sailing quietly on its breeze-ruffled surface. The avenue of trees threw sable shadows of branches on to the walkway below, tracing delicate patterns of leaves beneath John's shoes, the buckles gleaming in the moonshine, the points of light dancing ahead of him as he walked along. There were not many people about at this hour of the night, a few going for a rapid constitutional, but mostly couples, many young and in love, whispering into each other's ears. And then John heard the sound of hurrying footsteps and turned to see Commodore trying to catch up with him. He stopped walking and the slave panted up to his side.

'Oh Mr Rawlings, the Master thought there was something else I should tell you.'

'How did you get here?' asked John, astonished to see him.

'I came down the steps, Sir, and I held my breath on every one.'

'Why did you do that?'

Commodore rolled his great dark eyes. 'Because of the danger, Sir. They are cut out of the rock and are always wet. I would never have risked them but I felt there was something further that I had to say to you.'

'About young Augustus?'

'Yes. Well, I know of one person locally who would remember him. But the present Mr Bagot refuses to call on him, says he is a scoundrel and a wastrel and refuses even to see him.'

'So who is this interesting man?'

'Sir Roland Tavener, Sir. A most respected member of our community, whose only fault seems to be that his late brother Charles beat young Augustus into a pulp over an argument concerning Sir Charles's sister.'

'I met an old sailor in Bristol who told me that Augustus went to live with him when he ran away from home. Apparently young Bagot was very free and easy with the ladies.'

Commodore's great set of white teeth flashed vividly in the moonlight. 'You could say that, Sir. I would not disagree.'

'Tell me exactly how old was Augustus when he ran away from home?'

'Fourteen years, Sir, just after he found that rough bit of canine.'

'And he got a place to live and enough money to support himself?'

'Oh Master Rawlings, as soon as he was inducted into the Rat Pitt he never looked back. Old dog Sam earned him a fortune. But still he remained living in squalor.'

'But if you knew where he was, why didn't his parents try to get him back?'

'Well, he never told me his actual address, said he wouldn't burden me with the knowledge. So when his parents went looking for him – and they tried repeatedly, believe me – he would disappear with some of his raggety friends and not emerge again until he knew the coast was clear.'

'Did he hate his mother and stepfather so much?'

'No, but he was a naughty character, though I forgave him everything. It was just that he enjoyed the freedom of not having to go to school and being his own master.'

'So is it true he sired a couple of little bastards before he left Bristol's shores?'

Commodore looked at the ground. 'I'm not rightly sure of the number, Sir. But he did mention to me that he had given at least two damsels a belly-bump.'

'And you don't know who these damsels were?'

'Have no idea, Master.'

But the bending away of Commodore's head and the fact that he kept his eyes firmly on the ground made John a little suspicious that there might be more to the yarn than he was being told. However, he let the matter rest for the time being.

'So what age was he when he finally sailed for New Zealand?'

'Twenty-five, Sir. He'd had his birthday about three weeks before and told me he was still full of hugmatee.'

John smiled, thinking how well Commodore had mastered the

English language, slang and all. He looked at the slave's broad countenance.

'Commodore, tell me the truth. You were devoted to young Augustus, weren't you?'

The black man wept, suddenly and silently. 'He and I were like brothers. I could not have survived the ordeal of my horrific journey here without his friendship. He was an impish boy, I admit that, but I loved him just the same. That is how I know this new man is an imposter.'

'How?'

'When he first arrived here at Clifton, all perfumed and powdered, smelling like a molly-mop's marriage, the better to cover the stink of his armpits no doubt, he cut me dead.'

'What do you mean exactly?'

'I answered the door to him, standing upright and straight as I have been taught to do. He walked past me, never even gave me a second glance. We had been as close as blood brothers and even though the years had flown by, I know he would have recognised me at once. He is a fraud, Master.'

At that moment they were interrupted by a late walker, whom, as he drew closer, John recognised as the tight-trousered buck from the Rat Pitt. He drew level with them and stopped.

'Damme, but don't I know you?' he said, staring at John.

'We met in Bristol, you were coming out of the Pitt,' came the dry reply.

A grin split the young man's features. 'Oh yes. You were the miching malicho who gave me a dirty look. I thought it rather funny.'

'I'm delighted you found it amusing. Personally I don't like the sight of a handsome man with his apparel hanging half off and looking as pleased with himself as a fiddler's friend.'

'Don't you now? Well, Sir, let me tell you something. I don't like strangers making remarks about my appearance, be damned if I do.'

And with that he let fly a blow to the Apothecary's chin that had John reeling on his feet. Commodore moved rapidly between them.

'Now, now, Master Henry, don't be so hasty. Master John is not the kind of man to deliver insults. He spoke in jest.'

John had expected a string of rhetoric to flow from Henry's lips, but he turned to Commodore with affection.

'You old nigger-nogger, now you're giving me a hard time. I thought I spotted you earlier in The Hatchet. Is this a friend of yours?'

'Mr Rawlings, young Master, is a gentleman from London and an associate of Mr Huxtable. And he ain't no damn fool.'

At this Henry burst out laughing, nudged Commodore in the ribs, and said, 'Then I'd better make my apologies.' He swept his hat from his head and said, 'Forgive me for hitting you hard, Sir. Trouble is I'm a peacock when it comes to my appearance.'

Slightly mollified, John said shortly, 'Apology accepted. I'm sorry if I caused offence.'

But Henry had already turned back to Commodore and was saying, 'And who did I see the other night hanging round the kitchen and flirting with our Venus?'

Commodore smiled. 'She is a very pretty young woman, Master Henry.'

'Well you are not to misbehave with her. She's my mother's special piccaninny.' Henry bowed to John and raised his hat. 'Evening, Sir. Please excuse the mill.' And he walked off as fast as he had come.

John stared after him. 'What a strange young man.'

Commodore grinned in the moonlight. 'A strange family altogether, Master.'

'What do you mean by that?

But the negro merely shrugged his shoulders and said, 'Nothing at all, Sir.'

John slept fitfully that night and was late to breakfast, finding Sir Gabriel already at his repast, sipping delicately from a cup of coffee. Talking to him across the space between the tables was a man of florid complexion with eyes that seemed buried like winkles in the sand. He gave the Apothecary a small, sharp glance as he approached.

Sir Gabriel waved his hand. 'My dear Sir, I do not know your name but may I present my son to you?'

'Certainly you may,' the other replied grandly, with a condescending nod of his small, bewigged head. 'But first let me present myself. I am Sir Roland Tavener, baronet.'

'And I am Gabriel Kent. My son, John Rawlings.'

Sir Roland gave another deep nod, then peered even more closely at John. 'You have a different surname, I notice. Why is that?'

John let Sir Gabriel explain.

'I adopted John when he was two years old. I was married to his mother.'

'Ah. My late brother adopted a son also, but he has turned out to be a right jackanapes. Gambling, women, drink, he has experimented with them all.'

'I think a lot of young men do,' Sir Gabriel answered wisely.

'Unless they are apprenticed,' put in the Apothecary, 'because then they do it secretly.'

Sir Gabriel laughed unashamedly, joined by Samuel Foote who had just entered the room to get some breakfast. Sir Roland looked disapproving and raised his newspaper high.

Foote cocked an eyebrow in his direction and murmured, 'So is my arse! What a stuffy old windbag.' He sat down at Sir Gabriel's table. 'Well, what news from the Rialto?'

John looked a little downcast. 'Nothing, really. Mr Huxtable's slave, Commodore, would swear that our friend is a fraud. But who would take a slave's word against that of a white man?'

The actor nodded. 'It will all be different one day, you mark me. But meanwhile, friend John, I would continue with your enquiries in Bristol. You'll unearth something one of these days. Let one of the Bristolians come forward and challenge him. That will make him sweat, I warrant.'

John turned to his father. 'I don't know what to do, Sir. As you know, this visit was only meant to last a few days, but it seems as if it is going to take much longer.'

Sir Gabriel sighed with elegance. 'My dear child, when has one of your enquiries ever taken less? I am happy here. The water suits me and Lady Dartington plays a damn fine hand at whist. I am prepared to stay until your puzzle is solved.'

'If I were you,' said Mr Foote wisely, 'I would borrow a costume from the theatre and traipse round Bristol dressed as a sailor or something of that sort. Take your coachman with you and dress him up as well.'

'Now that,' said John, 'is a very good idea indeed.'

Eight

Before he set his – or rather Samuel Foote's – plan into action, John decided to call on Mr Huxtable. But the problem was how to get there. Sir Gabriel had gone riding forth in the carriage and there seemed nothing for it but to tackle the steps. John had been informed that they started behind the Colonnade and, strolling round there, he suddenly came to a complete halt as his eye took in the terrifying sight before him. He had never had a head for heights and now he took a few steps back as he contemplated the steep climb upwards.

The steps themselves were crude, rough hewn out of the rock, and as far as John could see were suitable for climbing only by mountain goats with a strong will. Furthermore, they glistened with damp and John could imagine the feeling as his feet slipped from under him and he clung on to whatever was at hand. He stood staring at the steps, wondering if his visit to Mr Huxtable was really necessary, then deciding that it was. A street child came and stood next to him.

'Go on, Mister, why doncher?' the cheeky little swine enquired.

'Because I'm afraid,' John answered frankly.

'Wot? A young feller like you? Why, I could climb them in ten minutes.'

'Then pray do so,' John answered, stung.

'Tell yer wot. I'll help you up 'em for a shilling.'

'Make it sixpence and you've got an agreement.'

So up they went, John feeling like an old codger, with the child pushing him from behind, shouting, 'Don't look down, Mister, for the luv of Gawd.'

The Apothecary would not have lied if he had said that it was one of the most frightening experiences of his life. He reached the top and his stomach lurched as he glanced down at that terrifying gorge yawning below him, the river a slash of blue snaking at the bottom. With a cry of fright he collapsed into a sitting position to try and pull himself together.

The urchin stared at him, wide-eyed. 'There's no need to take on so, Mister. They're only steps. Now where's me sixpence? I've earned it.'

Wiping the sweat from his forehead, John fished in his pocket and handed the child a coin. The boy took it, tried it between his teeth, then scuttled down the steps like a rat. Groaning, the Apothecary got to his feet and made his way to Mr Huxtable's house.

Commodore answered the door, noticing the beads of perspiration on John's upper lip.

'Don't tell me you climbed the steps, Master?'

John nodded, still slightly out of breath.

'Now you understand what I meant when I descended them last night.'

'I don't know how you did it. I think I would have died of fright.'

The black man smiled. 'I didn't go back that way. I hitched a lift from a coach going to the theatre.'

'That was still a pretty steep walk.'

'Anything rather than the steps.'

John nodded. 'I came to see Mr Huxtable.'

'He is out, Sir. Has taken the carriage into Bristol. But *he's* here.' He jerked his head towards the sitting room.

John froze. 'He must not know that I am in touch with his stepfather. I'll go at once.'

But already a heavy voice was calling out, 'Who's there, Commodore?'

'Say it's someone looking for somewhere else,' John whispered, but already he could hear heavy plodding feet making their way to the hall. He turned and bolted out of the front door at top speed, leaving poor Commodore to sort out the situation as best he could.

Feeling quite worn out with the recent memory of being shoved up the steps and then nearly meeting Augustus face to face, John walked across the Downs, an invigorating and pleasant experience, and ended up at The Ostrich Inn. The place did particularly well on a Sunday when there were excursions from Bristol to the Downs for people to take the fresh air, play bowls, or to picnic on the slopes of Nightingale Valley among the grazing sheep. Today the place was almost empty, yet John detected an atmosphere as soon as he crossed the threshold. It was as if everyone was on tenterhooks, behaving in an unnatural way. Furthermore, the landlord looked especially clean and was wearing a new stock at his throat.

'Dressed very finely this morning, I declare,' John said jovially as he stepped up to the counter and ordered a pint of ale.

'We have great company in the snug,' the landlord answered in a whisper.

'Oh, do tell. Who is it?'

'The Marchioness of Tyninghame herself.'

John looked suitably impressed but was raking through his memory to try and recall the name . . . and failed.

'I am sorry, I don't know who that is. But forgive me, I am not local. Just a visitor to the Hotwell.'

'She is not local either. But her husband was. Apparently he was a bit brutal and she left him. He actually divorced her. But I say too much. It is never good to gossip about one's patrons.'

The case was coming back to John now. The Marquis of Tyninghame's divorce had been reported in the newspapers. His wife had run off and left him without saying a word; he subsequently remarried and had a large brood of eight children.

'Isn't she of foreign blood?' John asked, vaguely scrabbling at memory.

'The lady is Austrian and a great beauty,' the landlord answered with a smug little smile.

'How interesting. I hope I manage to get a look at her.'

'I doubt it. The snug has a private door.'

'Oh dear. Well, never mind. I'll just have to do without.'

But at that moment the door leading from the private room opened and the lady herself stood framed within, gazing about her with huge light-green eyes, one hand holding a reticule while the other absently stroked the head of a little black boy who proudly held the hem of her dress. The Apothecary snatched his hat off and made a deep bow, even though she was looking in the opposite direction.

'Where is my coachman?' She addressed the landlord in a voice deliciously foreign in its undertone.

'He stepped outside, my Lady. Can I help you at all?'

'Please, I would like a glass of brandy.'

And she retired into the snug again without even glancing in John's direction. Slightly daunted, he retired to a corner and contemplated his tankard of ale, thinking about the woman whom he had just seen. She reminded him of someone and after a few moments he realised that it was Elizabeth. They both had that air of cool detachment, yet with his mistress one always suspected that underneath lay a moody, passionate heart. With this woman one sensed fragility, a delicacy that could easily be destroyed by the ugliness of the world. John longed in that moment to meet her.

The outer door opened and this time in strode the coachman, red in the cheeks and puffing very slightly. It was obvious that he had been in search of the boghouse because there was a slight whiff of it about his greatcoat.

'Has the Lady wanted anything?' he asked.

'She asked for another brandy and I served her.'

'Why does she need brandy at this time of day?' asked John, determined to get into the conversation somehow or other.

The coachman turned to see who had spoken. 'How should I know?' he said in a rough voice.

'Sorry, I meant no offence,' the Apothecary answered, adopting a humble face. 'I just wondered if she were ill.'

'No, she's had a bit of a shock, that's all. A child ran out in front of the coach and we had to swerve to miss her. 'Twas nothing more than a jolt.'

'You wouldn't like me to attend her? I am an apothecary,' John answered hopefully.

The coachman snorted. 'Another would-be suitor, eh? My Lady has had her fill of 'em. It is highly unlikely she will want any more.' And with that he ostentatiously turned his back.

The inner door from the snug opened again and the little black boy rushed into the bar.

'Oh please help. My Lady is so poorly. I'm afraid she is dying.'

With one of his hare-like leaps, the Apothecary was on his feet and positively sprinting towards the snug room from which feeble moans were emanating.

'Madam,' he boomed impressively, 'fear not. I am an apothecary and have come to assist you.'

And so saying, he picked up the slumped figure of Lady Tyninghame and placed her back in her chair.

The very touch of her gave an impression of gentle delicacy. John felt that if he held her too tightly her bones would shatter beneath his hands. Yet, saying all that, there was a similarity to Elizabeth in her wonderful facial structure and full, slightly wordly lips. But there any likeness ended.

John loosened her jacket at the neckline and felt in his pocket for the smelling salts that he always carried. The coachman, who had followed him in, regarded him with suspicion.

'I am merely giving her smelling salts,' the Apothecary said over his shoulder.

But Lady Tyninghame was regaining consciousness and looking around her with a pair of remarkable eyes.

'I'm sorry,' she said. 'I felt so enfeebled.'

'No need to concern yourself, Madam. It happens to us all at some time or another.'

The green eyes fixed themselves on John and in their depths he saw a flicker of something indefinable.

'Thank you so much for your help. May I know your name, Sir?'

'John Rawlings, my Lady. Apothecary of Shug Lane, Piccadilly, London.'

'Goodness, what are you doing so far from home?'

'I am accompanying my father to the Hotwell. He is taking the waters.'

'I too am making my way there. We were coming round the long way from Bristol and a child ran into the road and I thought we were going to hit her. Of course my wonderful coachman shouted and she sped away. But it left me feeling faint. So foolish of me.'

She smiled guilelessly and John wondered how such a fragile creature could have even contemplated running away from her husband, however brutal he might have been.

'And you, Sir,' she went on. 'What are you doing in Clifton?'

'I went to visit an old friend but unfortunately he was out, so I retreated to this excellent inn.'

She smiled naughtily, an impish look flitting across her features. 'And how did you get here?'

'Madam, I climbed the steps and have never been more frightened in my life.'

'The steps?' she repeated.

'Yes,' John answered, chuckling a little at the thought of the child who had literally shoved him to the top. 'Two hundred of 'em. And each one steep and slippery, carved out of the rock face.'

She gave a little shudder but a minute later was smiling again. 'Allow me to introduce myself. I am Violetta Tyninghame. I was the Marchioness but my husband wanted rid of me and so now I am just known as Lady. His second wife became the Marchioness, you see.'

'Vaguely, yes,' John answered honestly.

'Maybe I will tell you the story one day,' she answered. 'And then again, maybe I won't. But now to more practical matters. Is it your intention to descend the steps once more? Or may I give you a lift to the Hotwell?'

John put his hand on his heart. 'Madam, I swear that I would walk to Bristol and come back via Rope Walk – even if it took me six hours – than ever face those dreadful steps again.'

She stood up and transformed instantly from the vulnerable little creature prone to fainting, to a woman of stature and good breeding. Looking every inch a *grande dame*, she ordered her coachman to take them down the precipitous track known as Granby Hill. Once more John found himself subjected to that terrifying carriage ride carved out of the rock face, and was pushed flat on his back with both legs raised in the air as the coach hurtled perpendicular down the side of that vicious slope. But having arrived breathlessly at Hotwell, he helped Lady Tyninghame from her carriage and proceeded to a small ale house where he ordered a large brandy and fell in company with the deliciously dandified Samuel Foote, preparing himself for the performance that evening.

Sir Gabriel declared himself a little tired and preferred not to accompany John to the theatre, which was as well, his son considered. The play was *The Lame Lover*, in which Foote appeared as Sir Luke Limp, swathed in lace and speaking in pretentious Macaroni patois. This had the effect of reducing the audience to a roar of enjoyment. It would have been too much for Sir Gabriel, but John appreciated it thoroughly and screamed with laughter, behaving much as he did back in his apprentice days. After the show, Foote had invited him backstage to collect the costumes that he and Irish Tom were to wear on their excursions into Bristol.

As John stepped through the stage door he fell in love all over again with the theatre's atmosphere, reminding him vividly as it did of his affair with the great Coralie Clive. The smell of make-up and snuffed candles, combined with sweat and unwashed costumes, brought vividly to his mind the times that he and Coralie had sworn never to part. And where had that vow ended? Coralie had married a title, had a dead husband and a troublesome daughter, while John had twin boys he never saw and a wild woman for a mistress. But for all that, the theatre and its wonders appealed to him enormously.

'Hey, Rawlings, over here.'

He turned round and saw Samuel Foote emerging from his dressing room, still dressed as Sir Luke Limp and still in character.

'Odds, my deah fellah,' he lisped, 'did you enjoy my poor offering or didst thou take strong liquor and sleep through the entire performance?'

'Sir, I shouted loud as any man present.'

'Oh good,' said Foote, and kissed the Apothecary on the cheek and then, for good measure, on the other one.

'Come with me to the wardrobe and we'll fix you up as a big a villain as ever the streets of Bristol did see.'

'Well, I don't know about that. Just a ruffian will do.'

The door to the costume department opened to reveal tight rows of garments thrust together as closely as a crowd at a race meeting. There seemed little semblance of order, but John guessed that the small size of the theatre had forced the owners to use every last inch of space. However some minimal efforts had been made to sort them and at least the female attire was separated from that of the male.

'Why don't you go dressed as a woman,' trilled Samuel, peering through a gauzy sleeve at John, who was growing slightly uneasy. Much as he admired Foote and thought him one of the most amusing actors around, his feelings began and ended there.

However, John laughed and said, 'I wouldn't know how to behave and I don't need any lessons from you, though I thank you all the same.'

'Well, that's me in my place,' answered the actor, reverting to his normal character and leaving Sir Luke Limp behind.

John felt greatly relieved as he had a growing conviction that Foote had somewhat molly-mop leanings. Not that he really cared. The man was so clever, so charming, so amusing that he liked him whatever the circumstance.

'Here, this will do for you,' shouted the actor and pulled out a well-worn costume in a vivid shade of canary. 'And this will do for your coachman.' This time he produced an extraordinary garment that looked as if it had once been worn by a frog.

'Do they have to be so bright?' asked the Apothecary, drawing back a step.

'Absolutely. Stand out in a crowd. No good slinking through life like a slug.'

'But I thought we were meant to be in disguise?'

'No better disguise than drawing attention to oneself. It's the only way, believe me.'

'Indeed I do,' answered the Apothecary, a grin breaking out. But at that moment the door opened and Irish Tom appeared, filling the frame and looking very much like the Irish chieftan Brian Boramha.

'The frog green outfit is for you,' said John, and his grin widened at the expression of horror on the coachman's face.

'I thought green for an Irishman,' giggled Mr Foote.

'Do you mind my asking, Sir, but what is it meant to be?'

'Oh, it's something or other from the Harlequinade. It's probably Pantaloon's suit.'

'And you expect me to walk round Bristol looking like some poor old wretch dragged out from the theatre?'

'Precisely. It will give you an air of authority.'

Dumbfounded, the Irishman stared at the actor, tried to find words, but ended up saying nothing. John interjected.

'He's got a wonderful costume for me. I'll resemble someone with a fatal attack of jaundice.'

'I don't know whether to laugh or cry, Sorrh,' said Tom in his Irish accent.

'Oh, laugh,' said Mr Foote, reverting to Sir Luke Limp. 'By gad, but you're a handsome Irish fellow, so you are. Can I tickle you with a shamrock? And as for me, Sir, well I can hop with any man in town, so you'd better watch your step.'

And with that Samuel Foote fluttered his eyelashes and minced from the room, leaving John and the coachman staring dumbstruck after him.

They drove back through a silvered night; the tide was in and John could hear the water lapping at the river's rocky banks as they finally made their way to Hotwell. Rather than go straight to his hotel he made his way to the Long Room to see what company might still be up and about, but the place was deserted and after a moment or two he started to walk up towards Cumberland Basin and the Gloucester Hotel. Then he heard it. A faint wheezing rasp as someone close to him drew in breath painfully.

'Hello. Who's there?' he whispered.

There was no reply but the sound continued unabated. The moon had gone in but John peered through the gloom and gradually his eyes picked out a great lumpy figure sitting on a bench and gasping for air.

'Mr Bagot?' he said.

The sound continued but the figure turned its head. 'Who is it?'

'Rawlings. John Rawlings. We met briefly t'other day. Can I help you?'

'No, no. I'm all right, man. I'm just a bit short on breath.'

'Take a whiff of this.'

And before the other could disagree, John had squeezed into a place on the bench beside him and produced his bottle of smelling salts. Augustus inhaled and then slightly swooned.

''Zounds, but I am fainting.'

'No you're not,' John answered firmly. 'Breathe in deeply. You'll feel better in a moment.'

Augustus reluctantly obeyed, making great gasping sounds followed by a monumental fit of coughing. John patted him on the back, quite firmly, and in the general heaving that followed a piece of paper fell from the large tunic that Augustus wore over his breeches. It was a small torn square and on it was some writing. John could not help it. He bent closer to read it and at that moment the moon came out. On it were scrawled the words: WE HEAR THAT YOU ARE BACK. WE'LL BE COMING SOON.

Involuntarily, John gulped. It would seem that Augustus Bagot's return had already been noted. And though not couched in threatening terms, the last four words sent a shiver through his entire body.

Nine

By the time the Apothecary fell into bed that night, the clock had struck midnight. He had helped the enormous hulk into his coach – or rather Mr Huxtable's coach – and seen them set off on the long way round, over the toll road then up across the Downs. He thought rather grimly that if the coach had set off up the steep track of Granby Hill it would have fallen off and plunged into the Gorge below, tipped over by the huge weight of Augustus.

He had walked back through the sleeping spa and been let into the hotel by the night porter, who was slumbering in a small lodge near the front door. After that he had crept to his room but once there he could not sleep. That odd feeling was upon him, the feeling that all was not well with the world, that unseen forces were at work. Much as he did not like Augustus, much as he thought that he was an imposter trading off Mr Huxtable's goodwill, for all that he wished the fellow no harm. John merely hoped that he could find sufficient evidence to face the fat man with the truth and see him on his way. He heard the great clock in the hall strike one before he fell into an uneasy sleep with strange distorted dreams of a coach hurtling backwards until it fell into the Avon Gorge and disappeared from sight.

Sir Gabriel seemed fresh as a daisy at breakfast the next morning, while John felt dreary and liverish. His father, however, appeared not to notice and burbled on.

'My dear, I have made arrangements today to visit the New Vaux Hall Gardens.'

'And what are they, pray?'

'They are apparently the place to visit. They are situated at Goldney House, where the owner – after whom the place is named – has worked for years on his gardens and grotto. He has built scenery and so on and so forth and apparently the gardens rival those of Vaux Hall itself.'

'Oh surely not.'

'Oh surely yes. Anyway, you can come and see them for yourself. I have made an appointment to go with the Honourable Titania and her mother. Perhaps that might tempt you.'

'It certainly does. At what time are you leaving?'

'I have asked Irish Tom to bring the coach outside at eleven o'clock.'

'I wonder – if it does not inconvenience you in any way – if I might after this borrow him for a day or so. I intend to plunge into Bristol's murkier depths to try and find some people who knew Augustus Bagot and, quite honestly, I do not care to do such a thing on my own.'

'No, no. You must not. Let Tom accompany you by all means.'

Sir Gabriel had lowered his newspaper and was looking at his son anxiously.

'Don't be so worried, Papa. I know how to take care of myself.'

'If only that were true, my boy. You have been in more scrapes than I have years, I fear.'

John smiled wryly. It was true enough. And his latest predicament of not being able to see his twin sons was never far from his thoughts. He deliberately changed the subject.

'Have you by any chance met Lady Tyninghame yet?'

'No, who is she?'

'I revived her from a fainting fit in The Ostrich Inn yesterday.'

'Good heavens.'

'She is stunningly beautiful, an elegant creature. Yet as fragile as glass.'

'How intriguing.'

'Apparently she was divorced by her husband, the Marquis of Tyninghame, who subsequently remarried so she is no longer the Marchioness . . .'

'I'm not so certain of the legality of that,' interrupted Sir Gabriel.

'Be that as it may, she is now known as Lady Tyninghame. And I wondered if you had seen her?'

'Not here, no. But I do remember the case you mentioned. It was well reported in the newspapers of the time. Did she not have some young lover – a deal younger than herself – that the Marquis found out about and consequently showed her the door?'

'I have no idea, Father. But it sounds highly credible. She is a lovely woman and I can imagine anyone losing their head over her.'

'I am bound to run into her. After all, this is such a small place.'

'I would like to see her again too.'

Sir Gabriel looked askance. 'Surely you have enough complications in your life, John. Don't get into any more trouble, I beg you.'

John actually blushed, the first time in many a year. 'No, it's not that. It's just that I found her rather . . . kind. That is all.'

His father raised his newspaper, but not before he had given his son a thoroughly reproving glance. Feeling duly chastened, John finished his breakfast in silence.

The season at Hotwell was drawing to a close, running from May to October. Bath followed it immediately and many visitors moved on, liking the town's formality after the rustic beauty of Hotwell. But this late September day was fine and beautiful and John sat beside Sir Gabriel, who was once more restored to a good humour, following the hired post chaise of Lady Dartington and Titania. They were all proceeding to the New Vaux Hall Gardens, John rather apathetically, remembering vividly the real thing and how he had first met Sir John Fielding after the unfortunate incident in the Dark Walk. He little thought that there would be any such attraction at Goldney House.

Somewhat to the Apothecary's amusement, the carriages pulled up before the house where an ancient man who announced himself as the gardener sold them a ticket at a shilling per head. He then proceeded to take the visitors round the gardens, complete with walks boasting painted scenery and ending with a visit to the grotto. John, who was standing with Titania slightly behind their respective parents, smiled with sophisticated amusement.

The grotto had been built below ground, reached by descending some steps, and consisted of three archways supported by four columns deeply encrusted with shells; in fact there were shells everywhere, hundreds – nay, thousands – of them. John, who had seen a good few grottoes in his time, thought it rather a sad place, but the ladies obviously enjoyed it and made little cooing sounds of delight.

In the midst of this crustacean fantasy there was a small statue perched in the middle of an archway made of even more shells. It appeared to be a seated Cupid with what looked like his bow across his knees, discreetly hiding anything that might offend the faint-hearted, one hand holding an urn out of which poured a pretty little waterfall, the tinkling of which filled the air.

'What do you think?' Titania asked in a whisper.

'Well, I've seen better – and there again I've seen worse,' John answered.

Titania giggled. 'It's not as good as the real Vaux Hall.'

'Somewhat limited by space, I think.'

But there the conversation ceased because the gardener who had escorted them as far as the grotto could be heard speaking in the distance.

'Why my Lady, how good it is to see you again. I thought you had left us for always. What happy chance brings you this way once more?'

The voice that answered him was soft and gentle, yet had an underlying firmness of tone. John recognised it immediately. It was Violetta Tyninghame who spoke.

'Ah, my dear old Sixsmith, how lovely to see you again. I wondered whether you would still be here. Now take me to Cupid's grotto, if you please. I was very happy there once.'

'That were a long time ago, my Lady.'

'Indeed it was. But indulge my little fancy, dear Sixsmith.'

Before one of the quartet listening could say a word, there was the sound of footsteps coming down the small staircase and a moment later all four turned slightly to see a perfect vision coming towards them. She was dressed in lilac, a lovely rustling fabric, topped by a gracious hat with purple plumes. Unaware that there were people already in her chosen place, she paused at the bottom step and stood gazing before descending and sweeping one of the most elegant curtseys that John could remember seeing.

Lady Dartington raised her quizzer and stared through it. 'I do not believe we are acquainted.'

The newcomer smiled. 'Allow me to present myself, Ma'am. I am Violetta Tyninghame.'

'Tyninghame? Tyninghame? Now where have I heard that name before?'

Titania interrupted. 'Oh, don't bother with that, Mama. How do you do, Mrs Tyninghame. I am Titania Groves.'

John stepped forward. 'I hope I find you well, Lady Tyninghame.'

She looked at him closely and John realised that it took her a second or two to place him. Then she said, 'Oh, Mr Rawlings, my saviour. I don't know how I would have managed without you.' Turning to the others she added, 'I felt very faint the other day and it was Mr Rawlings who brought me back to my senses.'

John bowed. 'May I present my father, Sir Gabriel Kent.'

'How do you do, Sir?'

In answer, Sir Gabriel raised her hand to his lips and bowed deeply. 'The pleasure is all mine, Lady Tyninghame.'

Lady Dartington decided to be munificent. 'Are you staying at the Hotwell, my Lady?'

'Yes, I have come to take the waters.'

'In that case may I interest you in a game of whist one evening?'

'That would be most delightful.'

'Do you have friends hereabouts?'

'No, I am quite alone,' Violetta answered, and John thought he could detect a note in her voice that struck him to the heart.

Sir Gabriel stepped forward. 'Should you require an escort to any social function then I would be most happy to oblige, Ma'am.'

'My thanks, Sir,' she answered, and dropped a small curtsey.

They left the grotto while Lady Tyninghame remained, staring wistfully at the Cupid and remembering, John imagined, where

she and the young lover who had ruined her marriage had long
ago exchanged secret vows.

Changing for the evening and putting on a suit of fuchsia-coloured
satin with a high-cut waistcoat stiff with silver embroidery, John
decided that this night he would flirt outrageously with the
Honourable Miss Groves. Looking in the mirror while he tied
his neckwear in a startling bow, he decided that he had been
on his own long enough, that his affair with Elizabeth di Lorenzi
had run its course, that he must look elsewhere or else drift
uncertainly towards middle-age and solitude. Yet deep down, in
his most secret heart-of-hearts, he knew that still one letter, one
call from her, and he would be running to Devon faster than a
greyhound. So he deliberately set out to amuse Titania and made
much of her during the supper which they ate in the Old Long
Room, under the direction of Mr Barton, a youngish man with
a somewhat pimply face hidden by a layer of enamel.

It was a Tuesday and thus the night of the ball, so the place
was well attended. Sir Gabriel, on arrival at the spa, had paid a
guinea, the season's subscription for attending as many dances as
he might wish. So tonight he arrived in style, together with Lady
Dartington and one or two other acquaintances whom he had
met since starting his visit to the Hotwell. On entering the Old
Long Room he had been bowed to very deeply by Mr Barton,
who, with the mincing steps of a dandy, had led the party to
their table. John and Titania, as two of the youngest people
present, had been placed together, a fact which pleased both of
them.

Despite his longing to change his way of life, the Apothecary
found himself in an odd mood, everything seeming dreamlike
and unreal. As he whirled through the country dances and cotillions, he had the odd sensation of standing outside himself and
looking down at his frenetic activity on the dance floor. He was
quite glad, in fact, when an interval came and he was able to sit
down once more. Drinking a glass of brandy-based punch, he
looked round the room.

There were several people missing, including Samuel Foote
and the ravishing Lady Tyninghame. Also absent was that great,
fat loose fish, Augustus Bagot, and neither was there any sign of

Mr Huxtable, though John knew he did not often frequent such affairs. There was a roll of drums and Mr Barton stepped forward and pronounced in a shrill voice that dancing would resume in ten minutes. John turned to Titania.

'I believe the shops are still open.'

'Yes, they remain open late here. There is still a great deal of custom, you see.'

'I feel like a breath of fresh air. Will you walk with me by the river?'

'I should like to visit the milliner's first.'

'Shall we make a polite exit?'

Titania curtseyed. 'It sounds delightful.'

Meaningful expressions came over the faces of the rest of the company when John asked permission to escort Miss Groves to the shops. Lady Dartington looked rather cold but said reluctantly, 'You may do so, Mr Rawlings, but she is to be back in thirty minutes, mind.'

'I promise to take care of her, Madam.'

'So I should hope, young man.'

It was another bright night, a definite chill in the air but the universe packed with stars. John looked up and felt slightly giddy, but Titania was enthusiastically pointing out the Plough and nestling closer to John's protective warmth as she did so. He felt an overwhelming urge to kiss her and did just that, quite lightly and then with a little more enthusiasm. She snuggled even closer.

'I liked that.'

'You're a naughty girl.'

'Yes, I am rather.'

He laughed at her without derision and she smiled back and, standing on tip-toe, kissed him on the cheek.

'You are the most fascinating man I have ever met.'

'You say that to all the boys. How old are you?'

'Twenty-one.'

'High time your mother found you a husband.'

'I'm not so sure that I want one, thank you,' Titania answered loftily.

They walked on to the Colonnade, a pretty row of shops set back in a semi-circle, with pillars supporting a roof so that customers could shop in comfort should the weather prove inclement. Titania gave a gasp of delight at the sight of a new hat displayed in the milliner's window and was just about to go in when the night was broken by a most peculiar sound. There was a distant cry – of alarm, John thought – and then a ghastly scream, the sound of which grew ever louder. Then right over their heads, on the roof of the Colonnade, there was a terrible thump as something landed. John looked up and saw the ceiling begin to crack and crumble, and before his amazed eyes the vast rear end of someone appeared. He saw a huge pair of red breeches, torn asunder to reveal a naked arse.

'Oh my!' exclaimed Titania, reeling slightly.

There was a further fracture and a little more of the body appeared. With a lurch of his stomach John looked up and was able to recognise the broad end of Augustus Bagot. In that instant he was also able to take in one further fact. The great behind sagged like two white moonstones, unstirred and untouched. There was no mark at all on the buttocks, no mole, no port wine stain, no nothing. Mr Huxtable's quasi-stepson was a posturing fraud.

With an effort John pulled himself together and shouted for a ladder, and at the same moment the door of the apothecary's shop opened and a ginger-headed man rushed out and yelled, 'What ho! Is anybody hurt? I heard a crash.'

John gave him a swift glance and saw a large young person with broad shoulders and a shock of carroty hair tied back with a bright blue bow.

'Who are you?' he asked.

'Who am I? I'm the blasted Constable, that's who. And I'm also the apothecary, overworked and decidedly depressed.'

The man's gaze went upwards, and as it did so a further large proportion of the roof came away in a little explosion of dust and powder which fell on the ground of the Colonnade. The body slumped through as if it were lying in a hammock.

'I'm an apothecary too,' John said quickly. 'And I am at your disposal should you need my services.'

'Can you help me get the body down?'

'Are you certain it is a body? That he's dead, I mean?'

'No, not yet. But if he's fallen down the steps I should think it is more than likely.'

As he spoke the words John felt himself grow cold. The man could only be speaking of the terrible flight that he had recently tried to climb, and remembered with a nasty feeling of fear his sheer terror as he had looked downwards and seen the horrific drop below him. But what could have induced anyone to mount or descend that ghastly staircase in the pitch dark? There was no time for further reflection as a ladder was found from somewhere and the ginger-headed apothecary began to climb upwards. As he did so there was a further loud crack as in a flurry of dust and flying mortar Augustus Bagot finally descended to the floor below.

That he was dead there could be no doubt. The neck had broken and the head was turned at a ridiculous angle to the body. The eyes were wide open, staring, and the tongue was lolling out of the mouth. It was enough to make one faint, which several women promptly did, and even the beautiful Titania gave a little shudder and went as if to swoon. John rushed to her side but she shook her head and whispered, 'See to the dead man – and move him away if you possibly can.'

In the end it took eight strong men, John included, to move Augustus from the scene of the fall and into the compounding room of the apothecary's shop. The two men then made an examination of the corpse, but not before they had introduced themselves.

'Excuse the informality,' said the ginger-haired man, bowing, his long apron creaking as he did so. 'My name is Gilbert Farr, and you are?'

'John Rawlings, of Shug Lane, Piccadilly, London. I am here to take the waters and I vaguely knew the dead man.'

'And so did I. He came into my shop once and asked for opium to ease his pain. I gave him short shrift and told him to go to Bristol to find it.'

'And did he?'

'I don't know. Perhaps.' Gilbert shrugged like a horse easing its shoulders. In fact he had an equine quality about him, resembling a big, friendly chestnut stallion.

In silence the two apothecaries examined the body, then at John's request and aided by Gilbert's apprentice and a burly fellow who came in from one of the many inns, they turned the corpse over. It was John's unlovely task to examine the buttocks at close quarters. It was a revolting job and the Apothecary, who had seen some hideous sights in his lifetime, literally heaved as he looked at the vast amount of unclean flesh. But it was as he had thought. There was no sign of a birthmark anywhere. Augustus Bagot had been an assumed name. The dead man's true identity was unknown.

Gilbert Farr ushered the others present out and locked the door of the compounding room behind him.

'What next?' asked John.

'Now I write to the coroner and ask him to collect the body. I'll send the letter to Bristol tonight.'

'Tell me, are you the Constable for the whole city?'

Gilbert burst out laughing. 'No, thank God. It is only this small place of Hotwell that I look after. But it's enough. Did you know that two thousand people come here at the height of the season?'

'I hadn't realised it was quite so popular.'

Gilbert laughed again, a deep bellow. 'No, the constable of Bristol is frightfully grand. None of the citizens want to do it so they have a professional. He is puffed with pride.' He looked at his fob watch. 'Goodness, is it that late? Let's go for a drink in The Bear. Oh, but I forgot. You're with company.'

'I sent Titania home with a woman of her acquaintance so I am free as a bird. Yes, I'd love to.'

'What ho. I didn't envy you when you examined the victim's posterior. Were you looking for something?'

'Yes,' answered John.

'And did you find it?'

'No, Sir, it was not there. And tomorrow I must call on Mr Huxtable of Clifton to tell him that his so-called stepson was a fraud.'

'Good gracious,' said Gilbert, stepping back a pace or two. 'That sounds serious.'

'I think it is, very serious indeed.'

Ten

'I see,' said Horatio Huxtable, frowning very slightly and laying down his copy of *The Tatler*. 'You say that Augustus's claim was fraudulent?'

'Indeed I do, Sir.'

'And that he is dead?'

'I examined the body myself last night. And furthermore I examined the buttocks and there was not a sign of a birthmark anywhere.'

'I knew it,' said Commodore, who was standing in a respectful attitude by the door.

'So who was the imposter?'

John shook his head. 'I don't know, Mr Huxtable. But I intend to find out.'

'And you say he fell down the steps?'

'It would appear so, though I ask myself who would be lunatic enough to climb down them at night.'

'Who indeed?'

The Apothecary turned to glance at Commodore, who winked. 'I would like to examine those steps. Will you come with me? That is if you will excuse your servant, Mr Huxtable?'

'Of course I will excuse him. He told me from the start that that great fat oaf was a fraud – and now he has been proved right.'

Commodore bowed first to his master and then to John. 'It will be my pleasure.'

They left the house well wrapped against the day because there was a wind which had a biting tongue. It was the first week of October and the season was coming to an end. Soon most of the population of the Hotwell would move on to Bath and take the waters there, sacrificing the wild and rugged beauty of the alpine scenery for the indoor formality of the pretty town. But now John, even though his stomach seethed at the thought of those terrible, evil steps, was thinking that he must visit them once more. It was his duty to have a look just to see if any evidence had been left there. He turned to Commodore.

'I'm frightened, my friend.'

'So am I, Sir. There have been a lot of nasty accidents on them; I can tell you I was terrified out of my wits the other night as I came down. When I was a boy a little child went hurtling. He was climbing up but missed his footing and fell. Fortunately his father was a few steps behind him and somehow managed to break the boy's fall. Otherwise he would have been quite dead.'

'But has anybody actually been killed on them? Other than Augustus, I mean.'

'Yes, Sir. Several men and one woman. She, poor creature, was attempting to save time and climbed up in her long clothes, tripped and fell, gashing her head open on the bottom step.'

John shivered. 'Don't tell me any more. I've heard quite enough.'

The two men had been walking downhill since they had left the Huxtable home and had finally arrived at the rough path leading to the steps. John blenched at the sight of them and involuntarily stepped back. It was Commodore who put his foot on the top step and swore as his shoe slipped from under him and he fell backwards, landing hard on his bottom. John helped him up.

'What happened?'

'I don't really know. The top step seemed extra slippery, that's all.'

The Apothecary knelt down. 'Commodore, hold my legs and whatever you do, don't let go.'

He leant forward and felt the surface of the top step, then the second and the third. Finally, he went at full stretch and examined the fourth. Then for one moment he gazed the length of the treacherous flight and started to shake.

'Commodore, pull me up,' he yelled, and closed his eyes as the slave, with a terrific show of strength, obeyed his command. Feeling like a reeled-in fish, John got to his feet and stood gasping.

'Are you all right, Sir?'

'Yes, it was just the shock of looking down, that's all.'

'Did you find anything?'

'Yes. The top three steps have been greased with something.

Some kind of fatty substance. Taking a guess I would say it's goose grease.'

'Do you mean that a trap was set?'

'Yes, either for Augustus – or should I say Mr Unknown – or for someone else. But I think it has to be him because why would anyone else try to ascend or descend at night and in the dark?'

Commodore flashed a wonderful grin. 'You didn't hear me say this, Sir, but I raise my hat to them. They have rid the world of a thoroughly evil pest.'

'That's as may be, but I shall still have to report this to the Constable.'

'One must do one's duty, Sir,' the slave replied impassively.

John put his handkerchief into his pocket. He had rubbed the steps quite vigorously and some of the substance still clung to the fabric. He had a sample he could show to Gilbert Farr and discuss what it might actually be, but at the moment he intended to say nothing further. Stirring at the very back of his mind was a picture of Commodore's rapturous smile.

'How about a drink at The Ostrich, my friend? I think we need it after that experience.'

They walked across the Downs together, but as they entered the inn John was vividly reminded of that beautiful creature Lady Tyninghame. He turned to Commodore.

'Do you know anything about a Lady Tyninghame? I was able to be of some assistance to her in this very place t'other day.'

'Why, what was the matter with her?'

'Her coachman said that they had almost run a child down but the girl fortunately escaped with her life at the last second. The Lady felt very faint as a result.'

The black man turned his head so that John could only glimpse his face. He saw that Commodore was far away, locked in some secret thought. He wondered what it could be that held him in such a dark study. Eventually the slave turned to him, his normal expression returned.

'Enough to frighten anyone, I should imagine.'

'Yes. But tell me, do you know anything of the woman?'

'Oh, I most certainly do. I was two years old when I came off the slave ship and went straight to Mrs Vale's house, as Mrs Bagot formerly was. I can remember talk of the Marchioness when I was a small child. It seemed her husband was brutal and they say his brutality got worse when she was unable to produce an heir. But she was very popular with the people of Bristol, giving money to the poor and generally doing good works. They were all very sorry when he divorced her.'

'Where did they live?'

'Just outside the town, in a great house overlooking the sea. Near where the River Trym joins the Avon. It was called Bishopsea Abbas. I went there once.'

John looked up in surprise. 'Did you?'

'Yes. The Marchioness had come across Mrs Vale giving charity in Bristol and she invited her and Gussy to tea. We went by coach and bumped and jolted all the way. I was eight years old and at the height of my powers as a black boy. The Marchioness admired me and made much of a fuss of my fine clothes and sweet face. Then she let me play with her little black servant, Samson.'

'It sounds a pretty scene,' said John without sarcasm.

'It was. I still see Samson occasionally.'

'What happened to him?'

'He stayed on as a servant in the house when he reached puberty. After the divorce he left and went to work in Bristol. He was assisting in a grocer's shop when I last saw him.'

John nodded, sipping his brandy, thinking of all the many threads that were beginning to run through the story of the true Augustus Bagot and the identity of the false one. He shook his head. Whoever had, in the darkness, greased the top three steps knowing that Mr Unknown would tread on them had been doing the world a favour, there was no doubt about that. Yet John owed it to Sir John Fielding, who had spoken to him long and seriously on the subject, to report the matter to Gilbert Farr, the jolly young Constable of the Hotwell. John put down his glass.

'Commodore, I've got work to do. I must take the chaise to Bristol and then back to Hotwell.'

The black man gave his delicious grin. 'Not risking the steps, Sir?'

'No,' answered the Apothecary. 'I would rather be dead.'

Gilbert's shop was packed with customers. There were ladies asking for something for the vapours, young gentlemen whispering for condoms, macaronis calling loudly for something to relieve the headache. It was like the Tower of Babel and John listened, much amused, thinking that nothing changed, be it Shug Lane or the Hotwell. The world was the world, wherever or how far one travelled. With this thought in mind he moved to the back of the shop, looking about him with curiosity, until the crowd cleared. There was finally a lull and Gilbert called out, 'John – may I address you as such? – what brings you here?'

'I have something important to tell you; in fact two things.'

'Come into my compounding room. It's all right, the body has gone. The coroner sent his cart this morning.'

John grinned despite himself. 'I hope the bottom was reinforced.'

'I must confess it sagged a bit. Now come in, come in. Take a seat on that stool. Davy can look after the shop.'

Gilbert's apprentice, a smaller replica of his master, bowed to John and went through the dividing door.

'If you think we are alike, he is my brother. An unusual arrangement but we are obeying our father's wishes. Now what do you have to tell me?'

'Two things. The first of which I would have mentioned but was so busy dealing with the remains of poor Mr Unknown that it went out of my head completely. I found him the other night, sitting in a paroxysm of fear, heaving and shaking like a jelly. A note fell out of his pocket. On it were written the words "We hear that you are back. We'll be coming soon". Or something like that anyway.'

''Zounds! Do you mean that he had enemies?'

'So it would appear.'

Gilbert sighed, long and deep. 'Oh dear. I haven't really the time for this. Are you saying that you believe he was murdered?'

'I'm almost certain of it.' And with that the Apothecary produced his handkerchief and handed it to Gilbert.

'I'm afraid I don't understand.'

'It contains a substance that I rubbed off the top three steps of that terrible stairway carved in the rock.'

Gilbert sniffed, then tasted it. 'It's fat of some kind,' he said. 'Goose or duck grease.'

'To which even the meanest kitchen hand would have access.'

'You're right.' He scratched his head. 'I don't know how I am going to investigate this. I think I'll have to call in the Constable from Bristol.'

John nodded. 'That would probably be wise, but can you leave it for a few days? You see . . .' And then he told Gilbert of his plan to investigate the lowlife of the city to try to find anyone who had known the real Augustus Bagot.

'He also had children, you know. They say, if you'll forgive the pun, that he scattered his seed most liberally.'

Gilbert looked slightly amused. 'Did he really? Naughty fellow.'

'So there must be several outraged mothers and fathers – to say nothing of ruined daughters – who would like to see his head on a spike.'

Gilbert whistled between his teeth. 'I don't think you'll find too many angry parents in Bristol. It's a divided society, you know. Some very rich, others living on what they can steal. A bastard child is usually thrown out to die unless someone with a kindly heart should find it.'

'Is there nothing in between?'

'Yes, people like me who strive hard to make a living and then are taxed out of all sense.' He flashed a smile, lighting up his foxy features. 'And those who grumble about everything.'

John laughed as well, then said, 'It strikes me that the real Augustus must have been quite a decent sort of chap, the sort that one could rub along with, but the man who took his place was quite the opposite. I wonder whether he ever met the real one. But then he must have done or he wouldn't have dared try an impersonation of this magnitude.'

'But what did Mr Unknown stand to gain?'

'His mother's diamonds.'

'And that is all?' asked Gilbert, thunderstruck.

'They might be worth a mint.'

'And then again they might not.'

'There is also the fact that Mr Huxtable is not in the first flush of youth and might presumably leave his house and fortune to his erring stepson.'

Gilbert shook his head. 'But you say that the old man distrusted him from the start. Even sent for you to try and find the truth.'

John raised a dark eyebrow. 'I don't quite like the use of the word "even". You make it sound as if I were some kind of last resort.'

Gilbert, far from looking abashed, roared with laughter. 'Hardly that. Why, you'll have solved the case in a few days. But tell me, you don't propose to wander Bristol's underworld on your own?'

'My coachman will be with me. And before you ask, he looks like an Irish chieftan, a massive ox of a man.'

'Then that's as well.'

There was a shout from the shop. 'Mr Farr, Sir. I think you had better come. The place is full of customers.'

John stood up. 'It has been a most enlightening conversation. Thank you for your time.'

'Don't mention it,' Gilbert replied breezily, and with that he bowed to John and made his way back into the shop.

Eleven

The next morning John and Irish Tom took a boat into the city of Bristol. This was a small craft similar to the ferry that rowed passengers to and from the opposite bank. But this particular form of transport called in at the Hotwell when the tide was high and took its passengers past the confluence with the Frome into the Bristol docks. Dressed roughly, with new costumes supplied by the ever-helpful actor, the couple received barely more than a glance from the other occupants who were, John judged, mostly local traders.

As they rowed along he glanced up at the passing scenery and drew breath. Stupendous walls of rock rose on either side of the river, the highest being known as St Vincent, atop which stood a working pepper mill. Thick, dark foliage hung over the sides of the towering cliffs and in places John could glimpse flowery dells, while sheep grazed contentedly on the lower slopes. In the air was the high, tense smell of salt, and overhead seagulls wheeled and cried, swooping down to catch a fish and majestically rising again on their huge white wings. A thrill of excitement ran through him as he gazed and listened to the sounds of the river:

the rhythmic pulling of the oars, creaking in their rowlocks, the shouting of sailors across the green water, the chatter of the other passengers. He turned to Tom.

'I feel as if we are embarking on a great adventure,' he whispered.

The Irishman turned on him a rueful grin. 'Provided we can keep ourselves out of danger, Sorrh.'

'I think for the sake of appearances you had better call me John.'

'I will do that indeed, Sorrh.'

John merely shook his head at him and grinned.

They passed the ferry boat, rowed by a roguish fellow with a mop of flying dark curls fastened down by a scarlet bandana. He waved to the other boat and some of the passengers, John included, waved back. The Apothecary had rarely felt in higher spirits.

On landing, they made their way to The Seven Stars, a small but busy inn that lay at the heart of the commercial part of the city. Here they sat unobtrusively and listened to the chat that was going on all around them. The voices mixed in a mighty melange of accents, for it seemed that every nationality in the world was present. The great trading ships brought in their sailors and it was just as likely that one would hear a conversation in Russian as hear the Bristol dialect be spoken. But above all these guttural and incomprehensible languages, one voice rose high and clear.

'. . . and as I was saying to the Mayor of Bristol t'other day . . .'

A bell rang in John's head. Somewhere in his distant memory something stirred into life. He motioned Tom to remain silent and leant forward to listen.

'. . . one can't be too careful where one dines these days. I mean to say anyone can afford an ordinary, so one could be sitting with any thief or rogue. No, I tell you, my dear Sir, that I always dine at a more expensive type of establishment, so I do.'

Into John's mind came the mental picture of a watering ginger eye. He strained his memory to find the man who owned such.

'Allow me to be the first to inform you that Mrs Rudhall – she being the lady who lives at number fifteen, Park Street, in Clifton, don't you know – had her money lifted from her while she sat at dinner in Mrs Trinder's eating house in the Hotwell.'

The murder of the Earl of St Austell came thundering hideously into John's memory. Those two dreadful creatures in poke bonnets and brown shifts who had shot repeatedly into the crowd of merrymakers. And then, finally, came the name. He rose to his feet.

'Mr Pendleton?' he enquired in a polite tone. 'Mr Benedict Pendleton?'

The man with the highfalutin voice stopped short.

'Do I know you, Sir?' he asked, raising a dilapidated quizzer and peering through it until his ginger eyes appeared like two huge orbs.

John bowed. 'I believe we met once in the park. And then again, just possibly, in Devon.'

The other flapped a large white hand. 'Oh, la Sir, but 'tis almost impossible to recognise you. You're all pricked up like a villain, so you are. You quite frightened the life out of me.'

John bowed again. 'I do apologise. I am on my way to a costume ball. May I join your table, Sir?'

Pendleton nodded his head in ascent and a smell of sweet pomade reached John's nostrils. It was coming from the man's wig and once again triggered something in John's memory which he could not unfortunately place.

'I was just saying to my friend here . . .'

John bowed to the other person present who was made up like a poor man's macaroni.

'. . . that Bristol is hardly fit to walk abroad in. So full of villainous foreigners and the poorer class of person. One could be set upon at any moment.'

John could not help it. His infamous sideways grin appeared.

'It's nothing to smile about, Sir. I vow and declare one takes one's life in one's hands when one walks by the docks.'

'What are you doing out of London, if I may enquire?'

'I came to the Hotwell for the sake of my health, but met one or two old friends in Bristol and have been here ever since.'

'Do you go to Devon much these days?' asked John, carefully watching the man's face.

It was difficult to read because of the enamel make-up smothered thereon, but there could be no doubt that a fine sheen of sweat had appeared beneath the maquillage.

There was a small silence before Pendleton answered brightly,

'La, no. All my old contacts have gone. I am now quite the Bristolian.'

'But I could have sworn I saw you at the Earl of St Austell's wedding.' John was taking a leap in the dark and knew it, but the result was worse – far worse – than he could possibly have imagined. Pendleton suddenly clutched his chest and let out a groan of pain while a trickle of black kohl ran from one of his spicy eyes. As John watched in stupefied horror, the man fell forward onto the table in front of him. His companion, the elderly macaroni, leapt to his feet, pursed his carmined lips and uttered a little shriek. But he was not quite so quick as the Apothecary, who realising that something was terribly wrong rushed to Pendleton's side.

'Do you have pain in your arms?' he said, close to the man's ear.

'Yes, oh yes,' came an agonised whisper.

John wheeled round and shouted to Irish Tom. 'Tom, can you sprint to the nearest apothecary's and get some distilled water of lavender. And please be quick about it.'

He turned back to Benedict, loosening his grubby cravat and at the same time looking round frantically for the landlord. A very small man in a greasy apron eventually came over and said, 'Oh dear.'

'I'm afraid it is. Have you got a private room where we could carry him? I believe he's having a heart attack.'

'My, my,' said the little landlord, unperturbed. 'Follow me.'

John and the macaroni, who puffed and blew enormously, managed to drag poor Benedict Pendleton into a tiny snug, where John laid him out flat upon the floor, putting some rather worn cushions under his head. Pendleton opened his eyes, now totally ringed with black where he had wept with pain.

'Am I dying?' he gasped.

'I don't know,' John answered truthfully. 'But I have sent for some medicine which should be here very soon. That will help you.'

The Apothecary meanwhile ushered out the macaroni who was uttering constant small shrieks, and tried to tidy up the ravaged face of the sick man. Without his enamel, kohl and carmine, the beau looked even worse. His skin was ravaged with pits and there were bags beneath his tired old eyes. He was infinitely pathetic and John felt a moment of intense pity for the poor man, even if what he suspected was true.

Irish Tom came in, panting and out of breath, and thrust a bottle into John's hand together with some pads of lint. The Apothecary saturated several and laid them on Benedict's temples and under his nostrils, hoping that this might revive him. But it was to no avail. He grew weaker if anything.

'Is he slipping away?' asked Tom in a whisper.

'He's having a massive heart attack,' John whispered back. 'If I'd been called to him in London I would have taken a goodly dose of the tincture of hawthorn berries. In fact it may not be too late to administer it. Tom, show your kindness and go to that apothecary's shop again.'

Without a word of protest the coachman hurried out once more and John realised that he was feeling truly sorry for the afflicted man. A silence followed Tom's departure, broken only by the rasping breathing of the invalid. Then a hand reached out and clasped John Rawlings's shirt.

'Hear my confession, I beg of you.'

'But I am not a priest.'

'No matter. I must speak before I leave the world. I can't go unshriven.'

John looked round desperately. There was nobody remotely resembling a man of the cloth in sight and no time to send for one either. He leant over to hear the dying man's words. Most of it he had guessed correctly. Benedict had been a run-down, seedy, small-time crook, involved in petty theft and confidence tricks. His life's ambition had been to steal the Crown Jewels, but it had been a pipe dream only and he had never ventured further than the Tower's gates. His favourite ploy was to approach people in the parks of London and relieve them of their watches. But things had gone from bad to worse and he had eventually stooped to being a paid assassin.

'I know,' John said quietly. 'I was there when you shot the Earl of St Austell.'

Benedict's face became even more ravaged.

'I was starving and had fallen in with bad company.'

'Do you mean the ill-named Herman Cushen?'

Benedict's voice was very feeble now. 'Yes, he was behind it all.'

'I know he did not pay for the shooting,' John said quietly, but there was no answer. In fact so quiet was the wretched old beau that John actually put his ear to his chest to hear if there was a heartbeat. There was. Faint but nonetheless there.

'Where is Herman now?' John asked quietly.

Shockingly, Benedict's eyes opened fully. 'Here. In Bristol.'

'Whereabouts?'

The dying beau laughed, a ghastly sound because the death rattle was already in it. He said two words with his final breath – 'Queer bitch' – and then his miserable life came to an end, quickly and without further ado. John closed the staring ginger eyes and said, 'God, please forgive him his sins,' rather swiftly, because he was not at all sure of anything, then turned as the large and somehow terribly comforting frame of Irish Tom reappeared.

Several brandies later, Tom said, 'I know you've told me the story before, but could you tell me again, just to refresh my memory?'

John smiled at him, a little of his tiredness beginning to show. 'It was while I was staying in Devon, just after my sons were born. I was invited to the wedding of Miranda Tremayne and the elderly Earl of St Austell. Well, two assassins broke into the wedding feast and shot him dead – and several other people as well. They were dressed as women but it was fairly obvious that they were men in petticoats. To cut the story short, one of them was a young chap, later identified as Herman Cushen, who then went on the run and hasn't been seen since. The other was the man who has just died, Benedict Pendleton.'

'But how did you guess, Sorrh – I mean, John? What gave it away that he was one of the killers?'

'Little things. The smell of pomade, a suspicion that I had seen the fellow before somewhere, his mannerisms. Pure luck really.'

'I think it is a wondrous trick you have.'

'I've a good memory, that's all.'

'Well, I think it is time we explored the night life of Bristol, if it's all the same with you, John.'

The Apothecary stood up and stretched. He had left The Seven Stars once the physician had arrived, rather shaken by the day's events, and now wanted nothing more than a nice clean bed somewhere. But this was obviously something that was not going to happen. Irish Tom had the bit between his teeth and was ready to venture amongst the riff and the raff of Bristol, keen as a hound with a scent on the trail of the real Augustus Bagot.

They left the ale house in which they had been sitting and made their way towards the docks. They followed two macaronis who minced along in front of them, their three-foot wigs topped by tiny *chapeau bras*.

'Glory be to God and all the archangels,' said Tom, quite loudly. 'Have you ever seen such caricatures?'

'Keep your voice down,' answered John, *sotto voce*.

One of the pair, overhearing, turned to stare, and John was dazzled by the amount of make-up the fellow wore; everything that the paintbrush could throw had been plastered on his face, including a large black beauty spot.

'Are you addressing me?' he shrilled.

'No, no,' John answered hastily. 'My coach – I mean, my friend – was merely remarking on the coldness of the evening.'

The macaroni approached and as he drew nearer John could see that he was quite middle-aged. Raising his quizzing glass he stared at John long and hard.

'Look Gerard, I've think we've got a rum prancer here.'

Gerard wheeled on his high red heels. 'By Jove, I think you're right, Alastair. What a fine-looking boy, though filthy dirty and as poor as horse shit.'

'Just a minute . . .' exclaimed Irish Tom, putting up his fists.

'Tom, stop it,' ordered John, deliberately adopting a foreign accent and smiling at the pair of fops.

'I declare I think we'll take him to the Strawberry Fields with us. 'Twould be amusing, don't you know.'

'Please?' said John, spreading his hands and looking puzzled.

'Damme, he said please.'

The two creatures fell around the cobbles laughing, and while they were doing so John caught Tom's eye and whispered, 'This could be interesting.'

The Irishman shot him a look of disbelief and shook his head but kept quiet.

'Now look here, my Italian friend – you are Italian, aren't you? – how would you like to come and have a drink with us? Come on, *caro mio*, say yes.'

John calculated. The Strawberry Fields sounded interesting, a place of ill repute no doubt, but to go in dressed as a scoundrel and as the cat's-paw of two macaronis was far from ideal. He shook his head.

'No, Signor. Not tonight. I have other plans.'

'Oh, come now, pretty boy. We want your company, la so we do.'

John turned to Irish Tom, shouted, 'Run like hell,' and took off at speed, careering over the cobbles and wishing he were in better condition. The macaronis clattered after him but their high heels forbade any serious chase and soon the sound of their pursuing footsteps died away. John and Tom slowed to a stop and stood, panting for a moment or two before looking round them.

They were in a street probably worse than the one John had found himself in recently. This was a festering alley with houses leaning so close together that it seemed they were likely to collide at any given moment. Rats scuttled about in the darkness and played in the filth in the middle of the path. Flickering candles dimly lit the ghastly interiors, but in one particular house there was more light and the low hum of voices came from within.

'It's a bordello,' Tom whispered.

'I know,' John answered. 'Shall we go in? At least we can have a drink and ask directions.'

'But they will presume . . .'

'They can presume what they like, we've got to find our way out of this hellhole somehow or other.'

They approached the front door of the house and the stink of unwashed flesh, rum and sweat came in a vapour to meet them. John raised a handkerchief to his nostrils but made his way in with a determined step. A woman with a pair of very fine breasts was standing in the hallway. She pulled her top down a little as they approached, exposing one firm nipple, the colour of a raspberry.

'Hello gentlemen,' she said in a sing-song voice. 'What be your pleasure tonight?'

John raised his eyes to her face. 'I'm sorry, Miss, my friend and I have lost our way and wondered if you could direct us to the harbour.'

She pealed with laughter and answered, 'You'll find plenty of willing harbours round here, good Sir. Now what takes your fancy? Ginger, dark or purest blonde?'

Her double entendre did not go amiss and John chuckled and raised a mobile brow. 'Naught for me, thanks all the same. I am tired out already.'

But even as he spoke a well-built woman was coming down the stairs wearing nothing but a small black corset and a pair of white stockings. Over the top of the corset protruded a pair of enormous breasts. She flashed her handsome eyes at the two men and said, 'Now which of you is it to be? Or would you like me to take you on at the same time? I'm quite used to that, and good at it too. I charge more for the back door, mind.'

'Do you provide a scabbard for the sword?' John asked.

'Course we do,' answered the woman with the raspberry nipple. 'I can't risk my girls catching anything.'

John grinned. 'Go on, Tom. It will do you good. From what I hear you lead a fairly celibate life.'

'I do and all, John.' And no sooner were the words out of his mouth than Tom was whisked upstairs like a jack rabbit. The Apothecary smiled at his departing back and said, 'I really am tired, Madam. I would enjoy it enormously if I could just sit and buy you something to drink.'

There was a room to the right of the bar which had once been a parlour, John imagined. He and the madame – who introduced herself as Maud – sat there drinking rum, while she kept an ear out for visitors. She had been, John thought, studying her carefully, an absolutely stunning girl, but years of bodily abuse and alcohol had produced lines of wretchedness on her face and her mouth which, when not speaking, drooped down at the corners in a sure sign of discontent. But for all her miserable existence she had a certain braveness, a certain flair, that the Apothecary found himself warming to.

'So how long have you been in this business?' he asked.

'Whoring, you mean? Oh, since I was eleven. I was just a child when my mother put me on the streets to earn my keep.'

'That seems a bit hard.'

'She never wanted me. She was saddled with a bastard and she always resented my presence in her hovel. She was a whore herself. There is no other life for girls born into dire poverty.'

John's heart lurched as he thought of the unfairness of society, momentarily comparing the lives of Titania Groves and Maud. Nobody asks to be born, he thought, we just are, so nobody has any say over what strata of life they are going to come into. Savagely poor girls like Maud had no prospects before them except selling their bodies to any drunken vagabond with twopence in his pocket and a leer on his face. Spoilt pets like Titania – and his daughter Rose – had a good education and often their own pick of husband. What a tragedy it all was. He looked at Maud with enormous anguish. But she did not notice, too busy pouring two shots of rum into their glasses.

She raised hers in a toast. 'Here's to my father, whoever he might have been.'

'Don't you know anything about him?'

'My ma told me he was a gentleman, so I'm half a lady, me.'

'What was his name?'

'Gussie, that's what she called him.'

There was a prickling along the Apothecary's spine. 'Gussie who?'

Maud tilted her head back and laughed, looking younger and more vibrant than the drab with the raspberry nipple who had greeted them.

'I was never grand enough to have a surname. He was just Gussie. The only thing that Ma told me about him was that he was one of her regulars and that he had bright red hair.'

'Did she say whether he had a dog?'

Maud looked at him most oddly. 'Why do you ask that?'

'I don't know,' John lied. 'I just wondered.'

'She did once remark that he had some mongrel tagging along.'

'Did she mention its name by any chance?'

Maud put her glass down and gave him a long biting stare. 'Why do you ask so many questions? What interest could my father possibly hold for you? What are you, some kind of spy?'

John looked into the bleak blue eyes, regarding those and the colour of her hair, which under all the dirt and grime was obviously red.

'Yes, in a way I am a spy, but I promise you I am not a crooked one.'

And then he explained everything. About the letter from Mr Huxtable, the false Augustus Bagot – including a mirthful description of his general girth and deportment – and of John's search for the real man and anything known of him, which hopefully might lead to the killers of the false one.

Poor Maud sat fascinated, as if she had never heard a story before in her life. In the end a solitary tear formed in her eye and she said, 'Oh, the way you describe it all, it's like an adventure from another world.'

'Yes, but it happened right here and now. Maud, if you should hear anything at all, perhaps one of your clients might speak of something, please will you let me know?'

She did not answer but sat in silence, slowly sipping her rum. In the end she turned a thoughtful face in his direction.

'Would you like to meet my ma?'

'Very much. Is she nearby?'

'She's here. In this very house. In the attic. She's ill but she still goes out on the game. But I looks after her. God knows why. She didn't do much for me.'

'She could have put you to die.'

Maud's mouth gave a twisted half smile. 'Aye, she could have done that, I suppose.'

Twelve

Side by side they made their way up the twisting stairs, aided only by the flickering light of a solitary candle, passing various tatty rooms on their journey from which came the sounds of squeals and shrieks, grunts and groans, all of which served to remind John that he had been celibate for rather a long time. Eventually they reached the attic floor and Maud opened the door and slipped inside, motioning John to remain where he was. From within he heard muffled voices and one strident cry of 'Leave me be. I don't want to see nobody.'

'But Ma . . .'

'I told you, I don't know nuffink. I want to sleep.'

The door opened a crack and the Apothecary glimpsed a broken bed with a bundle of rotten rags lying on it. Within the bundle was a white face with fierce brown eyes and teeth to match. The most appalling smell hit his nostrils, of rot and urine and unwashed flesh. Gagging, John took a step backward. Maud appeared, her face sad in the candleglow.

'She won't see you.'

Thank God, thought John. Aloud he said, 'Can you ask her whether she believed Gus had come back?'

A shout came through the open door. 'That's what they're all saying up the town. That the sailor boy's returned. Bad cess to him, says I.'

'So they did not part on good terms?' John said quizzically.

'He left her pregnant. What can you expect?'

'Yes, you're right, of course. Anyway, your mother has told me all I need to know.'

'Has she?'

'You said she is still able to get up and sally forth?'

Maud gave a ghastly grin.

'Yes, you heard me. She plies her trade down Temple Street. Stands down by the fountains, she does.'

John was glad that it was dark on the stairs so that Maud could not see his expression. 'And does she get any customers?'

'A few. She only charges a penny, you see.'

John felt sickened by the very thought, and was glad when they returned to the ground floor to see Irish Tom, looking somewhat exhausted, waiting for him. They made to take their leave and John raised Maud's grimy hand to his lips.

'Goodbye and thank you for your help.'

She looked at him wide-eyed. 'You're not what you seem, are you? You're no rough sailor.'

'No, that's true enough. Now, where do you suggest we find lodgings? We want clean beds and some food in the morning.'

'You'll find some decent rooms at the Blue Bell. John

Hemborough runs the establishment. It's turn right, then right again.'

'Thank you, Maud.'

'And thank your girl for me,' said Irish Tom.

'Would you recommend her?'

'I think she should train for the circus,' answered Tom enigmatically, and with that they were off.

They woke the next morning and decided to make their way to the Rat Pitt in The Hatchet where once Augustus Bagot and his dog Sam had reigned supreme. Remembering the rough crowd who hung out there, the Apothecary felt fairly certain that this would be the place to pick up any gossip.

It was barely noon by the time they had strolled along via the harbour, but already the Rat Pitt was bursting with bloodthirsty boys, eager for some sport. The dogs made John wary, all on short leashes and all snipping, snapping and snarling. He gave them a wide berth as he and Tom took seats at the side of the arena. The Irishman, however, seemed ready for anything and was laying bets like a good 'un. John, feeling a bit of a mealy mouth, declined.

The rats were brought in in a sack which was unloaded onto the flat surface. A Master of Ceremonies of sorts shouted out, 'Dog Hercules, owner Philip Moncrieffe.' And there was a mighty roar as a simply enormous black devil was released, baring its teeth and growling. It set about killing like a maniac – which John suspected it was – but one cunning rat crept up its head and hung on to its ear, which it bit repeatedly. This made the dog even more savage, if such a thing were possible, and it killed without remorse. John was only glad that it was rats not children, for he felt sure the creature would have ripped their faces away in its maddened blood lust. Eventually a bell rang and the orgy was over. The dog was grabbed by its owner, the rat still biting its ear.

'Henry Tavener and Tray,' called the voice, and bets were hurriedly placed on the number of rats Tray could dispose of in a given time. John had to admit that his opinion of Henry had changed enormously, ever since that night on the river bank when the young man had greeted the slave Commodore with much affection. Until that time the Apothecary had considered him a brainless ass, but now he knew that the boy was kind and had genuine affection for people he liked.

He brushed right past the Apothecary but did not recognise him in his exotic sailor gear until John gently pulled at his sleeve. Henry stared at him, then exclaimed, 'Odds m'life, it's Rawlings. How the devil are you, Sir? And what are you doing in that get up?'

'I'm in disguise,' answered John, looking sinister.

'So you are. Why?'

'That I can't say.'

Henry looked conniving. 'Anything to do with that incident t'other night? When that fat old fool plummeted to his death?'

John tapped the side of his nose and assumed a wise expression.

'Oh, I see. Stand mum, is it? Well, I can do that.' Henry's voice became overhearty. 'Well, how now, good fellow. Want to know whether to bet on my dog, eh? Well, let me tell you he's a sure-fire winner. Aren't you, Tray boy?'

Tray boy let out a low sound which could have been anything between a growl and a yelp and allowed himself to be placed in the arena. A bell rang, the rats were unloaded and the dog started on its killing spree. Rats were falling like soldiers on a battlefield, except for the wily ones that climbed up Tray's face. There they hung remorselessly, taking bites out of his ear and attacking his eyes. Eventually the final bell rang and the count started. Eighty-three rat corpses produced a loud cheer and money changed from fingers to clinking fist.

'There, I told you he was a winner,' Henry announced triumphantly. 'Let's go and toast him.'

They made their way out of the Rat Pitt and clambered upstairs into the inn, leaving Irish Tom laying bets like a fury and in charge of Tray, who was bleeding fairly profusely from various bites.

'Henry, I think I can trust you,' said John when they were settled with their drinks. 'Fact is I need your help.'

'It's all to do with that fat chap, isn't it?'

'Everything to do with him.'

And John outlined the story as it had developed and explained why he was trying to find people who had known the original Augustus Bagot.

'In the hope that you might come across someone sufficiently angry to make an attempt on the second Augustus, believing him to be the first?'

'Yes, that's the story in a nutshell.'

'What did the real one do that might cause revenge to be sought?'

'Nothing too terrible. As a lad he haunted the Rat Pitt with a winning dog called Sam – somebody might have lost a great deal of money and be hell bent on pursuing him for it. He also made very free with the ladies and has two, if not three, little bye-blows running round Bristol. Thirdly comes the category of anyone who disliked him enough for some slight, and that could be anybody.'

'It's a tricky one to work out,' said Henry, staring into his tankard.

'I think I've located one of his bastards. A whore who is the daughter of the old drab who stands by the fountain in Temple Street.'

''Zounds, she offered herself to me once. I didn't stop running for a week. I can't imagine her killing him off.'

'You don't know,' John answered. 'Murderers come in very strange guises. One can never tell.'

'I think,' answered Henry after a pause, 'that the best person for you to speak to might be my uncle. He knows everything hereabouts as he was once a justice of the peace.'

'He retired?'

'Yes, got tired of seeing all his old friends in the dock.'

'I would like to meet him very much in another day or two. I think in the meantime I'll stay in this hideous disguise, found for me by Mr Foote no less, and rove round the dockyards, listening to gossip.'

'This Bagot fellow. How old was he when he sailed for New Zealand?'

'Well, he ran away from home when he was fourteen or so, and lived with the lowlife fraternity because his mother objected to his dog. I think he was about twenty-five when he actually sailed. Why?'

'I don't know really. I was just thinking.' There was a momentary pause and then Henry asked, 'How long ago did all this happen?'

'About twenty-five years.'

'So the fake Mr Bagot must have been fifty – or said he was?'

'Precisely. Why does it interest you so much?'

'Only because I am just twenty-five and according to my mother I was adopted.'

'Were you?'

'Yes, apparently I was her nephew – her brother-in-law's little bye-blow. I don't know who my real mother was. I was given to Lady Tavener when I was but a few hours old and a marvellous mama she has turned out to be. She even allows old Tray home, provided he sleeps in a kennel.'

'And I take it you know Commodore?'

'Yes, a wonderful chap. He's always been around and part of our lives.'

'Indeed,' answered John, thinking that he hadn't seen Henry look at him when they had first met in The Hatchet.

'And just in case you're thinking of our first meeting, I winked at him when you were not looking,' Henry said triumphantly.

John smiled, but within he was thinking intently. So far he had accounted for one of Augustus's little bastards – the poor, drab Maud – but where and who was the other one? Or, indeed, two.

He felt a strong need to discuss the whole matter with a good listener, and having collected Irish Tom who was flushed with winnings and alcohol, they went down to the docks and hired a boat that was plying for the Hotwell. They climbed aboard with some relief. Though the city of Bristol was raw with excitement and dubious pleasures, both men felt that they had earned a short respite.

Thirteen

'Pray continue, my son. So far I have heard every word you have said.'

'I think I have just about concluded, Papa. The fact is that I wanted you to hear all the points and then give me your comments.'

'Ah, I understand,' and Sir Gabriel lowered his ear trumpet and sat in quiet contemplation.

They were sitting quite alone in a small room overlooking the river. John had chosen the place – an annexe of the New Long Room – with due care, wanting desperately to hear his father's sharp and intelligent view of the events so far, and at the same time be in complete privacy. He could not have chosen better. The only sound was the lapping of the great river, the tide being full, and the distant hum of voices from the Long Room itself. Eventually Sir Gabriel broke the silence.

'It seems to me, my boy, that the best thing you can do is continue along the same path.'

'Meaning exactly?'

'That you must do your very best to find out who bore a grudge against the real Augustus Bagot. Though, come to think of it . . .'

'What?'

'That imposter might have made his own enemies. He certainly behaved in a rude enough style to have warranted a few.'

'But remember the wording on that note I saw. I definitely received the impression that it was written by someone from Gussie's past.'

His father looked wise. 'But that does not mean that they followed suit. It could merely have been an empty threat. Suppose that the person you are looking for is much nearer home.'

John gulped. 'You don't mean Mr Huxtable? Or Commodore?'

'Why not? I would have thought that they would have more reason than most to want the fellow out of the way.'

''Zounds, Father. It sounds as if this investigation is going to be a Herculean task.'

'I rather think it is, my dear. So for a start why do you not make two lists. One of people trying to murder the unknown man, and the second of people trying to murder the real Augustus Bagot.'

'But if I am going to enquire after both I am going to need a great deal of help.'

Sir Gabriel stroked his chin. 'What about Gilbert Farr?'

'He is very busy in his shop.'

'But he has a duty. After all, he *is* the Constable.'

'You're right, of course. I shall go and see him in the morning.'

'And now, might I suggest that you have an early night. The night life of Bristol has obviously worn you out.'

'You're right as usual, Father. I shall go to bed.'

'And I shall rejoin the others in the Long Room.'

It was a brisk walk back to the hotel, but as John passed the night porter he was surprised when the man rose to his feet with a certain urgency.

'Ah, Mr Rawlings, I'm glad I've caught you, Sir. I have a letter for you. The post boy brought it just after you had gone out.'

It had obviously been forwarded from London, and as John turned it and saw the writing on the outside he felt as if someone had given him a blow to the chest. He let out a gasp and took a step backward.

The porter, staring at him, said, 'Are you all right, Sir? You've gone white as a cloud.'

For a moment John could not answer, recognising the bold hand of Elizabeth, so like her in character, the letters so fearless and so clearly written. He managed to say, 'Yes, I am just a little tired,' before bolting to his room and breaking the seal open, holding the candle high so that he could clearly read what she had to say.

My dear John. It seems that we have spent a Lifetime without conversing, which might indeed be Deemed foolish Behaviour on the Part of two Adults who were Once so Close. Be that as it May I now wish to Speak with you on a Matter of Great Importance Concerning, as it does, Our Two Sons. I would ask You therefore to visit me In Devon at Your Earliest Convenience.

I Cannot state too Greatly how very much this would
Oblige your Old Friend and Humble Servant.
      Elizabeth di Lorenzi.

John drew a deep breath. A reconciliation at last! But what a
moment to pick. He sat down on his bed and thrust his head
into his hands, feeling overcome with deep depression. Then
suddenly, acting almost like an automaton, he flung himself upward
and hurried down the stairs and out of the front door, heading
for the New Long Room and the company of the man he loved
best in the world, Sir Gabriel Kent.

They talked long into the night, with small shots of brandy to
bolster them up. Sir Gabriel listened wisely and finally said, 'My
son, your first duty lies with your children and their welfare must
be the most important thing to you. Consult with Gilbert Farr
and explain your predicament. I shall offer him my assistance in
the case, limited though it might be. But you must not let a sense
of misplaced obligation stand between you and your flesh and
blood. If your two boys need you, if Elizabeth should need you,
then you must go to them forthwith.'

John gave him a kiss on the cheek. 'Thank you, Papa. If I say
you are always right it will make you sound like a saintly ass
and you are anything but that. So I shall go immediately to
Elizabeth and find out what is wrong.'

Even as he said the words the Apothecary felt his blood quicken.
It was as if she were once again in his arms, the smell of her hair
in his nostrils, her own wild, exotic perfume firing his senses.
He took a sip of brandy to distract himself.

Sir Gabriel was speaking. 'I believe that if you travel to Bath
you can pick up the Exeter stagecoach.'

'What a good idea. What time does it leave, do you know?'

'No, but the staff are bound to be aware.'

Finally, having been told that the coach arrived in Bath at ten
in the morning, from which it departed at ten-thirty, John sent
a message to Irish Tom to pick him up just after eight. Then,
with an air of mounting excitement, he retired for the night in
order to pack his trunk.

Fourteen

The ride to Bath was done at top speed, Tom being afraid of missing the connection at Bath. He made the two horses, which had been well rested during their stay in Hotwell, go as fast as they could. Sitting inside the newly upholstered interior, John was a prey to varying emotions. Riding overall was his sense of excitement, but this was tempered by a feeling of dread, of stark fear at seeing Elizabeth after this gap of two years. Not that he was afraid of her as a person nor, indeed, of her temperament, but for all that he feared her coldness, should she choose to be aloof and in high stirrup. But his natural optimism told him that she would not have sent for him at all if that were the case. He tried not to think of the worst that might have happened, as going down that alleyway filled him with mortal dread.

The scene in The Bear in Bath, a comfortable coaching inn, presented the usual excitement that greeted the arrival of the stagecoach. Hawkers and urchins ran about with useless things to purchase, while the passengers, weary and bleary after a night on the road, alighted to take breakfast within. Several people were making this their final stop, so to John's enquiry came the reply that there was a seat available on the outside at the rear. It was better than nothing and John accepted and clambered aboard. The horses, all four of them, were being led out by the horseman, and four rested replacements were standing by, ready to be backed into the harness. The coachman meanwhile had disappeared into the inn, and the guard, looking rather tired and grumpy, was leaning against the wall talking to one of the maids. Eventually though he heaved himself up beside John and looked at him rather suspiciously.

'Good morning,' said the Apothecary brightly.

The guard regarded him stonily but eventually relaxed a little and said, 'Morning.'

'I don't suppose you have many people to talk to on your journey,' John continued in the same jolly tone.

'It don't bother me much,' the guard answered. 'I likes me own company.'

'Well, that's just as well then,' John replied.

A few moments later the rest of the passengers came hurrying out of the inn and took their places, three hearty men clambering onto the roof and squeezing in beside the various trunks and boxes. Finally the coachman came aboard and gave a mighty crack of his whip which announced that they were off. There was a general shout and then they were asked to stop again for two late passengers, a rat-faced little man who leapt into the basket – which up to this point had remained empty – and his wife, a most dreary-looking female who appeared generally displeased with life. They immediately started complaining about the discomfort, the noise, the smell of the horses, the bumpiness of the road – in fact their entire journey was one long and continual moan. The Apothecary thought how miserable they must be and then realised that this constant stream of complaint was in fact their contentment. He nudged the guard who whispered, 'I'll shoot the buggers if they go on much longer,' and then lapsed into silence again.

They dined at Taunton, passed through White Ball and Collumpton, and finally arrived in Exeter shortly before eleven at night. John, thoroughly weary and feeling rather cramped for sitting so long in one uncomfortable position, made his way into The Half Moon and booked himself a room for the night. Now that he was drawing so close to Elizabeth he was full of excited fear, his stomach aching with dull pain, his nerve endings tingling with fidgety trepidation.

He slept well, despite his anxieties, and next morning hired a man with a trap to take him to Withycombe House. The weather had turned damp and soggy and John sat with his hat pulled well down and the collar of his greatcoat turned up. The city of Exeter looked dull and grey and when they got into the open countryside it was even worse.

The grass was flattened and had the dull sheen of raindrops, the fields were churning with gurgling mud, and the River Exe was beginning to swell with the excess water. When they reached the slope above which stood Elizabeth's great house, they could barely see it through the mist that was rising from the sodden ground. John's lurking feeling that all was not well returned a hundredfold.

The lodge keeper waved them through, recognising John and giving him a salute, before they proceeded up the drive. They turned a bend and the house came into view, its windows blinded by the slashing rain, the brick darkened by the driving downpour. They reached the front door and John pulled the bell, calling over his shoulder for the trap to wait until he had gained admittance. Everything became dreamlike and slow in motion as a footman appeared. He was new and stared at John blankly.

'Yes, Sir?'

'I have come to see Lady Elizabeth di Lorenzi. Is she at home?'

'Yes, but she is not receiving today. Would you like to leave your card?'

'But I must see her. She asked for me to come urgently. Please allow me a few minutes with her.'

The footman was opening his mouth but another voice broke across his.

'It's all right, Richardson. I know this gentleman.'

The sound came from the staircase, and as the footman turned, so did John. She was standing on the bottom step, dressed in a loose gown made of white voile, her dark hair hanging about her shoulders. And though she still looked beautiful, John could see that an enormous change had come over her. Gone was the wonderful woman who had ridden out fearlessly to hunt down her son's killers; gone was the woman who had whispered to him once, 'I long to kiss you'; gone was the flame, the passion, the magnificent creature with whom he had been so in love. In her place stood a much smaller person, a frail being, a woman on the brink of advancing years.

A cry broke from John, 'Oh, Elizabeth,' and it seemed to him that he jumped the distance between the door and the stairs and snatched her into his arms, the unrestrained tears scalding his cheeks.

She smiled at him, oh so sadly, and said, 'I was hoping you would not catch me like this.'

'My darling girl, what do you mean?'

'*En deshabille.* I planned to put on so much make-up that I would resemble my former self.'

Holding her tightly he could feel how thin she was. Though never remotely fat, now she was skeletal.

'Elizabeth, what is the matter with you?'

She looked up at him and gave him a smile that would haunt him for the rest of his life. 'I have cachexia.'

'The wasting disease? But why? What is the cause?'

'Let us not continue the conversation here. Let us repair to my sitting room and there I will tell you everything.'

The Apothecary nodded, too full of dread to ask any further questions. But when Elizabeth turned to mount the staircase he saw that she was too weak to do more than drag herself upwards. In a moment that felt as if his heart was breaking, he picked her up and carried her to her bedroom, then into the little parlour that led off it. Then he wept at the cruelty of life that could bring this terrible illness to a woman who had once stood tall as an Amazon.

A servant came in response to the bell and brought them wine and little cakes. Somehow or other John turned himself into the professional, used to seeing disease in all its forms, even though the effort was killing him.

'Elizabeth, tell me, have you seen a physician?'

She gave him a sad smile. 'I have seen not one, but two. And they are the best physicians of all.'

'Not the Hunter brothers?'

Elizabeth nodded. 'They were both staying down here and when I called for William, they both came. I am afraid that they found I had hard swellings . . .'

'Kernels?'

'. . . which they feared had gone too far for them to try and remove. Oh John, my dear, I am afraid that I am dying.'

For the first time in all their acquaintance she visibly broke down and clung to him, sobbing out her agony and suffering. John held her to his heart but deep inside he felt the turn of the knife. He had heard of this illness before, quite a few times, and knew that it was terminal, that the physicians and apothecaries could do little but relieve their patients' pain. What a joke for some evil entity to bring low a woman who had been so magnificent – that was the most bitter gall of all.

He cleared his throat and spoke. 'What have they prescribed for you?'

'Cinquefoil roots boiled in vinegar. And opium, of course.'

He said nothing, thinking of Elizabeth when first he saw her: supple, tall, beautiful, a world away from the shrunken creature that wept so bitterly in his arms. Eventually the storm passed and he dried her eyes, then she took the handkerchief and blew her nose.

'I feel better now you're here,' she said.

'I came immediately. I had a feeling something was wrong.'

She flashed a sudden grin and the old Elizabeth looked out from her face. At that moment the bedroom door opened quietly and a little boy with a mass of dark curls and eyes the colour of bluebells looked in. Seeing his mother was busy he closed the door again, but a second or two later it opened once more and this time he rushed in. Elizabeth stood up to meet him and he buried his face in her knees.

'Whyfore you sad, Mama?'

Before she could answer, the door opened yet again and an identical little boy with a serious face ran in after him and said, 'Mama is not well. I told you.'

So there they were, John's twin sons, so alike they could be the same person, but clearly with rather different personalities.

'Now which of you is Jasper and which one James?' John asked, rising to his feet.

They both stared at him, devouring him in a solemn gaze of bright blue.

'Well, speak up,' ordered Elizabeth. 'And make a little bow when you answer.'

The serious little boy did exactly as he had been told, bowing from the waist and almost folding himself in half as he did so.

'I am James, Sir.'

'And I am Jasper,' said the other, and imitated his brother's bow.

'You are my two favourite boys in all the world,' John stated, at which the twins looked surprised.

'Why?' asked Jasper; and James said, 'But you don't know us.'

'My sons,' Elizabeth interjected quietly, 'this man is your father.'

They looked at him solemnly but neither said a word, and John could tell by Elizabeth's attitude that it was better like this.

'Now run along my poppets,' she said. 'May I bring your father to your nursery supper? Or would you rather that it was just I who came?'

James spoke up. 'Please bring him, Mama.'

Then they hurried out and John could hear their nurserymaid calling. 'So that's where you've been hiding, the pair of you. Now come along.'

He turned to Elizabeth. 'Will you let me get into bed with you? Just to hold you close.'

'There can be nothing further. Those days are over for me.'

'My darling, I just want to be near you. That is all.'

They slept for a while, at first deeply – John being tired from travelling – but waking after a while and watching the shadows start to deepen on the walls.

'John,' Elizabeth whispered beside him, 'I want you to take the twins to live with you. If you do not have them they will go to my cousins and that is something I could not bear.'

'But my darling . . .'

'No, don't interrupt me. I shall be able to keep them for about another month. But after that time I will be beyond help. Say that you will let them grow up with your Rose – and with you. My dearest, wonderful John.'

The tears that were never far from his eyes threatened to overspill again. All he had ever wanted was becoming reality, but in such a terrible way. He would have given up practically everything to restore Elizabeth to her wild, beautiful self. Yet he knew through his studies that the ancient Greeks had discovered the terrible disease and named it after the crab that sits so plumply in the middle of the Zodiac. Later they had called it carcinoma, based on the Greek word for crab: *karkinos*. And this is what Elizabeth had, a carcinoma that was slowly but surely eating the life out of her.

'Of course I'll take the boys,' he whispered to her in the twilight. 'And I promise that I will give them as good a life as is in my power to give.'

'Then that is settled.' She pushed herself up on one elbow and stared down into his face. Close like this he could see the changes in her. The thick black hair was almost grey and was thinner than he remembered it. The lovely expressive eyes had become dull and misty. But it was to her general well-being that the greatest change had come. She had lost not only weight but inches. Elizabeth had become an elfin creature.

She made a great attempt at rallying, however, and having dressed and applied rouge, carmine and kohl, she led John to the boy's nursery where they were to have their supper before retiring for the night. Studying them carefully, John could see no visible difference in them at all and wondered how he was ever going to be able to tell them apart. Their hair was lovely – thick, dark curls growing in an identical manner – while their eyes were a blaze of blue.

'How do you know which is which?' he asked Elizabeth.

She smiled. 'It's very difficult to tell, especially when they play the game of being the other one.'

'What do you mean?'

'If one of them has been naughty he immediately changes character to his brother and then you are left with the decision of punishing both or neither of them.'

'Little devils! And they've already worked this out?'

'Indeed they have. But then I ask to look at their hands. And one of them – James – has got slightly longer fingers than Jasper. That's how you tell.'

'And then do you punish the miscreant?'

Elizabeth laughed, and for a minute John could have sworn she was well again. 'No, I haven't the heart. You see, I adore them. You gave me the greatest gift with that delightful pair.'

John put his arm round her waist, feeling delicate bones that were new to him.

'It was my pleasure, I assure you.'

She snuggled against him. 'I am so glad you are here.'

'I will stay as long as you like.'

'Two days only. Just long enough for the boys to get used to you. You are bound to be working on a case.'

'How did you know that?'

Elizabeth raised a bony shoulder. '*Plus ça change.*'

John smiled but could think of no answer, for once at a loss for words.

A surfeit of twins was in order for the next couple of days. They were very good, obedient and kindly, but he could not help but notice that they already had quite different characteristics. Where one – Jasper – was quick to see the funny side of things, to see the humour behind the humour as it were, the other was simply a good-natured sort. John silently summed them up as the cynical and the sweet. The two parts of a human being, he supposed. But they were both delightful children and he relished being in their company. He did not see as he walked through the grounds, a twin trotting beside him on either side, that the gaunt figure of Elizabeth was watching from her bedroom window with a drawn smile on her face. Nor did he know what it cost her in the way of agony and pain to rise and dress for dinner and to make what conversation she could in those frantic gay hours before she could retire for the night once more.

Yet this night, despite her haggard looks and forced laughter, he deliberately drew her into conversation as her usual hour of departure approached.

'Elizabeth, to hell with my other commitments. I want to be with you and look after you.'

She was silent for several minutes, deep in thought. Then she said, 'Very well. I will send for you. Promise me that you will take the boys back to London with you.'

'You know I will. And you promise me that you will call me in time.'

Something like her old smile crossed her features. 'When the right moment comes I promise to contact you.'

'Thank you. Will you stay with me tonight, just to hold me and let me know you are nearby?'

'You know I will.'

Later, he studied her by the shaft of moonlight across the bed. In that moment he prayed that just for half an hour she could return to her old passionate self, but he knew that this could never be. That hateful disease about which he knew so little had struck again at a person who John held dear. He decided at that moment that he would ask the Doctors Hunter to tell him all that they knew about this silent killer which came out of nowhere and seemed to pick its victims at random.

The next morning Elizabeth asked if she might stay in bed and John took the twins out for a ride. She had bought them two miniature ponies, on one of which James, the sweet child, allowed himself to be lifted. But Jasper, the cynic, actually raised his small foot into the stirrup and, despite his lack of years, swung himself up with enviable ease. John could not help but smile, wondering if they were going to have trouble with the boy later.

They walked down into the Exeter valley, taking in the greenness of the countryside and the colour of the cloud-strewn sky.

'Mama says we must call you papa,' announced Jasper. 'Why is that?'

'Because I am your father, that's why.'

James smiled. 'I thought we only had Mama.'

'No,' John answered firmly, 'there are two of us. I am your papa.'

Jasper said, 'My real papa is a prince, you know.'

'Well, until he comes you will have to make do with me, I'm afraid,' John said wryly.

'I see.'

'I like you anyway,' said James, as his brother decided to make his pony go faster, then fell off, cried a little and held up his arms to John.

'Help me up. I've hurted myself.'

'No bones broken,' John said as he quickly examined his son. 'You've just jarred yourself, 'tis all.'

But it was nice to feel the warmth of the little body in his arms and to feel the child's tears on his neck. John knew certainly at that moment that he and his twin sons would always be close, however their personalities developed in the future.

The next day he left them behind and returned to the Hotwell. His parting from Elizabeth tore his heart from his body, metaphorically if not literally. She, who had once been so beautiful and proud, the strongest woman he had ever known and loved, had been reduced to a wisp, a shadow, a creature so near death that only her own determination was keeping her alive. John had begged her to call him back so that she would not be alone to face the end.

She had given him a sad, dark smile. 'I will do what I think best, my dear.'

'Please don't say that. You frighten me.'

'The best way you can serve me is to look after our sons. You promise me that?'

'You know I do.'

He had kissed her hand and left, but his mind was full of foreboding and premonitions, which did not leave him until he returned to Bath. Here his spirits were raised by the thought of once more conversing with Sir Gabriel Kent and telling him of his two impish grandsons, soon to become part of the household.

Arriving back in Bath in the early morning, John accepted an elderly gentleman's offer of a lift to the Hotwell, and once there made straight for the hotel where he briefly washed and changed his travel-stained garments. Then he went out to seek Gilbert Farr. But he had forgotten that it was Sunday and that all the shops on the Colonnade were closed to observe the Lord's Day. However, a handwritten note had been placed in the apothecary's window reading: 'If any Personage should require Urgent Medical Attention he will find me between the hours of ten and twelve of the clock at number 7, Dowry Square.' It was a little early but John decided to risk a call.

A footman answered the door, stiff in both face and manner. 'If I may take your card, Sir.'

John fished around and found a rather tattered and dog-eared one which he presented with a flourish, and a second or two later Gilbert came running down the stairs. He was obviously dressing and was wearing a pair of smart breeches and a plum-coloured waistcoat.

'My dear fellow, how good to see you. You'll be pleased to hear that I have made some progress.'

'Really? What is it?'

'Come in, come in, and I'll tell you all.'

John was ushered into a small parlour full of knick-knacks, dominated by a large harp. He stared at it.

'My sisters play,' said Gilbert with a note of apology.

'Glad to hear it,' John answered, feeling stupid.

'But you'll want to know the news.'

'Very much.'

'It seems that Augustus Bagot – the imposter, not the real one – made an implacable enemy at the theatre.'

'Oh, who was that?'

'A dark and devilish young man called Wychwood.'

'Is that his surname?'

'Yes. He's Sir Julian Wychwood, apparently some young rake-hell, rolling in money, who comes to play cards at Hotwell and then moves on to Bath, where he fleeces all the gentlemen who sit at play with him. Anyway, to cut to the point he apparently asked some lad at the theatre to reserve him a box for the season, but as he had not yet arrived our friend Bagot took the box and refused to give it up.'

'That does not sound too great a crime.'

'You don't know young Wychwood. He is the sort of man who likes everything to go his way. He was incensed by this turn of events and even threatened to kill said Bagot if he could not get his box back. But he never did get it back. The theatre had a regular customer who refused to budge. Bagot said the box suited him.'

'Probably because it was sufficiently wide.'

'That and he had his private chamber pot in there, which he used to use during the performance. Apparently, according to that amusing fellow Foote, one night Wychwood stole in and emptied the contents all over Bagot, who was utterly enraged.'

John burst out laughing. 'That is a sight I would like to have seen.'

'The story gets better. Bagot lumbered to his feet, shouting his head off, at which Wychwood thumbed his nose, raced round the box twice and climbed upwards to the loge above.'

'He sounds an admirable young man.'

Gilbert's face suddenly became serious. 'Yes, but did he grease the steps? It sounds to me just the sort of prank he would indulge in.'

'For sure, but can you prove it?'

The Hotwell apothecary shook his head. 'No. And I don't see how I ever will. I think unless I can get a confession I will have to declare the matter closed.'

John sat silently, staring into space, his mind suddenly full of thoughts of his Elizabeth, a flame which had burned so brilliantly but which was now on the point of being extinguished forever. Then he realised that Gilbert was waiting for him to speak.

He nodded his head. 'I think you're right.'

'What shall we do then?'

John sighed, hating to admit defeat, then he said, 'Let's give it one more week before we give in.'

Gilbert made a sound of jubilation. 'I was hoping you'd say that. So what's the plan?'

'I'll go back to Bristol's underworld for a few days. Then, if I can't find anything there, I'll come back and try to meet Sir Julian Wychwood, perhaps even get him to confess.'

'For that, my friend, you'll have to have the luck of Old Nick himself.'

'In any event it will be an interesting meeting.'

'Interesting indeed,' answered Gilbert, and grinned.

As fate would have it the Apothecary did not have to wait long to encounter Sir Julian. That very day, having strolled out to take the air – Sir Gabriel having had to retire for the afternoon to come to terms with the fact that Elizabeth was dying – John saw that the street traders were selling their wares regardless of this being a day of rest. Naturalists had set up stalls offering minerals and jewellery made from Bristol diamonds, which were in fact quartz of magnesium conglomerate. Lace makers were selling lappet heads for ladies and ruffles for gentlemen, and it was at this booth that John spied Titania Groves examining the wares, and a tall man standing a few feet away from her, also looking at the goods for sale. Titania turned her head and looked at the stranger and, quick as a flash, he made a deep bow, stepped up to her, took her hand and kissed it lingeringly. Titania gaped, not being used to this kind of treatment, even in her social sphere. The man released her wrist slowly, then introduced himself, though John could not hear what he actually said. Titania smiled and dropped a curtsey, the man bowed and proceeded to buy her a lappet, which he then gave to her with a certain aloof dignity. The Apothecary was frankly amazed. He had never seen an approach like it. He looked at the fellow with much interest.

He was tall – well over six feet – and slim as a reed. His hair was dark, the colour of liquorice, his features attractively brooding, his eyes amber with somewhat hooded lids. In short, he was devilishly handsome – and he knew it. John watched Titania beginning to melt and decided, somewhat selfishly, to intervene.

'Good day, Miss Groves. I hope I find you well.'

'Oh, good day, Mr Rawlings. I had not realised you were back from your visit.'

John turned to the man. 'And good day to you, Sir. I do not believe we have met.'

Smooth as satin, the man bowed deeply. 'We have not,' he said. 'Allow me to introduce myself. Julian Wychwood is my name.'

John should have known it of course. Of all the attractive creatures currently at the Hotwell, this one crowned them all. He bowed very low.

'And I am John Rawlings, Sir. It is a pleasure to make your acquaintance.'

'Indeed,' replied the other, giving the Apothecary an unreadable look and bowing once more.

Titania, very rosy in the cheeks, said, 'Mr Wychwood insists on buying me this lappet. I told him it would not be proper to receive a gift from a stranger but he insists.'

Julian flashed a smile – predictably his teeth were strong and white – and said, 'Please Miss Groves. It would give me so much pleasure.'

John stood agape, completely outmanoeuvred by this charming stranger. He looked round for an ally and saw Lady Tyninghame walking alone, gazing in the direction of the river. Plucking his hat from his head he waved it aloft to attract her attention. She seemed slightly bewildered by his behaviour, but nonetheless came to join the group. Looking at her, John thought how delicate she was and a vision of Elizabeth shot through his mind. But he knew to think in such a manner would do neither him nor his lover any good at all. He deliberately forced himself to concentrate on the matter in hand.

'Lady Tyninghame, how very nice to see you. You know Miss Groves, of course. But may I introduce Sir Julian Wychwood to you.'

She gave a little gasp, the colour draining from her cheeks, leaving her white as a shroud. Automatically John put out his arm to support her. She seemed drained of animation and lay in the crook of his elbow for a good minute before her eyelids fluttered open.

'Excuse me,' she said faintly. 'I have been a little unwell recently.'

She straightened, turning to John with a gentle laugh and saying, 'This kind man is always helping me out. I do thank you, Sir.'

John silently handed her his smelling salts, but in fact he was slightly suspicious of this recent attack. It seemed to him that no sooner had she heard the name Julian Wychwood than she had collapsed.

While she was inhaling, he asked pleasantly, 'You have met Sir Julian before?'

She gave him back the bottle and said, 'Just once, many years ago. He would not remember me.'

'Did you know his family?'

'Only his father. His wife had died some years previously.'

The Apothecary mulled this over but merely said, 'Oh, I see.' But he didn't, feeling that one look at Julian Wychwood had been enough to make the lady faint. But then, he supposed, that might well be enough for any woman.

Julian, meanwhile, was gently kissing Lady Tyninghame's hand, not on the wrist like Titania's, but respectably on the back of the fingers.

She looked up at him shyly. 'I knew your father, Sir Julian. I called on him once.'

'Do you know I can recall the incident. I believe you came to tea with us. I thought you most charming, Lady Tyninghame – as indeed I do now.'

'I remember that you were frightened of a toy I brought you. A little wooden cannon that fired real balls.'

Julian smiled. 'I believe I hid my head in your lap and cried.'

Violetta smiled. 'But you were only a little boy.'

'And now I am grown to full height and twenty-five years old.'

'Quite the mature man.'

'I shall take that as a compliment, Milady.'

Miss Groves, a little annoyed by the lack of attention, said, 'I really don't think it would be proper to accept the lace lappet. I mean, we haven't been properly introduced.'

Sir Julian gave the slightest of shrugs. 'Perhaps a way round the dilemma would be for me to give it to Lady Tyninghame, who can then give it to you.'

Lady Tyninghame literally sparkled with merriment. She

clapped her hands and looked quite the opposite from the sickly woman of a few minutes before.

'Why, Sir Julian, what a splendid plan. If Miss Groves is agreeable, that is the way we shall proceed.'

Her caught her mood and as if he knew her well, put his two hands at her waist and twirled her round. There was something odd about the couple, but John could not grasp what it might possibly be.

Miss Groves, definitely piqued, said, 'Oh very well, if you insist. But there is no need, Sir, I assure you.'

'In that case,' Lady Tyninghame put in, making matters far, far worse, 'I shall accept it for myself with pleasure.'

She was elated, like a young girl, her loveliness enhanced by the bright, bold colour that had come to her cheeks. John thought that she was clearly delighted with the company of Julian Wychwood, whereas Titania looked ready to stamp her foot. He tried to lighten the mood.

'Shall we stroll round the Pleasure Gardens?' he asked brightly.

'You may do so if you wish but I have to return to Mama. So I will bid you farewell.' Having said that, Miss Groves dropped a curtsey to each of them and stalked off, bonnet high. Not in the least perturbed, Julian bowed low and presented Lady Tyninghame with the lappet of lace, which she accepted gracefully. John was about to make his excuses when Samuel Foote bustled up to them.

'Ha, young Wychwood,' he said. 'You've heard your enemy is dead.'

'Yes, and I can't say I'm sorry. What brute allowed him to occupy my box at the theatre?'

'Money talks,' Foote answered merrily.

'In other words, he gave you a larger fee than my retainer.'

Sam looked shocked. 'Not me. Oh no, Sir, not me. Some underling at the theatre lining his own pockets. Shocking, I thought. But what could I do? I am merely an actor fellow. But for all that, we all had a good laugh at your antics when you dumped his pot upon his head then climbed up to the box above. Stopped the show it did.'

Lady Tyninghame gazed at Julian with a slight air of reproof. 'What exactly did you do, Sir?'

Samuel raised his hat to her and gave a small bow. 'Samuel

Foote, at your service, Ma'am. As I was saying, this madcap friend of yours climbed over the theatre like a hero from a romance. It stopped the show while we watched him.'

She turned to Wychwood. 'I hope you didn't hurt yourself, my dear.'

Once again John was struck, even more forcibly, by the apparent closeness of two people who had barely been introduced. Something strange was afoot, he knew it certainly, but quite how he could investigate was impossible to conceive.

But now Sir Julian was speaking. 'I am afraid that I must bid you all adieu. My watch tells me that I am already late for my next appointment. My Lady, goodbye. Surely we will meet again soon. Gentlemen, farewell. I shall see you both around Hotwell without a doubt.'

He raised his embellished tricorne hat and his liquorice hair gleamed black in the sunlight. He made a flourishing bow, kissed Lady Tyninghame warmly on the hand and disappeared into the crowd. John stared after him.

'What an incredible young man,' escaped from his lips before he could control the words.

'I thought him rather charming,' said Violetta Tyninghame.

'He has a great air about him,' remarked Samuel, staring at the space that Wychwood had recently occupied. 'I knew an actor like him once. When he went on stage every eye turned to where he made his entrance. You could have heard a garter drop in the theatre. He was truly an overwhelming presence.'

'What happened to him?'

'He disappeared. Quite literally. One day he did not turn up to rehearsal and when one of the company went to his lodgings it was to find that he had gone.'

'Where to?'

'Nobody knew. To make it even more mysterious, all the furniture had gone as well.'

'What happened to him?'

'This is the peculiar part. One of our patrons – a rich young gentlemen – swore that he saw the actor one night in a theatre in Prague, where he was playing the part of Count Almaviva, of all things.'

'What's so odd about that?' asked John.

'It is an operatic role and none of us knew he could sing.'

The whole story seemed rather pointless to the Apothecary, but he smiled and nodded and pretended it was very interesting. Yet his brain was totally at another destination. All he could think about was the strangeness of the situation in Hotwell and, over-riding everything else, the fact that death was about to rob him of a partner for the second time in his life.

Fifteen

It was a bitter night, about ten of the clock, and John Rawlings was retracing the steps he had made on the night he had been waylaid by the macaronis. His thick cloak concealed a particularly garish suit in a violent shade of lime green. He had worn it in Devon and it held many happy memories for him, but tonight he wore it for a different purpose.

He had thought long and hard about the Strawberry Fields and had concluded that it was a club exclusively for nan-boys – a Miss Molly's paradise, in other words. He was also fairly sure, judging by remarks made by the dying Benedict Pendleton, that within its walls he would find that renegade from justice, Herman Cushen. Herman and Benedict had been hired to execute the Earl of St Austell and had made a good job of it, disguising their real target by ending the lives of two other people as well. But they had escaped and though one of them had been called to final justice to answer for his crimes, the other had totally vanished. Yet now John felt he was on his trail once more, a trail that had been cold for over two years.

With scant idea of where he was heading, John made a slow progress and was just about ready to give up when ahead of him he saw two fellows, chattering and laughing quite loudly in the empty streets. One of them had a particularly shrill voice.

'Come on, this way. I'm sure I remember where it was.'

'I thought we had to turn left.'

'No, it was quite definitely right. Now hurry along or we'll be missing the Roaring Boys.'

John sprinted to catch up with them and said, 'You are going to the Strawberry Fields, aren't you? You see I'm not too sure of my way.'

He put a slight lisp into his voice and swung his hips a little.

'Not sure of your way!' said the taller of the two. 'Oh, I don't think you'll have to worry about that too much. There'll be plenty of people there to show you how it's done.'

At this remark he bellowed with laughter, sounding rather like a mongrel letting rip. His companion joined him by braying like a donkey. John wondered for one infantile moment if they were all going to have to do animal imitations for their initiation ceremony.

The taller one seized his arm and whisked him over the pavements at a rate of knots, and they soon found themselves before an important-looking front door with a black servant in strawberry-coloured livery standing outside.

'Good evening, gentlemen,' he said, looking solemn. 'Is it your pleasure to sample some strawberries?'

'Indeed it is. Are you agreed fellows?'

'Agreed,' chorused John and the other one, and the door swung open to allow them into a large entrance hall. For a moment or two John's eyes were dazzled by the crimson draperies, the pot plants, the men lounging back on sofas and chairs, before his senses returned and he knew that the place was just as he had suspected. A male brothel. For all the girls, leaning voluptuously over the men or walking slowly up and down the room, presumably waiting to be picked, were boys in women's clothing. John stared, never before having seen such fawning, beautiful creatures with the manners and characteristics of the female sex perfectly imitated. Some of the nan-boys looked suspiciously young to him, probably no more than thirteen years of age. And how they postured and pouted, carmined lips blowing kisses, kohl-blackened eyes winking suggestively, eyelashes fluttering and then dipping beneath a black lace fan. And there, in the midst of them all, sporting a peacock dress with false breasts very much visible, but still ugly despite all the make-up, was Herman.

He glanced in John's direction and John swiftly turned away – but too late. Dragging his heavy dress behind him and with much shaking of the plumes in his wig, the wretched Mr Cushen was making a purposeful tread towards him. John steeled himself and faced him.

Herman's face was contorted into what he considered to be an attractive leer. 'Hello, my sweet. Are you feeling lonely? Want a little companionship for an hour or so?'

John answered in a piping falsetto. 'I would rather look round for a little while. See what's on offer.' He managed a high-pitched giggle.

'Certainly,' replied the other, with more than a hint of annoyance. 'Take your pick by all means.' He flounced off and John metaphorically wiped his brow. Heaven be thanked. Herman had not recognised him.

A boy of about fourteen, dressed gorgeously as a girl in red satin, offered John a flute of champagne, which he took with a shaky hand. Loving couples were now forming up to dance licentiously together, staring into one another's eyes, hands caressing sensuously. Fully aware that this particular branch of sexual activity was not for him, the Apothecary could still see the attraction of it for those whose natures inclined them that way. Where lay the difference he could not tell, and decided at some time in the future to discuss the whole matter with a learned physician.

Now all were being drawn into the dance, though John politely refused, claiming that he had hurt his knee. Instead he watched the nan-boys who had not yet been hired imitating the slave dancers from the east, posturing for their sultan, writhing about in quite the most formidable contortions. Incense filled the room and the music – played on a pipe – grew ever louder. Suddenly John had had enough. Very quietly, while all the attention was focused on the twisting bodies, he slipped out into the passageway, standing there a moment and cooling off. Then he made his way to the front door. But it was barred to him. The black servant stood there, his arm across the opening.

'Leaving so soon, young Sir?' he said, his voice very slow and deep.

'Yes, I'm not feeling too well.'

'Oh, that's a shame, Sir. Would you like to sit down somewhere?'

'No, no thank you. I think I'll just get some fresh air.'

'I wouldn't advise that, Sir. It's a very cold night and you might get a chill. Come with me to the parlour and I will get a servant to bring you a glass of cordial.'

'No, really . . .'

'I'm sorry, Sir. I insist.'

There was menace lying beneath his tone and John, with great reluctance, followed him down a narrow passageway and into a most opulent study. There were books lining the shelves and standing in piles on the floor. There was also a handsome globe and various maps of the world spread about the room. Indeed John could not think of a more contrasting place to find oneself in, having just left the fantasy of Miss Molly's honeymoon hotel. There was a large desk in the centre of the room with a handsome fellow of about twenty-five or so sitting at it. He raised his eyebrows as John was hurtled inside.

'Good gracious,' he said, his voice cultured and pleasant. 'What have we here?'

'Someone who wanted to leave, Master,' answered the negro.

'But people are free to come and go as they wish, Samson. I've always told you that.'

'I know you have, Master. But this cove was acting suspiciously.'

'In what way?'

'I can't exactly say. But there was something rum about him.'

The man behind the desk gave a little laugh. 'Well, I think it is very impolite of you, Samson, to presume such things. Allow me to introduce myself, Sir. My name is Peter Herbert.' He slid down from the desk and gave a little bow.

John stared incredulously. The man was a dwarf. Perfect in both body and face, his legs were no more than two feet long. At full height his head came to John's waistline. The Apothecary almost forgot to bow, he was so surprised.

'You look startled. Why, may I ask?'

'Forgive me. It is just that you are not the sort of person I expected to see running an establishment like this.'

Mr Herbert gave a short laugh. 'Do you mean the fact that I am a dwarf? Or do I look too straight-laced for such an enterprise?'

'Both really,' John admitted.

'Actually my mother owns it. I just stand in for her when she's out. I am by trade a book-keeper for the Merchant Venturers. Don't look so askance. My mama was a great courtesan in her day and was a very wise and kindly woman, believe it or not.'

'I'm finding all this rather difficult to take in,' said John. 'Do you mind if I sit down?'

'Of course, of course. Have a brandy. You've gone a little pale.'

The little man put a glass in the Apothecary's hand, then said, 'You don't look the type to be frequenting a nan-boys' brothel. What are you really doing here?'

'I'm just curious.'

'I see.' Peter Herbert sipped his drink, his legs swinging above the floor. 'I don't believe you,' he stated, then went on, 'I think you came here for a purpose. Now what is it?'

For no reason that he could pinpoint, John trusted him. Before he knew it he had told Peter the entire story of the Earl of St Austell's wedding feast and the two hired assassins. 'One of whom is now working here as a male prostitute,' he concluded.

The little man put his glass down and placed his fingertips together. 'This is a serious story. But I only have your word for it. Samson, fetch Curlylocks in here.'

A more unfortunate soubriquet for the wretched Herman Cushen John could not imagine.

Samson, who had been standing like a statue during this conversation, hardly breathing, left the room on the double but returned only a minute later with the message that Curlylocks was working and had been booked for the night. John was never quite certain whether this was the truth or a hastily made excuse, but whatever the reality Peter Herbert shook his head.

'Then I am afraid that I can do nothing to help you. To disturb a boy who is busy would be more than my dear mama could allow. Would you like to return tomorrow?'

John gave a hidden sigh, temporarily beaten. 'Perhaps. But if not tomorrow then another day.'

'Then it is possible we shall meet again. But if I am not here you will have the pleasure of my mother's company. Because if you are going to take poor Curlylocks away, she will have to be consulted first.'

It sounded terrible, John thought, imagining himself facing some ghastly old harridan. However he smiled bravely.

'I look forward to meeting her.'

'It will be an experience you won't forget.'

As Samson showed him down the passageway to the front door, John turned to him. 'Tell me, were you by any chance once a black boy to Lady Tyninghame?'

The man's face underwent a complete transformation. 'You know her? You know that sweet lady?'

'Reasonably well,' John lied.

'I was once her servant and I loved her. She was like a mother to me. But she had to let me go when that bitter time came for her. But you know all about that, of course.'

John nodded, wishing he did.

'I worked in various shops but in the end I came here. Master Herbert is good to me – and so is the old dame, though the poor soul thinks she's still a rare beauty.' Samson gave a short laugh. 'As to the boys, well, as long as they leave me alone I say good luck to 'em.'

'You're right. If that is their choice, if that is what makes them happy, then so be it.'

'Not everyone thinks like us, Mr Rawlings. The bigwigs of Bristol and their wives get very hot under the collar about such things.'

'The world never stopped turning for the opinions of the mighty. But Samson, do you live in or have you lodgings?'

'I lodge near The Seven Stars, Sir.'

'Then perhaps we can talk further somewhere else. Do you get any free time?'

'I get a day off once a month.'

'When is your next one?'

'Soon, Sir. This coming Friday.'

'Where will you be?'

'Probably in The Seven Stars.'

'I'll see you there at about noon.'

'Very good, Sir.'

And Samson opened the front door.

As he walked back to The Rummer Inn in All Saints Lane, the Apothecary's thoughts turned once more to Elizabeth. Looking up at the crowded stars that dazzled his eyes from the blackness of the heavens, he wondered about the reality of God. Was He really there, in charge of all the millions of potential lives that those glittering points of light might house? Or was He a myth, a legend, created to pacify mankind, to keep him from dreading too much the fear of death? John, humble mortal that he was, had no answer, no knowledge to help him. Only a small prayer to whatever it was that some part of Elizabeth's spirit would remain with him always.

Sixteen

Gone was the introspective thinking of the night before. John woke early, determined to find the answer to the puzzle of who had murdered the unknown man who called himself Augustus Bagot. Over a hearty breakfast he considered the options. If the murderer had held a grudge against the fat man, then there were several possibilities: Mr Huxtable, tired of the oaf who had taken up residence in his house; Commodore, the slave who had known the real Gus and who had loved him; and last, but very far from least, there was that most elegant and wickedly attractive man, Sir Julian Wychwood, who had fallen out with the pretender over a box in the theatre. Coming to the real Gus Bagot, who had lived and loved to the full in Bristol before taking ship to New Zealand, there was the definite possibility that he had caused someone great offence and the wrong man had answered for Gus's crime.

In that regard John had only been given one name, Sir Charles Tavener, who had beaten young Gus to a pulp because of his advances to his sister. Yet the note he had seen in the fat man's hand had been written in a rough script and the words 'We'll be coming soon' pointed to several people ganging together. And then there was the problem of Lady Tyninghame. A delicate creature with a strange and questionable past, yet what was her relationship with the dazzling Sir Julian Wychwood? Every instinct John had told him that there was a bond between them. Had Sir Julian been the young lover mentioned as part of the lady's downfall? With much on his mind the Apothecary ate a good meal and then ventured forth into the Bristol docks.

The first person he chanced to meet was young Henry Tavener, who was sauntering along with his dog Tray held firmly on a leash. He stopped and stared aghast at John's extraordinary outfit, provided by the wardrobe at the Playhouse.

'Are you in disguise again?' he asked abruptly.

'Yes. I am supposed to blend in with the inhabitants of the Bristol waterfront.'

Henry bellowed a laugh. 'Gadso, whatever did they have in mind? You look like a crushed mustard seed.'

John gave a wry grin. 'Thanks so much. You can borrow it if ever you feel the need. Merry quips aside, have you any gossip for me? I am desperate for leads.'

Henry looked terribly serious, an expression which ill became him. 'Do you know that since that conversation we had the other day, I am convinced that I am Gus Bagot's son.'

'Why is that?'

'It all fits too neatly. My mother refusing to tell me who my real mother was and being jovial about my uncle's little mis-demeanour. I'm sure that none of it is true and they probably bought me from some poor drab selling me at the dockside.'

'Oh surely not. I think your imagination is running away with you.'

Henry gave a hollow laugh, and by way of changing the subject John asked, 'Have you met Julian Wychwood yet?'

'Oh, you mean Lady Tyninghame's lover?'

John was instantly alert. 'Why do you say that?'

'I saw them at the ball last night. They were chatting so pleas-antly and she was looking at him with adoring eyes. And when the dance was done he offered her his arm and she clung to it like a dying bird.'

'What an odd description.'

'Yes,' said Henry, thinking about it. 'But that was how it struck me at the time. She's terribly frail, isn't she?'

'Yet she drew a bad hand of cards, I believe.'

'You refer to her tragic life?' John nodded. 'My Mama knows more about it than I do.' Henry paused, thinking, the effort of which made him frown deeply. 'I say, why don't you come and meet my mother. We live in Queen Square, but she's currently in the Hotwell for a few days. Tray and I were going to take the boat back. In fact, that is where we're off to at this very moment. Come and join us.'

'I've left my baggage at The Rummer.'

'Well, we'll go there and have a bumper and catch the following boat. They ply regularly when the tide is high.'

John pondered, and decided he could probably learn more from Lady Tavener than he could from nosing round Bristol.

'A capital plan,' he said, and watched as poor Tray, who had fallen asleep, was abruptly jerked back into action.

On the way back on the ferry boat they sat side by side, Henry sipping from a hip flask, John staring once more at the awe-inspiring scenery. It was truly like being in the Alps, he thought, the rugged cliffs rising on both sides, covered with furze, gorse and wildwood, with a flock of sheep bravely clinging on and chewing the fine grasses beneath their hooves. It was completely beautiful and the Apothecary found himself dwelling on the fact that one day modern man would undoubtedly ruin the terrain in some squalid way.

An hour later found him washed, shaved and dressed in a sober suit of dark blue ready to meet Henry's adopted mother, residing in her gracious apartment situated in Lebeck House. She looked delighted to see her son, but her face fell somewhat when she saw that he was with a friend.

'Mother, I want you to meet a new acquaintance of mine, Mr John Rawlings, an apothecary from London.'

'How dee do?' she said, and held out a pale, middle-aged hand on which the blue veins stood out.

John bent to kiss it, and as he drew closer the sparkle of jewels glittered in his eyes. Lady Tavener certainly had her fair share of diamonds and other sparklers. Having straightened up he made his best bow. She, meanwhile, had raised her quizzing glass and was giving him a thorough investigation.

She was a medium woman – in height, build, looks, personality and reaction to others. Only when her adopted son came near did she actually blossom and show animation. Now she laughed with pleasure as he threw her a fleeting kiss on the cheek and said, '*Maman*, dearest, I have met Mr Rawlings on several occasions and like him enormously. I do hope that you will too.'

'Anyone to whom you give your companionship is always welcome at my house. Delighted to make your acquaintance, Sir.'

'As I am yours, Milady,' answered John, and bowed once more.

It was about four o'clock and Lady Tavener had ordered a small round of sandwiches to keep away the fear of starvation between breakfast and dinner. With this she had a jug of lemonade, but Henry had already poured two glasses of dry sherry from the decanter which stood on the sideboard.

'You'll ruin your liver,' she said with a fond smile.

'Don't worry, I'll have an extra glass of the water tomorrow,' he answered, and whirled round the room to take a chair beside hers.

She turned towards John. 'Are you here for your health, Mr Rawlings?'

'Yes and no. I actually accompanied my father – you may have met him, Sir Gabriel Kent – to the Hotwell. But I have taken the health-giving waters and met some jolly company since I arrived.'

She sighed. 'Ah yes, Sir Gabriel. Now he is one of what I call the old school. You modern creatures do nothing but seek pleasure all the time.'

Henry laughed and said, 'But what else is life for? It's brief enough. We may as well make the best of it.'

The Apothecary sat in silence, thinking that in his short existence he had known much sorrow as well as much mirth, and he felt sad for Henry that he would spend his precious time on earth without ever touching the heights or the depths. But before he could wander into deep philosophy Lady Tavener spoke again.

'And what do you think of Bristol society, Mr Rawlings?'

'Very interesting. A somewhat mixed bag, I would say.'

'Isn't that true of everywhere? Are not we all a mixture of good and evil?'

'And some have evil done to us, would you not agree, Lady Tavener?'

'I would certainly.'

She poured herself another glass of lemonade and said, 'Poor soul, poor soul,' under her breath. Hoping wildly that she was talking about Lady Tyninghame, John remained silent and it was

Henry who said, 'Are you talking about the woman who has recently returned, Mother?'

'Yes, my dear. Violetta. Poor, sad creature.'

'Nonsense,' Henry retorted. 'I saw her in the Long Room t'other night looking as if she had just fallen in love.'

'What?' said his mama, sitting bolt upright.

'Yes, truly. She danced dance after dance with some dashing blade who is here to take the waters, or so he says.'

'Good heavens! Don't tell me the Marquis was right all along.'

John put on his innocent face and said, 'I don't quite understand.'

It was clear that Lady Tavener enjoyed a gossip as much as anyone, because she turned to the Apothecary and said in thrilling tones, 'I am speaking of a Lady Tyninghame, who was always thought of as a much maligned woman. She was married to the Marquis of Tyninghame, but he was cruel to her – they say he used to beat her mercilessly – and she left him. Rumour had it at the time that she had fallen in love with a much younger man who wanted to marry her. Apparently they used to meet at the grotto – which I have always personally thought a smelly little hole – and there used to hold hands. Be that as it may, the Marquis found out and divorced her, at which she wandered off, poor fey creature, and now she is back and in love again, or so it would seem.'

'An interesting tale,' said John.

So had the lover been Julian Wychwood all along? Had the pair been recently reunited? The Apothecary cast his mind back to the meeting last Sunday and vividly recalled the expression on Violetta's face when she had first heard the name of Wychwood. But did the ages fit?

'When did all this occur?' he asked.

'Do you know, I can't remember. But it was quite a while ago,' Lady Tavener replied.

There was a silence before Henry, snatching his mother's hand, planted a kiss on it.

'Thank you for the pleasure of your company, Mama, but Mr Rawlings and I must be off now.'

John stood up as well. 'Thank you so much for the sherry, Lady Tavener. Will we see you later at cards?'

'I shall certainly be going to the Long Room. I have arranged to meet my brother-in-law there.'

'Then our paths will cross again,' John answered, and gave a fulsome bow.

The evening was pleasant, but throughout dinner and the subsequent dancing the Apothecary had an uneasy feeling that all was not well with Elizabeth, that she was in the final stages of that dreaded disease called carcinoma. Thus, he excused himself early and walked briskly back to the hotel. He knew, had known almost certainly, that the porter would deliver him a letter. One look at it and he was aware of its contents even before he had broken the seal.

> To John Rawlings, Esq.
> Good Sir, I beg you to come at Once to Devon. Lady Elizabeth is near ye End and I write to You to Make Good Speed and come Forthwith.
> I remain, Sir, your Humble Servant,
> R. Sawyer (Steward)

In the fine clothes he had put on for the evening, John sprinted to the tavern which he knew Tom frequented at nights. He burst through the door and the Irishman, to his eternal credit, took one look at his master's face and rose to his feet. He asked one question.

'Is it Milady, Sir?'

John nodded, too out of breath to speak.

'Are we to go immediately?'

'Yes, now. How long will it take you to get the horses ready?'

'About fifteen minutes, Sir. Then we'll go at once.'

Exactly twenty minutes later they left. John had thrust some clothes into a portmanteau and penned a swift letter to Sir Gabriel. Then they were away into the darkness, heading for Bath and then Exeter, Irish Tom driving at a speed he had never attempted before. They changed horses several times, but the coachman stayed grimly at his post until after several hours of peering through the darkness, John suggested that they alight at Taunton

and take some refreshment. Looking at his loyal servant he saw
that Tom's eyes were red-rimmed.

'Tom, I'm going up on the box. You try and snatch some sleep
in the coach.'

'But, Sir, you've no experience. We might overturn and then
where will we be?'

'In the hedgerow, flat on our backs. Come on, my friend, I
insist.'

So it was John who took the reins between Taunton and White
Ball, where they stopped to change horses and exchange places
once again.

The Apothecary had not slept a wink but was not conscious
of feeling fatigued. The only thought in his mind was that he
should hold Elizabeth in his arms as she breathed her last. And
yet, despite this feeling of high alert, he must have dropped off
to sleep because he awoke abruptly as the horses began to pull
uphill and he realised that he was a stone's throw away from
Elizabeth's great house. He looked at his watch and saw that they
had been on the road for some fifteen hours.

'Tom,' he called out of the window.

'Yes, Sir?'

'Are you all right?'

'A bit tired, Sir, but holding on.'

'Good man.'

They clattered past the lodge and up to the house, and as they
approached John's heart plummeted. Every window was swathed
and dark, all the curtains in the place drawn. He knew at one
glance that he was too late. Elizabeth was already dead. An icy
calm possessed him, as if a small block of ice had penetrated his
soul. They pulled up at the front door and John saw that the
knocker was swathed in black material. Tom gave him a glance
of dread.

'I'm so sorry, Sir.'

'Not now, Tom, though I thank you most sincerely. I must
keep a cool head for the sake of the boys.'

The steward, Mr Sawyer, was sent for as soon as John was
admitted and came through from the servants' quarters to bow low.

'Sir, I am indeed sorry. Lady Elizabeth died yesterday. It was
all very tragic.'

John stood up straight, his long coat almost sweeping the floor, as the servants filed past him, the women fighting back tears, the men tight-lipped with grief. When all was done and he had thanked each and every one of them, he turned to the steward.

'May I see her, please. Is she in her bedroom?'

The steward's face assumed an expression that in any other circumstances John would have thought of as quaintly humorous.

'She is not here, Sir.'

'What do you mean? Where is she?'

'Somewhere in the sea, Sir. The body has not yet been recovered.'

For the first time John flinched and a servant placed a chair behind him.

'You mean she committed suicide? That she threw herself off the cliffs?'

A servant audibly burst into tears and was hurried out of the great hall.

'Not quite, Sir. Come into the Blue Drawing Room and I'll give you a glass of brandy to steady your nerves. As for your poor coachman, he looks quite done in.'

'I'm sorry, Tom. That was inconsiderate of me. Go and rest, for God's sake.'

Somebody took his arm and guided him to the Blue Drawing Room, then sat him down in a comfortable chair and poured him a large restorative drink. For a second his icy calm had been broken but he drew it back around him like a familiar old cloak. He looked up and saw that Mr Sawyer was still standing.

'Oh please sit down, my friend. You should be seated when you tell me what happened.'

Sawyer balanced on the edge of a chair and looked at John sadly.

'I'll relate the whole story, Sir, because I think you'll want to hear it.'

The Apothecary nodded silently.

'You'll remember her favourite horse, Sir. That big black devil called Sabre. Well, it was amazing to us all to see how it pined and weakened. It just stood in its loose box, head drooping. When one of the grooms tried to exercise it, it threw him, and him an experienced rider and all.'

'Does this have anything to do with her death?'

'Yes, indeed it does, Sir. Well, we called the horse doctor in and he said it would have to be shot. No life left in the poor beast at all. No-one told Lady Elizabeth, but it was as if she knew. She got out of bed and insisted that she be helped into her riding habit. Then she was assisted downstairs and out to the stables where she somehow climbed onto the back of old Sabre. They got the back from an old chair and put it behind her to support her. Then off she goes with a young groom to keep her company lest she should fall off. Sir, the groom is in the kitchen. Do you want me to fetch him?'

'Yes. I would like to know what happened.'

With Sawyer gone, the echo of silence rushed in at the Apothecary like a great wave. He wondered why he had not shed a tear, why he had not broken down, but knew it was because he had to hear all that there was to tell. And because somewhere upstairs in that great and quiet house there were two frightened little boys waiting to know their fate. But the sight of the groom unnerved him. The youth was wretched with weeping and was fighting to keep control of himself.

'Please sit down,' said John. 'And tell me how it ended.'

'I should have stopped her, Sir. I know it.'

'I beg you not to blame yourself. Whatever happened was at Lady Elizabeth's wish.'

'Well we rode out in the direction of Sidmouth House. I thought she was going to call on her old friend – ill though Milady was for visiting – so I stayed a few yards behind her. Oh Christ, Sir, what followed was so pitiful.' Tears sprang out of the groom's eyes but he continued the story in a halting voice. 'She suddenly calls out, "Come on, Sabre, you and I are both done for," and with that she kicks him into a gallop and just for a moment, Sir, it looked as if they were both flying towards the sun. They soared off the cliff top in an incredible arc. And then they plunged down and down into the sea.'

There was no sound except for the groom's quiet weeping. John sat like a frozen statue, then slowly he raised the brandy to his lips and drank deep.

'Go on.'

'I got to the top and looked downwards to the sea. I could see the great dark horse lying in the waves, quite dead. Of the Lady Elizabeth there was no sign. I think she was down in the deeps and gone from us.'

At last the Apothecary cracked. He just said two words, 'Oh no,' and then he wept like a broken man.

They fetched Irish Tom to him and the big fellow held John in his arms and let him cry himself out. Then eventually, when the storm was over, Tom said, 'What about your boys, John? Don't you think it best that you go and see them?'

'Yes, yes, you're right. Thank you, my old friend, you have witnessed me at my lowest.'

'Say no more about it, Sir. Now tidy yourself up and go to your lads. They'll be in a state of bewilderment, no doubt.'

A quarter of an hour later, washed, shaved and smelling pleasantly of his toilet water, John followed a footman up the grand staircase and to the right to the nursery. There he found a fire roaring and the nurserymaids busy about their work, while two little boys sat side by side, their faces very solemn. John walked through the door and two pairs of eyes regarded him. Neither child smiled or moved.

'Hello, James. Hello, Jasper,' he said, trying to sound jolly.

They stared at him. 'Hello,' one whispered back.

'Can I come and sit with you?'

'Yes, but we really want Mama. Is it time for us to go and see her?'

John's heart felt as if it were shattering into a thousand pieces. 'I'm afraid your mama isn't here,' he said, aware that the nurserymaids were looking at him with reproving glances.

'Where is she?' asked one child, John could not tell which.

'She's gone away.'

Simultaneously the twins started to cry, tears running down their sweetly innocent cheeks.

'Where has she gone?' asked the other one.

John was silent for a moment, trying desperately to think of the right answer, well aware that they were too young to understand the concept and finality of death. Then he had a flash of inspiration.

'She's gone to swim with the mermaids,' he said.

They stopped crying. 'Has she?' asked one.

'Has she really?' asked the other.

'Yes, she's gone on a great swim through all the seas in all the world. She'll be away a long, long time. So meanwhile I've come to look after you.'

'You're our papa, aren't you?'

'Yes, James and Jasper, I am your papa. Will you be happy with me?'

They looked at him appraisingly.

'We'll try,' they chorused.

John slept in the guest wing that night and had the most vivid dream. He was fast asleep yet he dreamt that there was a gentle knock on his door, which then flew open to reveal Elizabeth. She was wearing her riding habit and had a beautiful feathered hat on her head. She looked just as she had when first they met and she smiled and winked at him.

'I long to kiss you,' she said.

In his dream John sat up in bed. 'That is what you said when we first met.'

'But now I cannot do so,' she said, and a chill wind blew through John and he realised that she was transparent and that he could see the wall behind her. 'My will is with my lawyer in Exeter. The house passes in the entail to my cousin because my sons are born bastards. So from now on they will be with you. You will care for them, won't you, John?'

'I swear it.'

'It was clever of you to tell them that I am with the mermaids, because in a way, now I am. Goodbye, my love.'

The room was full of the scent of lilac in full bloom and she was fading before his eyes. 'Oh Elizabeth, don't go,' John cried out.

'Goodbye,' sighed a million sighs, and he woke to a guttering candle and the room full of deepening shadows.

Seventeen

The letter from Sir Gabriel had been kind but immensely direct. In it he had advised his son to remove the twins as soon as could be arranged and take them to London.

> They must start their new Life as soon as possible and their little Minds must be turned away from Withycombe House and their Treasured Recollection of Elizabeth. This may Sound Harsh, my beloved Son, but believe me, it will Be for The Best.

So John had remained in Devon for a week. The sea had not yielded up Elizabeth's body and though he himself had searched the shore line, rowing out in a boat and peering down as best he could, there had never been a sign of anything. She had gone to the deeps, as the young groom had said, and there she would lie, full fathom five, to quote the great poet.

The reading of the will had been brief. There had been minor legacies to staff and servants, but the bulk of Elizabeth's fortune, a not inconsiderable sum, had been left in trust until her sons reached the age of twenty-one. John had also been given a large portion 'for the housekeeping and education of James and Jasper Rawlings'.

His next task had been to tell the staff they were to remain until Elizabeth's cousin arrived to take charge, and to offer the two nurserymaids a job in London, should they both desire. Strangely, they had turned him down. They were country women at heart and could not bear the confines of town life, they said. But local enquiries had produced an applicant for the job: a big, fresh-faced local girl with skin like Devon cream and dancing hazel eyes, an unruly mob cap hiding her mop of curling black hair. She was called Hannah and John Rawlings took to her the moment they met.

The twins were told they were going on a holiday and thus

made no protest when Irish Tom drove John's coach round the carriage sweep and down the drive. John put his head out of the window and tears filled his eyes as the great house in which he had known the delights of passion, of fatherhood, of fun and laughter and quarrels, faded into the distance and into memory.

He had sent a messenger to Jacquetta Fortune to say that he was returning to London with his sons and a new maid and could she use the same rider for reply. Her answer was positive, saying that she was rearranging the rooms and asking him to contact her again when he reached Brentford. This John did, and thus the highly organised woman had prepared a tea for the two tots and had a big smile for Hannah, who had travelled on the box beside Tom, talking in her lovely Devon accent nearly all the way to town.

The twins were sharing a room next to that of their half sister Rose, who was currently away at school. Mrs Fortune had purchased two little beds and had done her best with the accommodation in the amount of time she had been given. So the total effect was pleasing and John left them happily fighting over who was going to get which bed. Jacquetta met him on the landing.

'They are a delight, John. And totally identical. But when the excitement wears off they will miss their mother badly.'

'I'm sure you're right,' he answered with a sigh. 'But we shall have to cope with that when the time comes.'

'But how?'

The Apothecary shook his head. 'I have no idea.'

But a visit to his shop proved to be a great event for his boys. One of them, James, shrieked with joy at the sight of the herbs hanging up to dry and the great array of jars holding various compounds. They both watched Robin Hazell, whom they obviously admired, pounding away in a mortar, and begged John to let them try. He found two smaller, little-used mortars, sprinkled a few herbs within, and left them sitting at the workbench, mixing away for dear life.

But it was Fred who caused the sensation of the day. Sweeping under the benches, he spoke to the little boys.

'Excuse me, young masters, I just want to sweep away the bits wot you dropped.'

Jasper, the bolder of the two, said, 'We haven't dropped anything.'

'Well, wot's them bits on the floor then?'

The twins sat speechless, lacking the language skills to argue, but James said, 'Where?'

''Ere, I'll show yer.'

And before John or Gideon or Robin could stop him, Fred had dragged Jasper off his stool and onto the floor where he pointed out the scraps of herbs with a stubby finger. At this level the twin was in his element, crawling round picking up any dropped detritus and licking it to find out what it was. James, seeing this, immediately joined in and as Gideon went to stop them, John touched him on the arm.

'Let them play, my friend. They're enjoying themselves. Besides, you have to eat a bushel of dirt before you die,' at which Gideon smiled and shook his head.

As he took them home that night, James said, 'Can we go to your shop tomorrow, Papa? I like it there.'

'What did you like best?'

'Fred,' the twins said in chorus.

Jasper asked James, 'Why did you call him Papa? *My* papa is a prince.'

At which Hannah spoke up sharply, 'Jasper, you can stop that this instant. That's your papa sitting opposite you and the only one you'll ever have. So get used to it or you'll get a smack on the bum.'

She glanced at John to see if he was annoyed with her outspokenness, but he merely smiled and directed his gaze out of the window. Jasper pulled a face but everyone ignored him, James being too sleepy to bother.

After that visit the twins talked about Fred incessantly until John was forced to ask the little chap if he would come to sup in the house and spend the evening with his sons. The boy abandoned at Thomas Coram's Foundling Hospital had been prepared for the visit by Robin Hazell, John's young apprentice. First he had been dumped into a tin bath and scrubbed vigorously, then dressed in some ill-fitting clothes which Robin had outgrown. Then he had made his way, walking in a new pair of shoes which Gideon had bought him.

He arrived on John's front door step looking such an eager scrap that John's heart bled for him.

'I hopes that I hain't too early, Mr Rawlings,' he said as he was ushered into the library where John was sitting alone.

'No, no,' John answered, feeling quite ancient as he looked down from his newspaper at the little bundle of hopefulness standing before him. 'You have caused quite a sensation with my sons and they have invited you to play with them. So I will have your best English, please, Fred.'

'Ho yuss, Sir. Me best.'

John sighed inwardly, expecting his sons soon to be adopting Fred's way of speaking. But it was a small price to pay for the child's good-natured company.

'Go on, my lad. They're having a cold collation in the nursery and Miss Hannah will be keeping order. So off you go and no getting into mischief, mind.'

'Oh no, Sir.'

When he had left the room John got up and looked out of the window, thinking how blessed he had been to find Sir Gabriel. Or rather for his adopted father to have found him. He had once begged on the streets of London, when he had been about the same age as his sons, until that fortunate day when Sir Gabriel's coach had run them down.

For that had been the start of the great love affair between John's mother Phyllida and the widower Sir Gabriel Kent. And John thanked God for it, for in what wretched alleyway might he have lived otherwise and what terrible street rat might he have turned into.

John found that tears were trickling down his cheeks at the thoughts that were going through his mind, and he wiped them away impatiently and sat down with his newspaper once more. But memories of Sir Gabriel brought the old grandee vividly to mind and he felt that he must soon return to the Hotwell to see how he was faring. Regular letters had advised John that the old man was in his element, paying court to the ladies over cards and attending balls and outings. But the season was drawing rapidly to a close and John did not want to think of his adopted father isolated in a spot that could become rather desolate once the fashionable crowd had moved on. He determined that as soon as the twins had settled in he would be off.

Before he did so, however, John took the opportunity of visiting the theatre and friends, calling on his old comrade Samuel Swann – who had now grown somewhat fat and somewhat self-important – and insisting on taking him out for the evening and away from Sam's wife and four noisy children. They decided to visit a tavern where they could talk over old times and chose The Old Bell in Fleet Street. There they settled down to reminisce, at which Sam said with a gusty sigh, 'How I miss the old days, John. Why is it that everything in life moves on? Why can't we live in one happy period for the whole of our existence?'

John shook his head. 'I have often thought the same thing myself. But alas it is not mankind's fate. And if it were, would we not get bored? Isn't it the newness of events that makes life exciting?'

'But the new things are not always pleasant.'

'How well I know that,' and John went on to explain to Sam, whose round face grew sadder and sadder, about Elizabeth's slow death from carcinoma.

'But she died as she wanted, Sam. She leapt over the cliff on her sick old horse and plunged into the sea below.'

'Good God. How brave. And how terribly, terribly wretched.'

'Better that than dying in pain, full of opium.'

'Was her body ever recovered?'

'No, strangely. The tide usually washes them ashore but not in her case. I told the twins that their mother was swimming with the mermaids.'

'What a delightful thought.'

'Perhaps it's true,' said John with a wry smile.

They talked over past cases and John found himself discussing the current one with Samuel, who quite literally quivered with excitement.

'Oh, how I wish I could come to the Hotwell with you. It would be so marvellous to be on the trail of a villain once more.'

John laughed. Samuel had always been so enthusiastic, but was known for putting his foot in it time and again, a fact of which he was blissfully unaware.

'I suppose you're too bound up with your family these days.'

Samuel gave a hearty laugh. 'I'm master in my own house, John. But Jocasta is not too keen on my being away. Says it leaves her with a great deal to do.'

The Apothecary smiled fondly, thinking of his rather large friend being completely under his thin wife's thumb.

'Oh, I quite understand, old chap. Can't upset the marital home.'

Samuel adopted a serious voice. 'Do you miss Elizabeth's company?'

'I miss her terribly. It was a tragic end to a great life. Yet in a way her actual death said all about the life she led. It was a triumph over suffering.'

'But how has it affected you, John? That's what I am asking.'

'I am a survivor, Sam. Whatever life throws at me I have the ability to overcome. Inside my heart I may weep but those looking on will never know how sad I am.'

And with that he drew the subject to a close.

When he returned home he saw that the parlour was still lit and went to see who was up. Jacquetta Fortune was sitting by the light of several candles, reading a book. John stood for a moment, studying her. She had certainly come to full bloom now, quite lovely in her blonde-haired way.

'Gideon not with you?' was on his lips before he had time to think what he was saying.

She looked up, surprised. 'No, I have not seen him this evening. In fact I have not seen him all day.'

John stood beside a chair. 'May I sit down?'

'Of course you may. You are master in this house.'

John gave a crooked smile. 'When I'm here.'

Jacquetta put the book down and said, very directly, 'Why did you ask about Gideon?'

John replied, equally truthfully, 'I know that he is in love with you. Is the feeling reciprocated?'

'Would you be annoyed if it were?'

'Not in the least. It is entirely a matter for yourselves.'

'Well then, I'll be honest with you and tell you that I intend to marry him. You see, I long to have another child and I must act soon before Mother Nature's clock ticks against me.'

'Thank you for being so frank. Tell me, do you love him?'

'Who could not? I know I am older than he is but it really doesn't matter to me. He has come into my life as my second chance, and I intend to take it.'

'And what about my business?'

'We will continue to devote ourselves to it utterly.'

'And will you go on living here?'

'Until we can find a house of our own.'

'So may I ask when is the wedding to take place?' John said.

'As soon as Gideon has spoken to you, Mr Rawlings.'

'To me?' John exclaimed. 'But why? I am not his father.'

Mrs Fortune looked a trifle severe. '*In loco parentis*, Sir. As you know, Gideon's father died when he was just a boy.'

John sat back in his chair, feeling as old as Methuselah. 'Oh dear,' he said aloud.

'Don't you approve,' Jacquetta asked anxiously.

'Of course I do. It's wonderful news.'

'Then why the long face?'

The Apothecary sighed. 'Oh, just because.' Changing the subject, he asked, 'How are the twins?'

'Slightly naughty. So I asked that little sprite Fred round to a cold collation – I hope you don't mind – and he worked his usual miracle with them.'

'What am I going to do about him? He can't go on in his menial position if he is going to be a playmate to my sons.'

'Why don't you take him as an apprentice?'

'But I already have one.'

'Surely there is no law that says you cannot have two?'

'But the child can't read or write.'

'He has made much progress in those subjects, Mr Rawlings. He is now almost literate.'

'I'll think about it, I really will. But now, Mrs Fortune, I intend to have a nightcap and I trust that you will join me in a toast.'

'I most certainly will, Mr Rawlings.'

John poured two glasses of brandy and then raised his. 'To your future happiness, Jacquetta. You most certainly deserve it.'

'Thank you, John. If I may make so bold, I hope that all will be well with you.'

Eighteen

Hannah, accompanied by a young, strong footman, showed the twins the sights of London in the daytime, and in the evening they played with their father, Mrs Fortune or, preferably, Fred. The Apothecary had been forced to weaken and had offered the boy an apprenticeship on the understanding that he would have mastered the art of reading and writing in the coming six months. Based upon this, John had given the fellow a tiny bedroom in the attic, little bigger than a broom cupboard, next door to that of Robin Hazell. Fred had been more than pleased, saying, 'It's me own place at last,' and had treated his minute sleeping quarters as if they were some grand bedroom in a huge mansion. He kept the room shining like a star and cleaned everything in sight. John, counting up the number of people who slept under his roof, had serious thoughts of buying a bigger house.

So, seeing that the twins were well settled, he decided that the time had come to return to the Hotwell. It was the last week of the season and he knew that Sir Gabriel would be getting anxious about leaving. Irish Tom, who had been lazing about the last few weeks, was called into action and, having cleaned and polished the coach, brought the equipage round to the front door in Nassau Street, lowered the step and watched John climb inside. Then Tom got smartly onto the box, cracked the whip and away they went.

They drove fairly fast – though not at the hell-for-leather speed they had driven to Devon – and arrived at Thatcham in the small hours, spending the night in a coaching inn. They had four hours' sleep and set off with fresh horses, arriving in Bristol some time before lunch. Tom picked his way along the riverbank to the Hotwell and pulled up in front of Sir Gabriel's hotel with a cry of triumph.

'We're here, Sir.'

'Yes by God, we are.'

The place was much emptier than John recalled it, a great

many of the *beau monde* having moved on to Bath, exchanging the rustic charm for the indoor formality and enjoying the contrast. After a quick wash and brush up, John found his father sitting on a seat by the river, which was at full tide and looked very pleasing. Next to him was Miss Titania Groves, delightful in green muslin and white lace. They looked up as he approached.

'Oh my dear,' said Sir Gabriel. 'What a terrible time you have been through.'

'I have indeed – and so have many others. But let us speak of happier things. How have you been enjoying yourself, Papa?'

'To be frank with you, I am now getting a little bored. The place is lovely, don't misunderstand me. But I shall be glad to see my own things about me once more.'

'And quite right too. You have stayed here rather a long time through no fault of your own.' John turned to Titania. 'Tell me, if you will, how many people that I met are still here?'

She smiled up at him. 'Well, everybody really. My mother, of course, and all the friends who sat down to cards. Oh, and Lady Tyninghame.'

'And Sir Julian Wychwood?'

Titania blushed apple-blossom pink. 'Yes, I believe so.'

Inwardly John grinned, though his features remained calm. 'I see. Then I will be in time to say goodbye to them all.'

'I think Lady Tyninghame is going within the next few days. She talked about moving on to Bath.'

'As are you perhaps?'

'Oh yes, Mama says it is a wonderful season. I would not miss it for the world.'

'I agree, it is very enjoyable, but miss it I must. Sir Gabriel and I are homeward bound.'

'Oh, what a pity.'

But John knew the little flirt was only toying with him. He felt fairly certain that she had given her heart to that wild seducer Wychwood.

'How is Sir Julian?' he asked casually.

'I believe he is riding on the Downs today. He says the air is very fresh up there.'

'How interesting. Does he ride well?'

'I saw him on horseback t'other day. He looked magnificent.'

She sighed, and John, glancing at Sir Gabriel, saw his father wink a brilliant eye. The old man rose to his feet.

'Pleasant though it has been chatting to you, I must now bid you farewell, Miss Groves. I feel a little fatigued and would like to rest before cards tonight.'

She stood up. 'Of course, Sir Gabriel.' She dropped a brief curtsey to him and to John and proceeded along the river path. John took his father's arm and was somewhat startled by the weight the older man put upon it. For the very first time the reality of Sir Gabriel's age came home to him in plenty.

They got back to the hotel and sat for a while, chatting about the twins and Elizabeth.

'So how are the boys settling into London life?'

'So far very well, but no doubt the day will come when they will beg me to take them home. Amusingly, they are both very much in awe of Fred, that little scallowag that bluffed his way into my employment.'

'You've told me of him before. You mean the foundling child?'

'That's the one. He is a sweet little person but his accent is atrocious. I have promised to apprentice him if he can master reading and writing come Christmas. However, the twins have taken him to their hearts and are very well behaved when he is around.'

'Then he is a valuable member of your staff.'

They talked a while longer and then Sir Gabriel made his way upstairs, leaving his son to peruse the papers, but he had only been reading for about ten minutes when he heard the sound of hurrying footsteps, panting breath, and a shock of carroty hair and a bright blue ribbon flashed into his vision.

'Gilbert!' he exclaimed, as young Mr Farr, complete with apothecary's apron, dashed up to him.

'My dear John, I am so glad to see you returned. I am afraid that I have made little or no progress with the investigation.'

'So what have you done? Closed the case?'

'Yes, more or less. Unless someone comes forward with a confession I do not know how to proceed.'

John shook his head. 'I am sorry that I had to abandon you, but I was called away to a matter deeply personal. And then I had to sort out its aftermath.' Gilbert opened his mouth to ask a question but John forestalled him. 'I would rather not discuss the matter, though I thank you for being concerned. But Gilbert, there is something I would like you to do for me.'

'And that is?'

'There's an escaped villain – an actual murderer – at loose in Bristol. He and an accomplice, who has subsequently died, shot several people at a wedding which I attended. He is now working in a nan-boys' brothel dressed in female clothing, which hideously unbecomes him. In short, Gilbert, he needs to be arrested by someone in authority.'

'You don't mean me?' asked Gilbert, askance, pointing a finger at himself.

'I most certainly do.'

'But what about the Bristol Constable, he—'

'Oh dammit, Gilbert, 'twould be a personal favour to me. Come on now. The killer has gone free for two years odd.'

John read Gilbert's thoughts as clearly as if he had spoken them aloud. It was not his affair, so why should he be involved with it? Yet on the other hand, he had sworn to do his duty when taking on the job of Constable, which was a downright nuisance and interfered with the running of his business. He turned to John.

'All right, I'll do it. When do we go?'

'Tonight, why not? I'm taking my father home in a few days' time. Speed is now of the essence.'

Gilbert pulled a face. 'I don't know why I'm getting implicated in all this.'

'Neither do I. But it will be a debt long overdue when we get that little wretch behind bars where he belongs.'

Gilbert sighed laboriously. 'Not my debt.'

'Oh, courage my friend. A case of murder is everybody's concern, surely?'

'I suppose you're right about that.'

'You know I am.'

It seemed that deep in his clothes press Gilbert had hidden a suit made of vivid puce satin, with a waistcoat of emerald green trimmed with brilliants. It had been created for a wedding of some family relative and had been treated with much hilarity by his nearest and dearest, to say nothing of his roguish friends. Gilbert had crept home in shame from the matrimonial celebrations, had hidden the aforementioned suit safely in the recesses of his cupboard and had never worn it since. But now, after a great deal of persuasion from John, who said it would be a most suitable attire for the evening's outing, he had dragged it out again and reluctantly put it on his back. John, meanwhile, had been to see the witty Mr Foote – catching him rehearsing at the theatre – and had borrowed a creation made of velvet and lace, a most effeminate set of garments which the one-legged actor, who always got the audience laughing when he appeared wearing it, insisted was returned the next day.

Thus rigged out, the couple were dropped outside the Strawberry Fields by Irish Tom and with shrill voices demanded entry. The door was opened by the black servant Samson, who looked with a certain surprise at John but made no comment. However, the dwarfish Mr Herbert must have left some instructions because instead of being shown into the main body of the building – from which emanated a great deal of laughter – they were whisked down the corridor and into that same room in which John had been questioned by the owner's son. But this time the little man was not there. Instead, sitting behind the desk, was a veritable harridan of a woman, who glared at them through a vast quizzing glass encrusted with sparklers.

It was impossible to see her face, which was so plastered with white make-up that it resembled nothing but a malevolent moon. Above the line of where her eyebrows had once been were painted two black lines, while her mouth had been so exaggerated as to look as if it was swelling up after a nasty punch. She wore voluminous red satin and many jewels, glittering when she moved her head, her fingers, and fighting a battle at her neck. Her voice when she spoke was surprisingly deep pitched.

'So you've come back for another taste, have you, my fine young Sir. And brought a friend with you. How cosy. But I can tell you that you're too late.'

John gazed at her uncomprehendingly. 'For what?'

'For capturing my little Curlylocks. He – she – has vanished. My spies tell me that he's taken a ship to the Indies, as a ship's cook and whore to the sailors, I don't doubt.'

John stared at her incredulously. 'When did this happen?'

The featureless face regarded him. 'What business is it of yours?'

Gilbert spoke up. 'I may be dressed outlandishly, Madam, but I am here on official business. I am the Constable of the Hotwell and I am here to arrest Herman Cushen for murder.'

'Well you can't. And now I require you to leave my property immediately. Out with you, I say.'

She reared up, a horrific sight, because as she stood she got taller and taller until she towered over them both.

'You're no woman,' shouted John, 'you're a man, damn you.'

The transvestite bared his teeth at them and, picking up a cast bronze lion that stood on the desk, hurled it with accuracy at John. It caught him a glancing blow on the temple but was enough to stop him in his tracks. At this Gilbert lost his temper and, jumping on to the desk with an agility that left John breathless, flung himself on to the great man-woman with a loud shout. Samson, hearing the fracas from the other side of the door, rushed in and threw a punch into the air which unfortunately caught John on the side of his jaw, just as he was struggling to his feet. Down he went to the floor again, listening to the sounds of Gilbert cursing and swearing as he belted the great creature with a series of blows which apparently inflicted no pain whatsoever. At this, Samson entered the fray once more and, picking up the bronze lion, leapt up onto a stool and crowned the almighty being with a savage downward thrust. The vast wig of curling blonde curls fell off to reveal an ugly brutal head covered by a mass of short black prickles. The owner of this unlovely sight stood swaying for a moment before buckling at the knees and crashing to the floor. The fight was over.

Samson looked round. 'I have been wanting to do that for years.'

John, still lying on the floor, said, 'But I thought the dwarf said that this flash-the-drag man was his mother.'

'I think Mr Herbert believed he was.'

'But that's impossible,' said Gilbert, getting down from the desk. 'The minute he stood up I realised it was a chap.'

Samson shrugged his shoulders. 'Then I don't know the answer, except that to a dwarf the whole world seems tall. But I do know that if we don't get out of here immediately we're as good as dead.'

They helped John up and made for the front door. 'Are you coming, Samson? There must be a better life than working here, surely?'

'Yessir, I'm escaping. I'll come with you to the Hotwell and try to find employment there.'

The slave closed the front door quietly, but for all his caution there was the sound of an inner door opening.

'Run,' he said. 'Go like the devil.'

The three of them took off at speed, only to hear the front door open behind them. 'After them,' they heard. 'One of them has killed Madame.' This was followed by a chorus of high-pitched shrieks and the sound of pounding footsteps.

John turned down a side street and, much to his relief, saw his coach standing at the ready. Irish Tom, hearing the hue and cry, peered into the darkness, identified John and shot off the box, lowering the step and opening the door. The three men clambered aboard, Samson losing a shoe in the haste. As they drove away they heard someone fling himself at the coach door, which opened a crack. Gilbert promptly trod on the pursuer's hand and the accompanying yelp of pain was drowned by the noise of the equipage taking off into the darkness of night.

Nineteen

They did not stop until they reached the outskirts of Hotwell, where the coach pulled up by a low-class ale house, The Bear in Love Street. John and Gilbert hurried in, in need of some liquid refreshment after their chase from the Strawberry Fields. Samson followed them warily, but grew more confident when he saw another black face inside.

The whistles and shouts at the appearance of the Apothecary and Gilbert Farr had to be heard to be believed. The entire crew of customers thought them effeminate to say the least of it and the lewd comments were enough to curl their most intimate hairs. But they put a brave face on it and made some merry quips in return before sitting at a table with Samson. They had started on their second brandy when there was another stir in the ale house as Samuel Foote appeared, flushed with success as he had just finished a performance at the Playhouse. He made a bold entrance, shouting, 'Unhand me gentlefolk, unhand me I say. I am but a poor player who struts and frets his hour upon the stage.'

The landlord, one Thomas Brotherton, yelled over the hubbub, 'Show some respect please, gentlemen. It's an actor from the theatre.'

There was a lessening of the uproar and Samuel, spotting John, came over to join them.

'You're both got up very fine,' he said, and turning to the Apothecary added, 'That costume suits you, so it does.'

'I promise not to spill anything on it.'

'You'll be lucky if someone doesn't heave their guts up all over you.'

'What a nasty thought.'

'I spoke in jest,' said Samuel, but his face bore a very serious expression.

Gilbert Farr said, 'We haven't been introduced, Sir, but I have much admired your work in the theatre. I was at the Playhouse this last week past and thought your performance admirable.'

Samuel rolled his eyes to heaven. 'An admirer. And such a young and attractive one, too.'

John said in a slightly warning voice, 'Gilbert Farr is an apothecary and is also Constable of the Hotwell.'

Samuel pursed his lips into a tiny O. 'My, my, I shall have to watch my Ps and Qs, won't I?'

Gilbert looked at him straightforwardly. 'It is a bigger villain than you could ever be that we seek, Sir. Or rather, we sought.'

Samuel stared at him. 'Do you mean the murderer of the fat man on the steep steps?'

'Yes.'

'Well the answer is obvious, my dear chap. It was that agile young man who swung round the theatre like a veritable ape. In other words, Sir Julian Wychwood. He had an enormous grudge against the fat feller for taking his box. He's your man.'

Gilbert looked astonished and John said, 'Have you any evidence, Samuel?'

'Evidence? Not as such. But I know human nature. Had to study it in order to perform, you see. I tell you that Wychwood is a trickster, especially with the female sex. And at cards, too, I'll warrant.'

'That's a bit heavy without any actual proof.'

'Pouff to proof. It is what one learns from life. That is the way of telling what a man is really like.'

They gave Samuel Foote a lift back to his lodgings in Dove Street, and when he was gone Gilbert said to John, 'Do you think I should question Wychwood?'

'Definitely. After all, Sam Foote has had a great deal of experience and he might just be right.'

'Should I make my visit formal?' asked Gilbert.

John considered. 'No, I think he might laugh. Try and bump into him – or even better come to the ball at the Long Room tomorrow night and I'll introduce you.'

'I will. And could you do me a favour, my friend? Could you quiz Mr Huxtable and his slave once more?'

'I can certainly do that. And what about Henry Tavener?'

'I think he's innocent, don't you?'

With these words they trooped off to their various addresses, but just as John was going into his hotel he noticed a hound in the street outside, nose upward, staring at the moon which hung low in the sky and was a deep sanguine red, a Hunter's Moon. The dog, which John recognised as Tray, had opened its muzzle and was letting out a doleful howl, a sound reckoned to shatter the nerves after listening for a minute or two.

'Tray, be quiet,' John called in an authoritative voice, but the wretched animal had now changed the unnerving sound to a continuous bark.

A window opened in the hotel and a head in a night cap poked out and said, 'Can nobody shut that wretched beast up. It's keeping us all awake.'

John called back, 'I'm sorry, Sir. I'll see if I can find its owner.'

'Thank you.' The head withdrew and the window banged shut.

Cautiously, John approached the beast which bared its teeth at him.

'Good dog,' he said nervously. 'Hush now. Be a good boy.'

The canine let out a low growl which made John shiver. It pulled back just as if it were about to launch itself at him when suddenly a hand rose from a bundle of clothes which John had not even noticed and attached itself to the dog's collar.

'Quiet, Tray, you miserable little bastard,' said a voice, and with this reassurance John walked forward.

The forlorn object turned out to be Henry Tavener, as drunk as a wheelbarrow, lying on the ground, his hose muddy and laddered, his cravat smeared with vomit. It was not a pretty sight. Henry smelt disgusting, but for all that John took a deep breath and forced himself to pull him into an upright position. Forgetting that Henry still had his hand under Tray's collar, the Apothecary was somewhat amused to see the dog jerked onto its back legs at the same time.

'Wha?' said Henry.

The Apothecary answered, 'Release your dog, Sir. You're choking it.'

'Eh?'

'Oh, never mind,' and John slipped Henry's nerveless fingers from Tray's neckpiece, at which the wretched animal gave another loud howl and belted off into the darkness. Slowly and extremely uncomfortably, John led the shambling wreck to his mother's lodging in Lebeck House, where he found all the candles lit and two anxious people waiting up.

This was his second encounter with Sir Roland Tavener and all he could say was that the man did not improve upon acquaintance. The winkle eyes were buried deep and he still had that supercilious manner which John had found rather irritating when they first met. But at this precise second he had a sobbing Lady Tavener in his arms, over whose bulky form it was almost impossible to appear upper crust. John could not help but smile at the look of consternation which filled the little eyes as they regarded Henry, who was making horrible noises again, scarcely able to stand.

'My God, boy, what have you been doing?'

There was no reply as John rushed the wretched young man

out into the kitchen and held his head over the sink. From the living room he could hear Lady Tavener wailing, 'Oh Roly, that it should have come to this.'

'The boy's a drunken sot, mixes with the wrong sort, always goes round with that mangey cur of his. To think that a son of mine should turn out like this.'

'Hush Roly, he might hear you.'

'I don't care if he does,' answered Sir Roland, deliberately raising his voice.

The wretched Henry, his vomiting at an end, now wept. 'You see,' he said to John. 'That's what my father thinks of me. Oh God, I wish I were dead.'

'How can you say that?' John asked angrily. 'You, who have had a life of privilege, while other poor creatures claw an existence out of nothing. You should make something of yourself, get out of that sordid Rat Pitt for a start and give both yourself and your dog a bit of peace. Go into business – there's enough of it hereabouts for you to find something that would appeal. Buy a ship and export glass, made of that blue shade. Import wine in return. Come on, lad, you'll make a fortune.'

Henry's bottom lip trembled. 'You're just saying that.'

'No, I mean it. But the answer lies in your own hands.'

Lady Tavener walked in at that moment. 'Henry, you look awful.'

'I feel awful, Mama.'

John cut in. 'The fact of the matter is, Madam, that Henry is worried about his parentage. He has it through his head that his real mother was a whore, who stood on the quayside with the other mongers and sold him to the nearest bidder. Is this true or not?'

'And what business is that of yours?' she asked haughtily.

Henry straightened up. 'Please, Mother, for once in your life tell the truth. Don't let me go on suffering like this.'

She hesitated and Sir Roland walked in. He had apparently overheard all of the previous conversation because he said loudly, 'Go on, Beatrice. Tell him the truth.'

'Oh, but Roly, I cannot do so. Think of my reputation.'

'I would have thought,' said John with force, 'that the time has come to stop thinking of one's good name and put your wretched son's interests first.'

'Well, I'll say it if you won't,' said Sir Roland. 'As you know, you are mine and the woman who says she is your mother *is.* In other words, she and I had an affair which Charles knew all about and approved because he was impotent. But she was always worried about what people would think and so the story of the adoption was put about.' Just for a second the winkle eyes looked large and jovial. 'But people guessed Henry was mine and that's an end to it.'

'So you're not the son of a whore,' John said tactlessly.

'No, Henry, you are not. Unless you regard me as such,' Lady Tavener said with a rusty pink spot appearing in either cheek.

Before his son could say a word, Sir Roland spoke up. 'It was all done to please brother Charles. He'd had an accident some years ago which affected his prowess, yet he knew Beatrice longed for a child and so the whole plot was conceived – as did she! – to grant her wish. So, Henry, it's time for you to grow up and stop imagining things.'

For answer the poor young man threw himself into his mother's arms, weeping vigorously and ruining her maquillage. After a moment or two Sir Roland gave him a half-hearted pat on the back and beckoned John into the other room where he poured out two large brandies. John, who had already had quite a few, sipped it tentatively.

'Well, let it be hoped that this will pull him together and make a man out of the little swine.'

'Don't be too hard on him, Sir,' John answered. 'He really cared about his parentage, you know.'

'Probably an excuse to do nothing about his lifestyle.'

'Have you thought about taking him into business with your good self?'

Sir Roland huffed. 'I am a Merchant Venturer, Sir, and very highly regarded.'

'But surely that wouldn't prevent you taking him into apprenticeship or similar. Indeed, it might be seen as a highly philanthropic act.'

Sir Roland paused, letting the vision of this form in his mind. 'Indeed, perhaps you are right. I will give it my consideration.'

'I was hoping you might say that,' John answered, getting to his feet. 'Well, I must be off. If you will give my good wishes to Lady Tavener and Henry . . .'

'Certainly.'

'Good night,' and John bowed his way out, thinking what a great many pompous people made up the population of the world.

Next morning he rose early, had only a piece of bread, butter and cheese, and took his coach up past the Playhouse and along to Clifton village. There was still a hill to climb but at least he wasn't perpendicular.

He found Mr Huxtable at home, reading the newspaper, a pair of spectacles on his nose, his feet up on a footstool. Commodore answered the door and looked surprised to see the Apothecary again after such a long time had elapsed. Horatio stood to welcome him.

'Ah, my dear Mr Rawlings. How very nice to see you again. I do hope you haven't had too disturbing a time.'

'It was rather terrible, I must confess, but I'm afraid that is not the reason for my visit.'

'Is it about the man who claimed to be my stepson?'

'Yes, I regret it is.'

'Why, am I suspected of pushing him down the steps?'

'It is a hideous puzzle because no-one knows whether he had an enemy from his early life or if he made a recent enemy who did the deed.'

'Yes, I see. Well, that would put me in the picture, and Commodore too, I imagine.'

'Yes, it would. Mr Huxtable, please know that I am only asking this question because I am assisting the Constable, a pleasant chap called Gilbert Farr who is terribly overworked in his apothecary's shop. Were you at home alone on that night?'

'I understand, and the answer is no. I went out to a card party arranged by a neighbour, and as the late pretender had left the coach behind, that is how I travelled.'

'And Commodore, did he go with you?'

'No, he went off courting his lady love. One Venus, who is Lady Tavener's slave. And I am sure that is where he went because

Lady Tavener's housekeeper complained that she had to throw him out.'

'Late?'

'Late.'

John leant back in his chair, relieved. He liked Horatio and had grown to admire Commodore, who had been brought to this island as a frightened little boy and who had responded so well and grown into a considerable man. He was glad that they both had people who would speak up for them if it became necessary. His thoughts roamed to Samuel Foote's assertion that it had been Julian Wychwood. He conjured up a mental picture of the man, so darkly seductive and probably controlling a violent temper. Mr Huxtable's voice broke into his thoughts.

'Would you like some coffee?'

'I would adore a cup,' said John, and really meant it.

An hour later he left and called in at Gilbert's shop on the way back. They discussed the evening's arrangements and John, facing the prospect with a grim smile, went to have a plunge bath at the Hotwell spring in preparation.

Twenty

The plunge bath was not an altogether pleasant experience. First of all he had to enter the bath room, which was small and smelt very slightly of some unknown odour. Then, in exchange for his shilling, John was handed the key of the door and, having locked himself in, removed his nether garments, turned round, took hold of the iron rings fastened to the wall and stepped back. There were three shallow steps but still it was an unnerving experience, walking backwards in the semi-darkness into tepid liquid, wondering when his feet were going to touch the bottom. Though John had been assured that the water was changed after every bather, he only hoped that this statement was true.

He dipped his head down several times and then tried to relax, but the puzzle of the death of the false Augustus Bagot kept going through his mind. Who had greased those top steps? Had it been someone from Bristol's lowlife, thinking he was the Augustus of old, or had the killer been lurking among the people staying at the Hotwell? He considered them all and realised that any one of them could have crept out in the darkness, applied the goose fat and then gone on to whatever rendezvous they had arranged. Whereas it would have been almost impossible for the old whore who stood by the fountain in Bristol city, or her child, sired by the young Gus, to have got there without transport and carrying naught but a lantern. No, he felt positive that the killer was near at hand – but who was it?

After ten minutes John had had enough and, climbing up, wrapped himself in a towel, unlocked the door and made his way to the small changing room. Having dressed, he decided he needed refreshment and stopped at a tea shop and went within. The woman who resembled a haystack was sitting at a table with a small, frightened female who looked like a very small shrew.

'So you see, Mrs Lightpill,' the larger woman was saying loudly, 'I have the morning free. Sir Geoffrey – bless him, bless him – has his cousin visiting and he – that is, I mean to say, the cousin – has taken the old gentleman out in his conveyance. I do believe they are intending to move on to Bath – that is Sir Geoffrey and the cousin, the Honourable Anthony Longbotham – which means that I shall have to pack up my things and travel on. Ah, there is no rest for us ladies who act as confidantes to the elderly. Bless them.'

She moved her arms rapidly and a wisp of hair fell out of her hat and bobbed in the breeze. Mrs Lightpill looked terrified but merely nodded her head. Miss Thorney continued relentlessly.

'Talking of ladies, I saw the strangest thing t'other night. You know that little village of Clifton? Well, I was invited up there to partake of a little cold collation with my friend Miss Wilson. She is a companion to the Honourable Mrs Anstruther – such a martinet, I fear. Anyway, as I was saying, I was invited to sup. Well, my dear Mrs Lightpill, I was fair put out by the thought of how to get there. Anyway, Sir Geoffrey most kindly lent me his coach because he was retiring early, having a bad attack of the gout. He is a martyr to it, my dear, a martyr. Well, I was saying, I had the most terrible journey there up the steepest of hills. I was thrown about like a shipwrecked spar . . .'

She laughed suddenly and very loudly, a noise which made Mrs Lightpill jump with fright.

'. . . but eventually reached the top. We drew level with those horrid steps – you know the ones, carved out of the rock – and there was a woman at the top on her hands and knees, scrubbing them. I could hardly believe my eyes.'

John, who had been trying not to listen, suddenly strained his ears. Mrs Lightpill, who had not said a word up till now, whispered, 'Why was that?'

Miss Thorney, mistaking her, said impatiently, 'Because it was such a silly thing to see. A woman of quality scrubbing steps in the darkness, the only light thrown by a watchman's lantern. I think she must have spilled something or other.'

Mrs Lightpill went pale but said nothing.

'I knew she was a woman of quality by the cut of her cloak. Very grand it was. Anyway, as soon as she heard the carriage she dived into the shadows and I went on to Royal York Street. Miss Wilson lives at the very best address, you know.'

'Well, who was it?' Mrs Lightpill asked eventually.

'Who was who?'

'The woman scrubbing the steps?'

Miss Thorney looked thoroughly put out. 'Well how should I know? Her face was hidden by her hood. It could have been anyone.'

Mrs Lightpill nodded meekly. John stood up and made his way to Miss Thorney's table, at which he bowed very courteously. She looked startled, though Mrs Lightpill looked relieved.

'Ladies, good day to you. I trust you will recall me. I am John Rawlings, son of Sir Gabriel Kent.'

'Oh yes, of course.' Miss Thorney nodded her head vigorously and some more of her hair fell down. 'Won't you join us? We're quite put out for a little male company.'

John bowed again and said, 'The pleasure would be entirely mine. May I get you ladies some more coffee?'

'Too kind, too kind,' gushed Miss Thorney.

The order placed, John turned to her wearing his honest citizen face. 'Forgive me, Madam, but I could not help but overhear what you said just now. Pray tell me, how can you be so certain it was a woman?'

Miss Thorney heaved her shoulders and went a bright poppy red. 'Because as she stood up from the scrubbing her cloak slipped back and I saw the outline of her . . .'

'Yes?'

'Well, her womanly things.'

'You mean her breasts?'

Miss Thorney gave a subdued squeal and whispered, 'Yes.'

So this was news indeed. The woman putting goose fat on the steps had been witnessed. But who was she? In his mind, though he continued to smile and nod at Miss Thorney, John ran through the list. There was Augustus's bastard, Maud; her ghastly old mother; Lady Dartington; Lady Tyninghame; Lady Tavener; and the Honourable Titania Groves. None of them seemed a remote possibility. Inwardly the Apothecary groaned. Surely it was not possible that a stranger had entered the equation at this late stage. Abigail Thorney's voice broke in on his thoughts.

'Well, I must be going, Mr Rawlings. I have all Sir Geoffrey's packing to do before he leaves for Bath. And a great many items to be given to the launderess,' she added in a sinister voice. 'Are you coming, Mrs Lightpill?'

The tiny woman spoke. 'No, I will remain here for five minutes, Miss Thorney, if it please you.'

'Oh very well. Suit yourself.'

John rose to his feet and bowed yet again and Miss Thorney swept off, the last of her hair descending with a thrust of her head. Mrs Lightpill smiled at John and he smiled back.

'Miss Thorney can be very commanding,' she murmured.

'Indeed she can,' he answered, and patted her little gloved hand.

It being so near the end of the season, the last celebrations were now in place, and so it was with the ball held in the Upper Long Room. It was to be a special occasion and there was an air of some excitement among the guests gathered to celebrate the event.

John was dressed very finely in crimson satin with white waistcoat, and Gilbert Farr had made a great effort and appeared looking mysterious in midnight blue. But neither of them could hold a candle to the elegant Sir Julian Wychwood, who made a great flurry over his entrance, dressed in silver brocade with stark black adornment. Women turned their heads to stare and men looked at the floor as the saturnine seducer walked the length of the floor and bowed before Miss Groves. She blushed like a rosebud and allowed him to lead her out for the first dance.

'I've something to tell you,' John whispered urgently to Gilbert.

'Be quick. I've got to join the dancers.'

'It's—'

But too late. Lady Dartington was bearing down on him, quizzer raised. 'Ah, Mr Rawlings. Where have you been? I have not noticed you this last day or two.'

He made a fulsome bow. 'I have been hither and yon, my Lady.'

'Are you going on to Bath?'

'Unfortunately no. My father and I are returning to London to settle in for the winter.'

She lowered her voice. 'I hope that wretched fellow is not coming.' Her eyes indicated Sir Julian, who was stepping out in a sprightly fashion with Titania. 'He has quite turned my daughter's head. But fortunately he seems greatly attached to Lady Tyninghame and she to him.'

'Yes, I had noticed that.'

'If you ask my opinion she is head over heels in love with him – quite unsuitably, I might add.'

'Why is that?' John asked politely.

'Because she is a deal too old for him. There is much talk of it behind the fans.'

'Gracious!' John answered, looking suitably shocked. 'And what of him? Does he have an equal *tendresse* for her?'

Lady Dartington gave what would have been the equivalent of a snort in a person of lesser degree.

'I should hardly think so. He is using the poor fool for what he can get out of her.'

John nodded and attempted to look wise, though he was having some difficulty in subduing a smile. The Hotwell, like every other place on earth, was alive with gossip and scandal mongering. He gave a short but polite bow.

'Excuse me, Lady Dartington, I spy my father over there. I really must join him.'

Tonight the great beau shimmered like a dark flame, his high old-fashioned wig sitting well upon his head, his strong features alive and interested, yet John saw to his immense sadness that the old fellow was at long last starting to slow up, that the great fire which had been his father was beginning to burn low. An irrepressible sob caught in the Apothecary's throat as he considered Sir Gabriel's mortality. Yet the face of his son showed not a trace of these thoughts as he bowed before his father and said, 'Good evening, Sir. May I mention how very fine you look.'

'As do you, my boy. As does everyone. What a well-dressed company there is here tonight.'

John was about to answer, but as the dance ended a sudden hush fell over the room and the Master of Ceremonies announced, 'Lady Tyninghame.'

She was both fragile and lovely to a heart-breaking degree, clad from head to toe in lavender satin with lilac adornments, the material swirling round her slim form and accentuating her delicate features. The Apothecary almost clapped as she walked into the room unaccompanied. Immediately Sir Julian, dark beast to her pale beauty, was at her side, kissing her hand and making a great to-do of greeting her.

Sir Gabriel looked at John and raised a finely chiselled eyebrow. 'A love match?' he said.

His son looked thoughtful. 'I'm not so sure,' he answered.

The next dance was called and though Sir Gabriel decided to remain seated and consume a glass of punch, John felt obliged to bow before Miss Abigail Thorney, who was sitting amongst a collection of mothers and spinsters, trying to look animated. She went the colour of a beetroot and stood up, knocking a thin woman half off her seat as she did so.

'Oh, Mr Rawlings,' she gushed. 'Do you really want to dance with me?'

'It would be my pleasure, Madam.'

She danced like a haystack as well, this one caught in a violent wind. Whirling about, clapping her hands with excitement, she laughed so much that she did not notice the other dancers smiling as well. John rather enjoyed himself and cavorted vigorously, until, with a great chord from the orchestra, Miss Thorney fell over and was helped up by various gentlemen amidst cries of 'Oh, how foolish I am,' and 'Please excuse, silly me.' Afterwards John escorted her to the punch bowl and ladled her a glass while she looked round the room, smiling contentedly. And then her eye was caught by something and she began to stare fixedly. John, following her gaze, saw that it was trained on a couple who stood a little outside the rest of the happy dancers. It was Lady Tyninghame and Julian Wychwood, talking earnestly, she gazing up into his face, which she suddenly put both hands up to and pulled towards her to kiss him fondly on the cheek.

Miss Thorney let out an exclamation of surprise. John smiled. 'I agree. It is rather public a place for a caress.'

She looked up at him, her expression concerned. 'It's not that, it's just . . .'

'What?'

'I don't know. For a split second I thought . . . But it's only silly me. Please pay no attention.'

'But what startled you?'

'Just for a moment she looked awfully familiar. But then she has been around here for the season, so that would explain it.'

'Yes,' said John, but looked terribly thoughtful.

Another dance was called and this time he partnered Titania Groves. But in the middle of all the whirling and stamping he thought of Elizabeth and how much she would have enjoyed the occasion. She was always in the background of his mind, but John was a born survivor, which meant that though he had come face to face with personal loss twice in his life, he would not and could not let it bring him down. He felt as deeply as those who made a great show of sorrow, wearing their widowed state like a mourning ring for the rest of their days, but he could not join them. He was too strong a character to allow it.

The dance ended and he made his way to where Lady Tyninghame and Sir Julian had been standing together. But the doors leading from the Long Room were open and he realised that they had stepped out onto the balcony together. Feeling slightly dishonest but for all that extremely interested, John paused in the opening and listened.

'You are beautiful,' came a voice, not Julian to Violetta but the other way round.

Julian laughed in the silvery moonlight. 'Come now, my dear, surely that is going a little far?'

'No, darling, I mean it. You are outstanding. In all my wildest imaginings I never thought you could be so fine.'

'Flattery will turn my head. But I must say I enjoy it.'

'Surely you must get enough of that from that Titania?'

'I've told you already, I like her well enough but that is all there is to it. The most wonderful thing about this season was meeting you. And of all places in this funny little spa.'

'Fate brought us together, Julian. I really believe that.'

But there the eavesdropping ended as some other dancers made their way out and John was forced to relinquish his place in the doorway. That Violetta and Julian were lovers he was now certain. But what of his other ideas? At the present time there was no answer to them.

Probably because he had thought of Elizabeth during the dance, he dreamt of her that night. He was in a boat, far out at sea, which was hit by a sudden squall. It began to founder and in the dream John was washed overboard. He started to swim but after a while ran out of energy and felt his head go under the waves. Then a pair of strong arms seized him round the waist and bore him back up to the surface. He turned and saw that Elizabeth was there, swimming with him, holding him up.

'So you *did* become a mermaid,' he said in the dream.

'Oh yes,' she said, and smiled her gorgeous smile, 'and I'll always swim beside you.'

John woke abruptly, scared for some strange reason because the dream had been a reassuring one, and then realised that there was a persistent tapping at his door. It was not loud and threatening but a constant sound which sent a chill down John's spine.

'Who's there?' he called.

There was no answer, but the sound continued, growing a little more urgent.

'Who is it?' he called again.

This time someone spoke at the other side of the door and John was able to make out that it was a man, but whoever it was said their name so softly that John could not catch it. Reluctantly, he got out of bed, lit a candle and threw a loose silk gown over his night shirt. Then he went to the door. Outside stood a shadowy figure.

'Come forward,' John ordered. 'Step into the light that I might see your face.'

Samson took a pace in, his tall frame filling the doorway.

'Master,' he said.

'What is it?'

Samson sank onto one knee. 'Master, I've come to confess.'

Twenty-One

John stared at Samson. 'What for?'

'Why, for the murder, Sir. The murder of Augustus Bagot.'

John gaped. 'Why you of all people?'

Samson looked at him without a flicker of emotion. 'I did it, Sir. That's why I've come to confess to you.'

'Well you'd best enter and tell me about it.'

Samson's large frame threw an enormous shadow on the wall as he gingerly sat on the end of John's bed, while the Apothecary parked himself on the one chair that was in there.

'Tell me the story from the start,' he said, 'including what he did to upset you.'

The answer was astounding. 'He came into the Strawberry Fields and made a thorough nuisance of himself.'

'In what way?'

'Drunk as a lord and pestering all the nan-boys.'

'I thought they'd be used to that.'

'He did it too much. It was offensive. It was my job to throw him out and I did so.'

'Unaided?'

'No, with help from the madame, who knew how to pack a punch. We left him lying in the gutter.'

John grinned. 'That's a nice thought. But was this enough to make you want to murder the man?'

'People did not speak well of him in Bristol.'

John thought to himself that he wished he knew which Augustus Samson was referring to, but kept his own counsel.

Samson continued, 'Well it all built up in me until one night

I borrowed Mr Herbert's horse and rode to the Hotwell over the Downs. Then I greased the top three steps and the rest you know.'

The story was as full of holes as a colander, but John merely nodded.

'Well, thank you, Samson. But tell me one thing. Why was it so urgent that you had to wake me up? Surely it could have waited until tomorrow morning?'

The black man frowned, clearly thinking, then eventually said, 'Well I didn't want you going after the wrong person, Sir.'

So that was it, a strange midnight confession, and one which John could hardly credit. He now felt certain that the killer was Julian Wychwood, enraged beyond measure by the loss of his box at the theatre. And the woman who had greased the steps? Could it possibly be Titania Groves, not realising what she was doing, perhaps told that it was a jape, and more than willing to earn herself good points in her lover's eyes?

John showed Samson out, then lay down on his bed, wide awake and staring thoughtfully at the ceiling. Every character staying at the Hotwell flitted before his eyes and eventually formed into a grotesque dance before he fell asleep again.

The morning found him strangely refreshed and longing for his breakfast. Sir Gabriel was lying in so he ate alone, very heartily. Then he went for a walk by the river to get some fresh air. Ahead of him, sitting in a shady arbour, he spied Lady Tyninghame, looking pale and pensive. Of Sir Julian Wychwood there was no sign and John decided to seize the opportunity. He bowed before her.

'Good morning, Madam. I trust that this day finds you well.'

She gave him a wistful smile. 'As well as can be hoped, Sir.'

Something in the way she spoke rang a faint alarm bell in John's mind and he said, 'Why? Is anything wrong?'

'Not with the day, no. It is truly beautiful for the time of year. But I am afraid that I am suffering at the moment.'

'What with, Madam? If I may ask.'

'I have such a bad reaction to food. It rather frightens me. I find I can manage only a few mouthfuls at a time. My appetite has completely gone.'

John's professionalism was aroused. 'Are you taking anything to restore your loss of hunger?'

'A decoction of the roots of Goat's Beard. But I do not find it very effective.'

'No, no, Madam. The inner rind of the Barberry tree boiled in white wine. That will do you far more good. You must drink a quarter of a pint every morning. I will ask Gilbert Farr to make you some up.'

She turned on him a sad, sweet smile. 'I really don't know if it will be any use, Mr Rawlings. You see, I had a difficult labour and my appetite never returned after that.'

'Labour!' John exclaimed. 'But I had not realised you had had a child, Madam.'

She gave a bitter laugh. 'No, not many people do. But that was the reason my husband threw me out. He knew that the child could not be his.'

'Good heavens, may I ask why?'

'He stopped sleeping with me some months before. Called me a slut and a drab and never laid a finger on me again, except to beat me of course.'

'What a horrible story. I am so sorry that you have had to suffer like this.'

She smiled once more. 'None of it mattered to me because, you see, I had at last met my soul mate. My own true love, and that meant I was so happy that I no longer felt the pain.'

John was silent, not quite sure where this was leading.

Lady Tyninghame continued, 'I think you know who it was I fell in love with.'

John stared in astonishment. 'Sir Julian Wychwood?'

Violetta laughed aloud. 'You speak of my sweet son. I have found him again after all these years. He is such a joy to me.'

'Your son,' said John, the breath knocked out of him. 'Good God!'

There was the sound of footsteps running along the river walk and the next second the man himself appeared. He turned on John fiercely.

'What have you said to Milady? How dare you upset her!'

'I have said nothing,' the Apothecary answered firmly.

'Don't argue please, my dears,' cried Lady Tyninghame. 'I was merely recounting the past to Mr Rawlings.'

As if this was a cue for people to arrive, a mass of activity suddenly took place on the riverside walk. Sir Gabriel could be seen, his usual black and white garb crisp in the morning sunlight. He walked alone, but a few paces behind him one could glimpse Lady Dartington and Titania, and walking behind them with his dog in tow came Henry Tavener.

Julian pulled a dark face at John. 'Not a word, d'ye hear me?'

Lady Tyninghame called out, 'Greetings, Sir Gabriel, come and sit with me, do.'

The old man made a few gallant strides and bowed to the assembled company before taking a seat beside Violetta, whose hand he kissed. Lady Dartington gave a loud sniff on seeing who was there and went walking past with Titania, who made sorrowful sheep's eyes at Sir Julian, but Henry Tavener joined them saying, 'I feel in damn fine spirits thanks to you, my dear Rawlings.'

'Why, what did he do?' asked Lady Tyninghame.

'Proved to me that my parents really were my parents, or rather that my mother is my actual mother.'

There was a silence while everyone tried to work out what he meant, then Lady Tyninghame said, 'I have found my son, only recently, and I want you all to know that I love him more than life itself.'

She turned to Wychwood, who stood behind her in what one could only think of as a protective manner and, placing both arms around his neck, pulled his face down that she might kiss it.

'My darling,' she said.

He kissed her in return and Lady Dartington, walking ahead, gave a loud sound of contempt and, nudging Titania, said, 'I told you so,' in a highly audible voice.

Violetta smiled gently. 'May I tell you the whole story?' she asked.

'Dear madam, if you should so desire then please do so,' Sir Gabriel answered.

'Years ago I was married to a beast of a man who set about me with a riding crop on my wedding night. I will spare you the details but I endured years of pain, and then I met a young man who changed my life completely. His name was Augustus Bagot.'

For the second time that morning John rocked on his feet. 'You don't mean . . .'

'No, the young and beautiful Gus. He was seventeen, I was twenty-five, but we loved each other with great passion. Eventually I became pregnant and my husband – who had thrown me out of his bedroom because I could not conceive by him – knew damn well that the child could not be his. Poor little Gussie was frantic but had nothing to offer me. You see, he was just a child really. Poor little boy.'

Everyone sat transfixed and John, looking round, saw that tears had started to flow gently down Violetta's cheeks and were echoed by a moistness of eye in, of all people, Henry Tavener.

'Anyway, I had a little money of my own so I booked a passage to the Colonies and set out on that long sea voyage quite alone except for a maid. Funnily enough she was terribly seasick and I was not, not at all. And then, when I arrived in Boston I met a man who I had glimpsed on the boat. His wife had died on the voyage and he was desperate to start a new life so we joined forces. I could not marry him because I was not divorced, but he was a good, kind man, totally uneducated, a labourer who had come to the Americas to start a new life, but a loving spirit.'

She wept in earnest now.

'We moved in together and ran a boarding house. And then, one day, he suddenly died – I think of hard work. A few days later I gave birth to my son and, with the utmost reluctance, I gave him to a couple who longed for children but who were unable to have any. Their name was Wychwood. Josiah Wychwood and his employees set up in the fur trade in Hudson Bay and were so successful that the couple returned to England and he was made a baronet.'

'And you, Madam,' asked Sir Gabriel, 'how did you fare?'

'Funnily enough, I made a great success. Women running things on their own were not so oddly looked upon in the Colonies. I gathered enough money to come back home and to find my own lovely boy again.'

So the identity of both Bagot's little bastards had been revealed. At last. But there were still many questions to be answered. Had Julian greased the steps to avenge his mother? Because, if so, he had picked the wrong Augustus. And why, when she had loved her little Gussie so much? Why would he seek revenge?

Sir Julian spoke. 'Come, Mama, you must be tired. Let me buy you some tea.'

She rose to her feet, then smiled and bowed her head graciously, before strolling off with her son in the direction of the river.

Sir Gabriel turned to John.

'Well, what did you make of all that?'

'It was a fascinating story. Rather like a novel, don't you agree?'

Sir Gabriel smiled and said, 'All it needed was a pack of baying wolf hounds . . .'

But the rest of his words were drowned out by the sounds of a man shouting in pain and a woman's voice, screaming loud and long, then suddenly coming to a halt as if something had been shoved over her face. John and Sir Gabriel stared at each other in consternation, then the younger man began to run in the direction of the noise.

Julian Wychwood was lying on the path, blood oozing from his head, a stone with the tell-tale signs of being used as a weapon abandoned nearby. Of Lady Tyninghame there was no sign whatsoever. Julian was coming round as the Apothecary ran up and lifted the young man's head and shoulders.

'Where's your mother?' he asked rapidly.

Julian furrowed his brow. 'I don't know. I was attacked by some villain wearing a kerchief over his face. He dragged her off. That's all I can tell you.'

'Did he have a coach nearby?'

'I didn't see. I'm afraid I lost consciousness for a few minutes.'

John examined Julian's head. 'That's a nasty gash you have there. I'll take you to the apothecary to dress it, then go in search of your mother.'

Somehow he managed to drag the wounded man to his feet and the two of them staggered back down the walk to see Henry Tavener running towards them.

'Just the man,' John shouted. 'Julian's wounded and must see the apothecary at once, and Lady Tyninghame's been abducted.'

'Which do you want me to do?' Henry asked ingenuously.

'Take Julian to Gilbert Farr quickly. And if you see my father tell him I've gone to find Lady Tyninghame.'

And with that John hurried back to the place he had found Julian. Close to where the body of the young man had lain were tracks, a few inches apart, of something that had been dragged from the riverside walk. Following them, John saw the wheel marks of a waiting coach and drew his own conclusions. The indentations had been caused by the lady's heels as she had been seized under the arms and dragged backwards. And John deduced from the direction of the wheel and hoof marks – of which there were two sets – that the coach must have been heading for Bristol along the track that led by the river. Just for a moment or two he stood hesitating, then he took off for the Hotwell at speed.

Twenty-Two

By the time he found Irish Tom ten minutes had passed. Then there was the time-consuming preparation of the coach and horses. In fact, when they eventually set off for Bristol they were nearly three-quarters of an hour behind their quarry – and John had no idea where to head for.

'But where do you think they'll be, Sir?'

'To be honest with you, Tom, I haven't a thought. Where do you think you would take a woman you had just abducted?'

Despite the awfulness of the situation, Tom gave a rich Irish chuckle. 'Now that would all depend on what purpose I had in mind.'

John mulled this over. 'The abduction was rough. He's probably holding her for ransom.'

'But who would pay?'

'Well, her son of course. That is if he had the money.'

'Has he?'

'Tom, I don't know. He always seems fairly well-to-do but one can never judge by a person's appearance alone.'

'How right you are, Sir. The kidnapper could be beside the book in his choice of this particular lady.'

They drove into the heart of the city, passing the houses of the great and the rich. But there was no sign of anything untoward and eventually John instructed the coachman to drive among the dark and foetid side streets where he would not normally walk. The smell and the sullenness of the people that he passed depressed him, and he was just opening his mouth to send Tom on a course to the docks when he noticed something. Outside some most disreputable hotel was parked a carriage that looked remarkably like Lady Tyninghame's.

'Tom, drive past that place again.'

'I can't turn the coach round in this midden.'

'Well, we'll have to go forwards and try to find the street again in this maze.'

But somehow, with various clicks of his tongue and softly spoken instructions, Tom persuaded the two pretty horses to back slowly up the street. John leant out of the window to get a better look.

He had only seen Lady Tyninghame's coach once, parked outside The Ostrich Inn on Clifton Downs, but he had noticed the interior, done out with softest violet velvet. This coach had similar furnishings.

'I'd swear it's hers. Let's go and enquire.'

They left the coach in the yard, right next to that of the abducted woman. John, peering within, said, 'Yes, it's definitely hers. Look, there's one of her gloves.'

'That could belong to anybody. Are you sure, Sir?'

'Positive. Now are you coming in or would you prefer the fresh air?'

As the air was rank with every kind of ghastly smell imaginable there was little choice. The two men made their way inside.

A heap of rags stirred itself behind a battered table. 'Want a room?' it said.

'We are looking for Lady Tyninghame,' John answered coolly. 'Do you know if she has been brought here? Probably against her will.'

The rag bag, which turned out to be female, gave him a long, hard stare from eyes as black and as cold as a bird's.

'What name did you say?'

'Tyninghame. She possibly arrived here under protest.'

The old woman shook her head. 'Nobody come 'ere like that.'

'Well who has come here then?'

'Just a buttock and twang. 'E was black.'

The two men stared at one another. 'Did he give a name?'

'No, just the money. Names ain't necessary in this establishment.'

'Very well. May we book a room for an hour?'

The rag bag growled a laugh. 'I'd never have taken you two for nans.'

John flapped his hand. 'You can't always tell a good quean, dearie.'

Irish Tom, in turn, did an extremely clumsy hip waggle and said, 'Will you take me upstairs, Johnnie, me sweet boy?'

'How much?' John asked.

'Two and sixpence.'

'Expensive,' he answered, handing over the cash.

They made their way up a dirty spiral staircase, quite large and showing evidence of former glory. John guessed that this neighbourhood had once known better days. Halfway up they paused, hearing voices coming from a room leading off the landing. Standing stock still in the dingy gloom they heard a woman say, 'We've come a long way, you and I.'

A man's voice, deep and mellow, answered, 'I said once that I would give you anything in my power and I really meant it.'

'You've proved that,' she answered, and gave a laugh, the like of which John had not heard in a long time. It was harsh and cruel, a laugh that held in its depths a wealth of something – he searched for the word and came up with it. Evil.

'Who is it?' whispered Irish Tom, close to his ear.

'Guess,' John muttered back.

'It can't be . . .'

But a door had opened above them and a man's figure, dressed in a flowing red robe, appeared.

'Who's down there?' he called.

John put his finger to his lips as the two men froze. The man took a step forward. 'Anybody there?'

But he got no further. A figure came hurling past him, screaming like one of the furies. It too was dressed in scarlet, and scantily at that. It flung itself at John, nails raking, lips pulled back like that of a snarling, savage dog. He saw a gob of spittle at the corner of her mouth, heard her scream, 'You bastard, I always suspected that you were spying on me,' before she clawed his face relentlessly.

He reeled back under the impact and would have fallen to the ground had not Irish Tom put out a strong arm and broken his fall. She was kicking and rending for all she was worth, but somehow John managed to get hold of her hair and pull her away from him.

She swung in the air as he lifted her off the ground.

Where was beauty now? To where had disappeared fragility and charm and delicacy? It was as if two entirely different women dwelt in the brain of Lady Tyninghame.

John could not resist asking her, 'But why are you like this? What demon possesses you? Only this morning you were all sweetness and light. And now I come to think of it you were a bit *too* sweet when you told the mealy-mouthed story of your life. Tragic? I don't imagine so.'

The face which he had admired so much for its fragile loveliness contorted to that of a gargoyle.

'Put me down,' she screamed. 'You're hurting me.'

John obliged and was rewarded for his pains by a cracking blow between the thighs. He doubled in agony.

Irish Tom, who had been brought up as one of nine children in the slums of Dublin, had had enough. He fetched a blow to Lady Tyninghame's chin that must have reduced her world to spinning stars before she fell unconscious to the floor. It was only then that Samson — for it was he who lurked above in the red robe — had the courage to creep slowly down the stairs.

Tom turned on him angrily. 'Look what you've done, you grinning fool. Your precious Lady Tyninghame is nothing more than a slut and the devil's daughter. See what she's inflicted on my master, damn her eyes.'

If he had expected a fight, Tom was proved wrong. Instead, Samson dropped to his knees and picked up the prostrate form of Violetta Tyninghame, cradling her in his arms and stroking her hair back from her face.

'What have you done to her?' he demanded, glaring at Tom over his shoulder. 'She's totally unconscious.'

'I gave her a clout, that's what. And I'll give you one yourself if you don't stop your moaning.'

This was the moment when the rag bag who had let them in climbed the rickety staircase and pointed a pistol at them.

'Out, the lot of you. I don't have brawlings on my premises. You, darkie, pick up your lady friend and get out. As for you, you Irish bog-lander, you can escort your molly-mop out and I never want to see your face again.'

Once outside Samson made a run for the coach but was stopped by Tom's foot, John being in too much pain to do or say anything. With Lady Tyninghame just beginning to recover consciousness, Tom glared at Samson, who still held her in his arms.

'Now come along the pair of you. I am making a citizen's arrest and am taking you straight to the Constable of the Hotwell. You'll travel in my coach and stare down the barrel of my pistol the entire journey. John, you drive.'

In pain though he was, there was something reassuring about sitting on the coachman's box and driving along beside the docks and eventually the River Avon. The tide was just coming in and the ships were beginning to feel the swell of it, rising off the mud and starting to bob at its pull.

John thought that maybe Violetta Tyninghame had a condition whereby she could change her personality completely, a kind of splitting of the mind. As for Samson, he had more or less told his story. A little black boy, a sexually aware adolescent, an exciting lover. The rest they were yet to discover, as indeed they would, John thought, as he drove the coach to the front door of Gilbert Farr's shop.

His pain gone – almost – he jumped down from the box and threw open the door. All was very much as he had left it. Irish Tom, who seemed to have grown another few inches since John last looked, was holding his pistol with a 'one false move' look on his face. Samson was holding Violetta in his arms, making soothing noises and stroking her hair. She had returned to her normal, somewhat sugar-sweet self, her eyes closed, her face serene. Looking at her, the Apothecary diagnosed a mental illness, recalling the clawing, spitting virago who had kicked him so viciously in his privy parts.

Ordering Tom to stay exactly as he was, John went in and fetched Gilbert Farr, who immediately handed the running of the shop over to his younger brother.

'Did she admit to greasing the steps?' Gilbert asked.

'Not yet,' John said.

'But what was her motive for all this? Is she mad?'

'Yes, Gilbert, it is my honest opinion that she has a mental affliction. And do you know something else?'

'No, what?'

'I don't think she has any memory of it.'

'You mean that she can commit murder and then, telling her truth, deny it?'

'Precisely.'

Gilbert locked the prisoners in his compounding room with Tom and pistol to guard them. Then he sent a fast rider to fetch the Constable from Bristol, complete with his van for escorting prisoners. Two warders took away Lady Tyninghame, subdued now and playing the role of bewildered innocent; indeed so well was she acting that the two men from Bristol gaol hesitated about taking so great a lady into custody.

So it was from Samson that the bitter facts were revealed. As he told his story, weeping and shaking his head, John felt immense pity for the man, who had been duped and seduced at the age of fifteen.

'She was always cuddling me when I was a child, saying I was her beloved black boy, the best boy in all the world. She wouldn't let me go when I grew hair, Sirs, she kept me and went on holding me close, just like when I was a child. Then one day, I can remember it distinctly, my cock came up and she was excited. She took me to her bedchamber and told me what to do and I did it and she loved it, said I was largely made and the best she'd had.'

John and Gilbert looked at one another, not sure whether to laugh or weep.

'But the master – the Marquis – found out and beat the living guts from my body and sent me away. Then he set about her.'

'So was that true that he attacked her on her wedding night with his riding crop?'

'No, Sir, it was when some little spying chambermaid reported the fact that I was in her bed every afternoon.'

'I see,' said Gilbert. 'Please go on.'

'Well, then she met Gussie Bagot and she really lost her heart and her decency.'

John raised one of his svelte eyebrows, but said nothing.

'Well, they were always at it, day and night, couldn't get enough of one another.'

'But what about you?' asked Gilbert.

'I was allowed a crumb from the sliced cake. But very occasionally.' Samson started to weep. 'You see, I loved her with all my heart. There could never be another woman for me, not even when she betrayed me.'

'So is the rest of the story true? Did she cross the Atlantic and go to Boston?'

'In parts it's true. But she went alone, there was no maid, and she did marry that poor old man she met.'

'So she's a bigamist.'

'Oh yes,' said Samson sadly. 'But fortunately he died before she returned. And there's one other thing.'

'What?'

'She couldn't give that baby away fast enough. She hated him, and all that wild talk about loving her son is completely made up. She asked me to kill him when I hit him with a rock. But I hadn't the heart, not even for her.'

Gilbert remarked quietly, 'I pity you loving such a terrible creature. Life must have been a veritable torture.'

'It was — is — like being utterly insane. Like being possessed by the devil. For that is what she could turn into in one of her lunatic rages.'

'Did Lady Tyninghame put goose fat on the steep steps, and why? She must have known by this time that the man who claimed to be Augustus Bagot was nothing of the sort.'

'Oh yes, she knew all right. But in her crazy mind he insulted the very memory of Gussie by being such an obnoxious and terrible creature. So, she thought, he must die for the impersonation.'

'God's breath, she was completely demented,' John said. 'But why turn against Julian Wychwood, whom she claimed to love so much?'

'She considered that his very presence reminded her of the man she once loved.' Samson put his head in his hands. 'Oh God, I don't know. She must have seen the world through the eyes of pure hatred.'

There was a profound silence, broken only by the sound of the wretched slave's sobs.

'Where is she now?' John asked eventually.

'On her way to Bristol prison.'

'Then God have mercy on her.'

There was a sudden scuffle outside and Julian Wychwood thrust his way into the room with a small guard hanging onto his arm like a dog. For once the smooth seducer looked ruffled and slightly dishevelled, with an unbecoming bandage on his head.

'What has happened to my mother?' he asked, and John saw that not only was his forehead wet with sweat, but that there were tell-tale signs of dampness beneath his eyes.

'She is on her way to Bristol.'

'Why?'

'Pending questioning by a magistrate.'

Julian thrust the guard to the floor with an impatient flick of his arm. 'Then I must go after her. She will need my help.' The guard, who turned out to be Gilbert's brother, tried to scramble up, but Julian downed him once more with the toe of his boot. He looked round the room, gave a truncated bow, said, 'Goodbye,' and then he was off, and before either John or Gilbert could move they heard the sound of his horse's feet on the cobbles outside.

'Will he catch her up?' John asked.

Gilbert shrugged his shoulders. 'Possibly, but he'll have to ride like a demon.'

Once Samson had broken down and told them the whole story of forbidden love and a woman with a diseased mind, he, too, had followed in her footsteps and been transported to the gaol. And then the two apothecaries were left, staring at one another.

'I could do with a drink,' said Gilbert.

'Let me buy you one in The Bear. Irish Tom's already gone there.'

They settled themselves with a pint of ale and sat in silence for a while. Then John said, 'I can't understand a mother not loving her child, can you?'

Gilbert answered, 'I think the woman concerned cannot be judged by normal moral standards. She is a unique being. You have seen her in a blinding rage, Samson has confirmed that she is prone to them, but will a magistrate believe it? Just you wait and see. I'll bet you a guinea that she gets off.'

'But I will give evidence. And so can Tom.'

'If you are even called to the hearing, my friend. There are wheels within wheels in Bristol.'

'Meaning?'

'That the name of Tyninghame still wields great power. It would not surprise me in the least if the Marquis would not want the whole thing hushed up.'

'But why?'

'He may have been made a cuckold, but to have had that inflicted on him by a black servant of fifteen years would be more than his dignity could allow.'

John was speechless. 'I think things might be different if she came up before Sir John Fielding.'

Gilbert smiled enigmatically.

'Just you wait and see.'

Twenty-Three

A mist crept up from the sea that night. It smoked softly along the River Avon and by the time it reached the Hotwell and, later, Bristol, it had turned into a thick, impenetrable mass. To the solitary figure waiting outside Bristol Gaol it did no favours. An occasional drop descended from the brim of his fashionable hat, and the horrible light thrown from the single lamp made his skin look jaundiced and ill. The man who was regarded by most as darkly handsome and sinisterly attractive looked both small and pathetic in those horrible circumstances. And if truth be told, that was exactly how he felt.

Sir Julian Wychwood looked at his watch, drawn from his waistcoat pocket, and as he did so it was echoed by the prison's mournful chimes. Two o'clock in the morning and not a soul penetrated the thick enveloping mist which lay over the land. Julian had not taken shelter in his coach for he felt sure that his beloved mother could be released from another door and he might not see her slip away in the gloom. That is why he stood outside and let the fog drift around him.

The whole episode was cloaked in mystery. As far as he was concerned, some unknown assailant had knocked him semi-conscious, during which time he had glimpsed through a hazy eye his mother being dragged backwards into her own coach. After a frantic search, the next he had heard was that she had been taken to Bristol Gaol pending a magistrate's enquiry. None of it made any sense to him, and so here he was, his clothes growing gradually damp, his face getting more pinched as the endless minutes ticked away.

Eventually, at quarter to five there was a great rumbling of bolts and turning of keys in the great door that guarded the entrance. Julian drew closer and eventually a ghost-like figure emerged, stepping out and gazing round blindly, putting a hand up to its face to protect it from the vapour.

'Mother?' called Julian.

She turned to him uncertainly, gazing at him with eyes that seemed blinded by the mist. 'Julian?' she said in a quavering voice.

'Yes, I'm here. Oh, my dear, sweet woman, what have they done to you?'

'It has all been so horrible, Julian. I have been crowded in a cell with whores and other creatures. I thought I would die of shame.'

'But what was it all about, Mother, why should you – the victim – be placed in gaol?'

For answer she laid her finger across his lips. 'Shush, my love. I'll tell you the whole story when I have settled down. Now, is that your carriage I see in the gloom?'

'Yes it is. Allow me.'

She looked so fragile that he picked her up in his arms while she made little birdlike noises and snuggled against his chest.

'Where d'you wanna go, Sir?' asked the driver, who had been sleeping best he could and felt thoroughly despondent.

'To the Hotwell?' answered Julian, but his mother cut across him.

'No, if you please, there is somebody I must see up at Clifton. If you could possibly drive me there first.'

'But Madam,' answered the long-suffering driver, 'there is a very thick fog tonight and the way is dangerous enough as it is. I think you should leave it until morning.'

'I am not asking your opinion, I am giving you orders,' answered Lady Tyninghame, in a tone of voice which Julian had never heard her use before.

'But Mother . . .'

She turned to him, sweet as a sugar mouse. 'Oh please, Julian, darling. It is urgent. I really do need to go. I'll tell you all about it when we get there. Surely your coachman will be able to pick his way?'

He suddenly felt exhausted, as tired as his coachman obviously was.

'Oh, go on, Saunders, for the love of God.' It was a plea, not a command.

'If you like to take the risk, Sir,' and Saunders made a harumphing sound to express his displeasure.

They set off into the invisible night, the horse picking its way and occasionally shying with fright as an object loomed up out of the fog. Lady Tyninghame fell asleep, leaning against Julian. He was aware, more than ever, of her fragility, of the fact that she could snap like a wishbone. And yet again he puzzled over the fact that she had been so desperate that she had given him away immediately. For surely she had planned to marry the old man she met on the ship?

Or so it appeared to Julian as they plodded through the fog for hours, forever climbing. Eventually Saunders cried out, 'Gawd, I think I can see the lights of The Ostrich.'

'Which one?'

'Not the one at the docks, the one on Clifton Downs.'

'So we're there.'

Violetta stirred into wakefulness, yawning and saying in a tired, tiny voice, 'Are we at Clifton, sweetheart?'

'Yes, Mother. You slept all the way here.'

'I was so exhausted. I have been through such an ordeal.'

'You promised to tell me about it but you slept all the way instead.'

'Never mind, dear child, I will do so tomorrow when you are refreshed. Now, let us get out for a moment.'

'You said you wanted to see someone, but I must remind you that it's six o'clock in the morning.'

'Well, I am getting out. Nature calls me. And surely you will not let your mother go unescorted.'

Reluctantly, Julian stepped out of the carriage, breathing in the foggy air and wondering at how different and strange everything appeared in these misty conditions. His mother had entirely vanished and, looking up at the coachman's box, he saw that Saunders slept where he sat. He suddenly felt terribly alone, as if he were standing on the edge of the world with no-one to guide him. He tried to thrust on his natural persona, the devil-may-care young man that women found irresistible, the rake that girls adored and men tolerated. But instead he felt frightened and lonely. Like a child again. And then his mother's voice spoke out of the fog.

'This way, Julian. Walk forward a little.'

Christ! Where was she?

He called out, 'Where are you? I can't see you.'

'Another few paces, sweetheart. Go straight ahead.'

He did as he had been bidden and then paused as his foot detected a different surface beneath his shoe. It was rock. He was standing on rock. But where in Clifton was there solid rock in the shape of a step? And then Julian knew and he stopped short.

Now her voice was right behind him. 'Go on, you unwanted little bastard, who disgusts me by the very fact you're alive. Climb down in the fog. Let's see how you like that. Let's see what you're really made of.' And she pushed him, hard.

Fortunately she did no more than unbalance him so that he slipped down one of the steps and clung on to the second with his knee. She pushed again. This time Julian raised his right arm to fend her off; he was hanging on for his very life with the left. And then he heard running feet in the fog and he called out with all his strength, 'Help! I'm on the steps! I'm being attacked!'

A dog came flying out of the fog, a fearful-looking hound. 'Go on, Tray,' said a voice. 'Kill.'

Lady Tyninghame gave a scream of genuine fear, and as she buckled to her knees Julian could hear the noise of growling followed by what sounded horribly like a booted kick. She gave one last scream as she plunged downwards into the mist, towards the Avon Gorge, the sound dying away as it hit the wall of vapour that lay below. Julian, panting, put up his right hand.

'Help me up, I beg you.'

A strong arm came down and hauled him upward till Julian sat once more upon the grass, weeping like a child.

''Zounds, no more of that, I pray you. I never thought to see such a sight.'

'It's just that I'm shocked. My own mother tried to kill me.'

'Oh, is that what all the fuss was about. I know I accidentally kicked something in the fog. Hope I haven't hurt her.'

'I think, Mr Tavener, that you have.'

'Damme, what terrible mistakes one can make in misty conditions.'

And with that, Henry Tavener and Julian Wychwood, to say nothing of the good dog Tray, lurched towards The Ostrich and banged on the door until they gained admittance and could discuss the situation at length.

Twenty-Four

The day that an inanimate and shapeless mass was hauled out of the mud by a pair of local fishermen was the day that John Rawlings and Sir Gabriel Kent left Hotwell for the last time. Overnight, what had once been a spa of great natural beauty and delights had become cold and desolate. The season was over, the fine company had moved on to Bath. Instead of the buzz of excitement that had been in the air, there was now an almighty silence. To make matters worse, the tide had gone right out, filling the spa with the stink of rotting fish, rotting detritus, rotting boats and another sweet, sickly, unidentifiable smell that wove amongst the rest and became part of the melange that they formed.

Sir Gabriel raised a handkerchief to his nostrils. 'What a place of stinks is Bristol and its environs.'

'Are you glad to be leaving?'

'You know that I am always delighted to return to my own home.'

'I hope that you will allow me to escort you there.'

They drove on for another few yards and then Irish Tom pulled the horses to a stop.

'There's something going on, Sir. The Constable is here and they are stopping the coaches.'

'Do you mind if I have a look?'

John stepped down from the carriage and saw that Gilbert Farr in the midst of five or six other men was looking at something lying on the mud banks of the river. John knew, even from a distance, that it was a body. He also knew that there was very little of it remaining, having been crushed to pulp by the fall. The second Augustus Bagot had had his fall broken by the roof of the Colonnade, but this poor creature had not been that fortunate. She had crashed down on to the river bank from a great height and thus there was very little left of her features. The size of the pulped mess told John that it was female, but it was Gilbert Farr who cried out in some distress, 'Oh God, it's Lady Tyninghame. This mushed object is the hat she was wearing when she went to prison.'

So the fat man had had a kind of revenge, thought John. She had died in exactly the same way that he had. He walked up to Gilbert.

'Anything I can do, old friend?'

Gilbert shook his head. 'Nothing. She's as dead as a door nail. It must have been as I thought. The Marquis pulled a few strings and got her out of gaol, but what happened after that Heaven alone knows. She must have caught a coach back to Clifton and crashed down the steps in the fog.'

'But what was she doing up there?'

'Your guess is as good as mine.'

'And why didn't she fall on the Colonnade?'

'I imagine it was because she was too light a weight. But whatever happened she's past help now.'

'Well at least let's hope she rests in peace, the poor tormented soul.'

Walking briskly back to the coach, John started to tiptoe as he saw Tom, who was standing beside it, put his finger to his lips.

'Your father's dropped off into a nice snooze, Sorrh. I'd let him rest if I were you.'

John laughed, just a trifle grimly. 'In that case, I have no option but to find an alehouse. The sight of those remains made me rather queasy, to be perfectly honest.'

The nearest was The Seven Stars, that drinking house in which one could hear practically every language in the world being spoken. Today, however, it was less crowded and John managed to get a seat at a table and was just settling down to consume a glass of canary when a whispering voice spoke in his ear. John jumped with nerves and on looking round could see no one but a strange bundle of rags unfolding itself beside him. A second or two later, the sibilant creature, who previously had told him so much about the youthful Gussie, had taken a seat opposite him.

On this occasion, he was slightly smarter in that his face and hands were clean and he had on a salt-stained jersey, which was less ragged than his terrible coat.

''ullo, Guv,' he said. ''ow are you? Did you find out any more about our Gussie?'

'Plenty,' John answered, moving a little as the man's particular brand of body odour came creeping towards him. 'I discovered the identity of his two little bastards – two persons far removed from one another socially – and I also found out for sure that the fat imposter was just that – a fake.'

'I could 'ave told you that.'

'Yes, but I had to have proof positive.'

The whispering man gave a chuckle and asked John to get him a large brandy. Once he had it in his hand, he peered into its depths and said, 'Want to know something?'

'Yes. What?'

'I saw Gussie recent. I was on a ship plying between here and Bordeaux for wine, and bugger me but if he weren't there, standing on the quay. "Gussie," I calls out, loud and clear, and he looks up and waves, just like his usual self, though there are flecks of grey in his unruly mop now. Anyway, we repairs to a tavern and I tells him all about the fat man impersonating him. He laughs. "You don't mean old tubby Cecil, do you? Do you know, I met the blighter once and he had a very peculiar interest in me. I was a bit in me cups and never thought to ask him why. What was the reason, do you know?" he says. So I says, "Your mother had died and left you a fortune in diamonds. It was in all the newspapers. Didn't you see them?" At that poor Gussie cries a bit and says, "I was a naughty boy in my youth, I neglected my parents something shockin'." Then he revives and asks about Commodore. I told him he was a big fellow these days. So Gussie suddenly sits up straight and says, "I'm going to England. I'm going to see them all and get those diamonds. I am going to apologise to my poor old step-papa for all the trouble I caused. I'm going to be an upright citizen in future."

'Well, I thought to meself, That'll be the day, but I just chuckles and says, "Good." Then I asks him about his dog, old Sam. He shakes his head. "Gone to the great kennel in the sky, alas, but I got a new one called Tinker. He's a winner, I can tell you." Then Gus stands up, looks at his watch, and says, "I'm late, I'm late, got to be at the snail races. See you in England, you old devil." And he's gone, quick as a flash. He's a lovely fellow, old Gussie. They don't make them like that any more.'

They certainly don't, thought John, but inwardly he was pleased to hear the news. Pleased that the red-headed reprobate was returning to Bristol and was going to liven things up once more.

Walking back to the coach, he decided to tell Sir Gabriel nothing about the arrest and subsequent death of Lady Tyninghame, sparing his father the details of her terrible end. So, as he got back into the carriage, Sir Gabriel awoke and asked, 'Who was the poor dead soul?'

'Just a drab from Bristol who decided to finish it all.'

'Poor woman. Who can have such a wretched life that they feel they must end it?'

'Perhaps she was mentally ill,' answered John, and refused to discuss the matter any further, concentrating instead on the various landmarks along the way that told them they were approaching home.

They reached London the next day and went straight to Nassau Street, the front door being opened by a footman who, though keeping a solemn face and demeanour, winked one eye at them to show that some secret lay within.

The house was strangely quiet and John, sensing this to be part of the surprise, went from room to room calling, 'Rose, where are you? Sweetheart, are you here?'

Sir Gabriel, somewhat fatigued by the journey, made his way to the library door, and as he opened it there was a squeal of laughter and he was assailed by Rose and her two little half-brothers with a great hug that sent the old man reeling on his feet.

'Grandpa,' she shouted, and kissed him heartily a dozen times.

'Ganpa,' echoed the twins in unison, and kissed his knees.

John hurried to join them, and Mrs Fortune came out of the parlour, also laughing. How happy everyone was; one could sense joyfulness as if it were a tangible thing, passing from one person to the next. Eventually, though, Rose escorted Sir Gabriel to a chair and poured him a sherry while he was reintroduced to the twins and took them to sit upon his knees. He smiled at them both.

'Which is which, John?'

'Do you know, Papa, I am never quite sure.'

'I'm Jasper,' they chorused, then giggled and said, 'I'm James,' simultaneously.

'You little scamps,' said the great beau, and began to laugh at them once more.

Later on in the evening, when the twins had been washed and fed and were ready for the night, Sir Gabriel said something very strange.

'Do you know, my boy, I am at last ready to join Phyllida.'

John looked up, rather shocked, for he had never heard his father say anything like that before.

'What do you mean?'

'That I have been in this world so long, seen fashions come and go, people change, countries at war, then at peace, that I now feel I am finally ready to depart.'

'But, Father, I don't like to hear you say those words. They have an air of finality about them. Where would I be without you?'

'My son, you are a grown man. You do not need your old father tripping along beside your every step.'

A voice spoke up from the corner, where Rose had been sitting so quietly that her father had completely forgotten her presence.

'If Grandpa feels it is time, then surely he has that right.'

John did not know how to answer because an enormous truth lay in what she said. If a very old man had decided he had done enough living, then who had the authority to try and persuade him otherwise?

'Do you believe in Heaven and Hell, Grandpa?'

Sir Gabriel took a sip of sherry and answered thoughtfully, 'Not as such, no.'

'Then what do you believe?'

'In an altered state. A state where everything is so changed that this time and this place are completely unimportant.'

'Then how will you recognise Phyllida if you meet her?'

'I should think that a love as great as ours will transcend everything.'

'But Grandpa, how do you explain my gift? Where does that enter into your altered state?'

Sir Gabriel laughed. 'This is a deep conversation, child.'

John opened his mouth, not sure whether to speak or not, but Rose said, 'Because I do have second sight. It is a fact.'

'I am not denying it. But how that fits into anybody's conception of life after death I have no idea. It would take a far more worthy theologian to explain it.'

'I think a worthy theologian would be the last person to explain anything to do with matters relating to the psychic mind,' put in John. 'And now, Miss Rose, it is time you went to bed.'

'Oh, Papa.'

'You can "Oh, Papa" me for the rest of the three minutes you have left. It will make no difference.'

She obeyed instantly, made much of delivering smacking kisses to Sir Gabriel's powdered cheeks, gave her father a quick cuddle, then left the room without further demur.

The two men stared after her.

'A really delightful child.'

'She is indeed.'

'And *is* it true what she says about having second sight?'

'I'm afraid that it is. Sometimes it worries me.'

'Why is that?'

'Too much knowledge on such very young shoulders.'

Sir Gabriel stretched his long legs before him.

'I should imagine, my boy, that she has also been given the gift of learning how to cope with it.'

The next morning they set off for Kensington. It had originally been intended that John alone would accompany his father, but Rose had begged – with tears – that she should be included in the party. So Irish Tom, who had grown as close to his master as it was possible for a servant to get, had helped John raise Sir Gabriel into the carriage, lifted up Rose, giggling and smiling, and finally closed the door behind them before clambering up onto the box.

They had a pleasant drive through London, Tom going all the way down Piccadilly to Hide Park Corner, passing the Tyburn gallows, that melancholy place of execution, and passing through the toll gate to Knight's Bridge, where they stopped for a while for refreshment and nature's call. Then they turned up The King's Old Road to Kensington, which had been opened to the public and was quite the fashionable place, the *beau monde* gathering in numbers to be seen out exercising their horses and waving gaily to one another.

Eventually, the creatures walking slowly now, they turned up Kensington Church Street and Sir Gabriel gave a great sigh.

'My dear, I can tell you that much as I enjoyed myself at the Hotwell – and met so many charming and interesting people – it is indeed a pleasure to be back home.'

John jumped out of the carriage as it stopped at the top of the row, but to his astonishment Sir Gabriel was almost too weak to walk down the step. The Apothecary had to pick the old man up and carry him to the street. It was then that the first terrible thought crossed his mind and refused to go away again. Was a visit from the Grim Reaper destined to come to him three times this year?

He imagined Elizabeth's last terrible act, leaping towards the sun like Icarus; the death of Lady Tyninghame, whom he had once thought so delicate and delightful; and last night his own father speaking of dying. And yet, practical person that he was,

he knew that it awaited all, had attended dying patients in the
past and no doubt would have to do so again.

Sir Gabriel was apologising profusely. 'My dear boy, can't
think what came over me. Must have been a sudden cramp in
the legs. Caused by too much dancing at the Hotwell, I shouldn't
wonder.'

'Yes, I wouldn't be at all surprised,' answered the Apothecary
seriously. 'You had quite a few dances with various ladies, I
noticed.'

Miss Rose, bright as a new-minted coin, said, 'Would you
grant me the honour, Sir?' and sank in a low curtsey.

Sir Gabriel took the proffered hand, bowed deeply and executed
a few stately steps of the minuet before laughing and saying, 'I
think, my sweetheart, that I'd best go indoors before one of my
neighbours thinks I have taken leave of my senses.'

'Very good, Sir,' and she offered Sir Gabriel her arm.

They made a stately entrance, John following behind, and Irish
Tom assisting, the servants coming out of the front door with
cries of welcome.

They passed a quiet but splendid evening, Rose behaving herself
beautifully, and Sir Gabriel resplendent in a flowing white robe
and black turban, its only adornment the huge zircon stone that
had been mined in Russia and exported to England.

'I love it when you are *en deshabille*, Grandpa.'

'Why is that, my child?'

'Because you always look so imposing, and I particularly like
that jewel you wear in your headgear. It is so brilliant and alive,
like gazing into the heart of the sea.'

'Ah, my pretty Rosebud, you have such a beautiful way with
words.'

'I believe it is a magic stone.'

'Then it shall be yours after I die. I have not mentioned it in
my will, but remember what I say, John.'

Somewhere in the depths of his soul the Grim Reaper grinned
and John shifted in his seat.

'Anything wrong, John?'

*Yes, everything is wrong. I can't bear the thought of losing you, of no
longer enjoying your friendship, your love, your wisdom. Father, you who
have been so good to me. Why must you be taken from me?*

Aloud he said, 'No, I am feeling in good health. What about you, Rose?'

'Blooming,' she said, and laughed loudly at her own joke.

Sir Gabriel rose to his full height, an awe-inspiring sight, and said, 'Well, I am rather tired. I think I'll to bed. It's all this travelling. It takes it out of one so.'

Rose jumped to her feet. 'Can I get you anything, Grandpa?'

'A glass of cold water, if you would carry that up for me, my dear?'

'Of course.'

She clattered off in the direction of the servants' quarters and Sir Gabriel said, 'That is a wonderful child you have there, John.'

"I thank God for her. And for the twins. They are quite agreeable little monsters.'

'They are fine boys, but I have only met them a few times. Tell me, my son, do you miss Elizabeth?'

'I miss her every waking hour. Oh, Father, if you could have seen her towards the finish. It was pitiful. She was like a twig, a shrivelled leaf. And then to put an end to the pain by taking that dying horse of hers and leaping over the cliffs into the sea . . .'

'To me it sounds a happy release for them both.'

'That is what I think too. And somehow it has made it easier for me to cope with her loss. Because, if I was another sort of man, I could wrap myself in grief and never emerge again.'

'Thank God you are not. For that would be to the detriment of your children. When Phyllida died, it was only having you, John, that kept me sane. But thank heavens you were young and active and it was all I could do to keep up with you.'

The Apothecary burst out laughing, despite the seriousness of the conversation. 'Now that I don't believe. You always were and you always will be the great leader of fine living.'

Sir Gabriel chortled and yawned. 'My bed calls. Stay up, my son. Have a glass of port. Relax after all your recent adventures.'

With the room quiet, John stared into the fire, wondering how his future would evolve. He hoped that one day he would meet a woman who would rock him to the soles of his feet, so much so that he would ask her to marry him and his life would go off at a different tangent. But sweet though Emilia had been, as much power as Elizabeth had possessed, it was difficult to imagine anyone following in their footsteps. With a deep sigh, John poured himself another port and listened to the creak of the house as it settled and the longcase clock chimed 'The British Granydears' on the hour.

The following day dawned very brightly, full of that warm sunshine typical of an October day. Sir Gabriel again chose to remain *en deshabille* and wore a black robe decorated with small silver flowers. His turban was silver, fastened together by the great glittering zircon.

The year previously he had bought some new garden furniture and now he chose to sit on a cast-iron seat decorated with a pattern of fern leaves. It had been placed in the shade of a tree and as the clock struck noon Sir Gabriel ordered a bottle of champagne and three glasses. John looked at these last and asked a silent question.

'My boy, a drop or two of alcohol has never done anyone any harm. Remember how I let you have little sips of wine?'

'But Rose is a girl.'

'The same applies.'

She came into the garden at that moment and John, looking at her, felt astounded by the way she was growing up. Perhaps because he had not seen her for several weeks, he appreciated again the beauty of her skin and the wonderful flick of her black lashes over eyes that were a startling hyacinth blue. In another few years she would have the whole of London at her feet. And just for a moment John had an image of himself with grey hair and an authoritative manner, regarding with raised brow the line of would-be suitors.

Sir Gabriel was ordering the servant to pour two glasses and himself filled Rose's tumbler, just a quarter full. He raised his.

'To my son and granddaughter. I would like to thank you both for the enormous happiness you have brought me. You have both been quite exceptional.'

They drained their glasses and had another until the bottle was empty. Then Sir Gabriel closed his eyes and dozed, while Rose, who had been sitting next to him, lowered her head into his lap like a little kitten. His old white hand, adorned with great rings, lazily stroked her hair. John must have slumbered for a while because when he opened his eyes it was to see that everything had grown very still. The hand stroking Rose's hair was quiescent and the old man slept very deeply indeed.

In a second John jumped up and, kneeling at Sir Gabriel's feet, felt for the pulse in his neck. There was none. Weeping came instantly. The father he had loved for ever – or so it seemed to him – was gone from him.

'Oh, Papa, my beloved Papa,' he cried, the tears pouring down his face uncontrollably.

Rose's black eyelashes opened wide. 'Oh, my dearest Father, don't be sad.'

He wept in her little arms. 'But I loved him, Rose. I loved him with all my heart.'

'But he's gone to find Phyllida, that's all.'

He looked at her through a mist of tears. 'And will he? Will he find Phyllida?'

'Oh yes,' she answered seriously. 'For they have been finding and seeking one another since the beginning of time.'

Twenty-Five

Never had the circle of life been brought home more forcefully to the Apothecary – and never, indeed, had the superstition that bad or good luck comes in a cycle of three. He had stayed in Kensington and organised a rather hectic – and rather beautiful – funeral for Sir Gabriel Kent, the last of the great beaux. Not many of Sir Gabriel's older friends came because he had, in fact, outlived them all. But people with whom he still played cards, neighbours – including the jolly Mr Horniblow from next door – and people who had served Sir Gabriel in shops and liked the old man's style, all came aplenty. Then there were John's friends: Joe Jago, representing Sir John Fielding, Serafina and Louis de Vignolles, Samuel Swann, looking terribly sad. And last, but a million miles from least, came Jacquetta Fortune on the arm of Gideon Purle, followed by Robin Hazell and Fred, terribly small, new hat held hotly in hand.

Despite the solemnity of the occasion, John had striven hard
to make it as joyous as possible. On the morning of the burial
he and Rose had visited Sir Gabriel for the last time. John had
placed a kiss on the old man's cold cheek and Rose had placed
an autumn rose in the coffin. Then the lid had been nailed down
and the mourners – nearly eighty of them – crowding outside
the house had walked in procession to the church at the end
of the lane. Dispensing with tradition, John, Joe Jago, Louis,
Samuel, Gideon and Nicholas Dawkins, the Muscovite, bore the
coffin on their shoulders for the short journey to the church.

John had had sets of mourning gloves of finest kid made for
all the mourners, and could not help but smile at Fred's look of
pure joy as he had placed them on his hands.

'Me first pair,' he had whispered to Robin Hazell, who had
winked at him but remained silent.

After the miserable ceremony of throwing earth on the grave
– most of John's friends threw flowers – they walked back to the
house and enjoyed a wake, which went on rather a long time.
So it was that John, quite solitary, walked down to the graveyard
where Sir Gabriel now lay next to his tragic little daughter-in-
law, Emilia Rawlings. He stood for a long time, staring at them
silently, thinking how different everything would have been if
Emilia had not been brutally murdered by a jealous, crazed soul.
Then he realised the futility of such thoughts. Things were as they
were and it was up to him to make the best of them for the sake
of the young people. Sighing, he scattered rose petals on both
graves, said 'Adieu,' to them and, bracing his shoulders, walked
out by the church and into the waiting carriage in which his
daughter sat quietly alone.

So the cycle of life went on. The week after the funeral there
was a wedding in St Ann's, Soho. Mrs Fortune, now at the peak
of her beauty, was walked up the aisle by Nicholas Dawkins,
whose wife had made the happy introduction between Jacquetta
and John. And what a family affair it was. Gideon, John's former
apprentice, was the happy bridegroom, and though one or two
of the more gossipy members of the congregation might have
mentioned that the bride looked a deal older than the groom,
the general jollity of all present overcame such remarks and all

proceeded merrily. Afterwards, the guests trooped down to the grave of John's mother, Phyllida Rawlings, and Jacquetta laid her wedding bouquet by the headstone.

The breakfast was held at number 2, Nassau Street, and there was much feasting and drinking, followed by dancing. Serafina stood in front of John and asked him to dance. He made a face and pointed to his mourning clothes.

'Oh, sweetheart, do you think Sir Gabriel would have minded? Why, he would have been the very last. I can almost hear him saying, "Come along, my boy".'

John got to his feet and bowed. 'How right you are, my beautiful friend.'

They joined the long line of dancers and whirled into 'Man in the Moon' with great enthusiasm. And the Apothecary could have sworn that, narrowing his eyes very slightly, he could see a stately figure dressed in stunning black and white, cavorting close by.

Later that evening, when all the children were asleep, the last guest had left and the house had reverted to its usual peaceful state, John managed to look at the day's post. One letter in particular drew his attention because it had journeyed from Boston, come all of that long and fearful journey across the Atlantic. John turned it for a moment between his fingers, wondering who it could possibly be from. Then he noticed that on the outside of the envelope was printed the sender's name, one Josiah Hallowell, The Orange Tree Tavern, Boston. More than a little excited, John undid the seal and read the contents.

Sirs,

I was recently introduced by a Niece of mine to a Delicious Sparkling Water which had upon it the name and address of J. Rawlings, 2, Nassau Street, London. My Niece recently crossed the Atlantic Ocean to live with me in the Colonies and brought said Bottle for me to sample. I must tell you now that the Long and Arduous Journey did not affect the Quality of the Water at all, but I found it both Delicious and Thirst Quenching.

To come to the Point, dear Sirs. I wonder whether it would be possible for one of your Representatives to make the Journey to visit my Establishment in Boston with a view to entering into a Business Agreement whereby your good selves would ship out to us so many bottles Per annum. Of course it would be a Long and Tedious Journey but you would be assured of the Warmest of Welcomes when you Arrive. Written in the Hope of Hearing from You Soon.

> Respectfully Yours,
> J. Hallowell.

The Apothecary sat for a long time in the darkening library, thinking about what he had just read with an amused smile teasing his lips. Then he began to think seriously about it. Though his business was doing quite well, it was actually small, more a cottage industry than anything else. It would be impossible to send Gideon, newly married as he was, and Mrs Fortune – or rather Purle – was out of the question. He could hardly send Robin Hazell, and John actually laughed aloud, though not unkindly, at the thought of choosing Fred as his emissary. That left himself.

The Apothecary suddenly sat bolt upright. Why not? And then he thought of his young children and his heart plummeted. Very well to send himself, aware of all the dangers of the voyage, but to subject the twins to such a hazard would be unspeakably selfish. With a sigh, John picked up a book and tried hard to concentrate. But before his eyes rose a vision of a vibrant new land, full of an exciting mix of peoples striving to build a life. He could almost hear the bells of Boston ringing and smell the sharp, salty aroma of the harbour. The call to adventure which dwelt within him, never far below the surface, rose up and John seriously began to consider the prospect of going.

For once the courthouse next to the Public Office in Bow Street was empty, and on making an enquiry as to the whereabouts of Sir John Fielding with the Runner on the desk, John was told that court proceedings had risen early and that Sir John had left for his country house in Brompton, near Kensington. Irish Tom obediently turned the horses in the direction of Piccadilly and trotted away briskly.

They found Sir John sitting outside in a very finely wrought iron chair with arms and a strong back. He was totally relaxed, his great wig removed, showing his short cropped hair beneath, the ribbon which covered his eyes also gone so that he looked like a man asleep which, perhaps, he was. However, as the carriage clattered along the small lane leading to the house, Sir John stirred and sat upright, a fine figure clad in a white cambric shirt, his coat carelessly spread on another chair, his socks and shoes removed so that he could wriggle his toes in the autumn sunshine.

He went very still as John dismounted and approached. 'Give me a minute,' he called. 'Let me identify you from your tread.'

John pulled a face at Tom and advanced slowly, walking with a slight limp.

'It's Lord Suffolk,' the Magistrate cried triumphantly. 'And you're suffering with an attack of gout.'

John burst out laughing, put on a gruff voice and said, 'You're right, Sir John. M'gout has swollen m'foot up like an air balloon, so it has.'

'John Rawlings,' said John Fielding, 'you do one of the worst imitations I have ever heard. And I've heard a few, you can believe me.'

John bowed before him, while Tom went off to the servants' quarters, Meanwhile, Sir John had called out for a jug of punch and two glasses.

'Well, my lad,' he said to John, 'you find me *en deshabille* but delighted by the pleasure of your company. It is a long while since we last met. Let me say how sorry I was to hear about the death of Sir Gabriel. The world will miss him.'

'It will indeed, as do I. I don't think anyone could ever quite replace him in my affections.'

'Quite rightly so. Now tell me your adventures. And miss out nothing. I long to hear a bit of gossip away from the courts.'

The punch arrived and, having sipped from his glass, John embarked on his tale, while Sir John listened in that intense silence of which only he was capable. Crouching forward slightly, his body rigid, the look on his face severe, John knew that he was imparting the details of the death at Hotwell to the keenest brain in London. Eventually the Magistrate spoke.

'So it was the wretched Lady Tyninghame all along?'

'I came to the conclusion, Sir John, that she was mentally impaired in some way. It was as if two people lived inside her. The most terrible thing was that she tried to kill her own son. Or so Gilbert Farr, the Constable, wrote to me recently.'

'I remember a case I had before me some while ago. It concerned a Frenchman named D'Eon. To come to the heart of the matter, rumours flew that he was a woman impersonating a man. I thought otherwise. I believed him to be a man who truly believed that he was a woman. Not quite the same as the Tyninghame case, but I am quite positive that such mental disorders can sometimes be found.'

John nodded, then said, 'There is something else that is of concern to me.'

'I had wondered if there was.'

'I have had a letter inviting me to go to Boston on a matter of business. I would like to go, but how can I? How can I leave my children?'

The Magistrate thought for a few minutes, then said, 'Can you not take them?'

'But the hardships of the journey . . . Would it not be wrong to expose them to such?'

Sir John scratched his chin with a long, shapely finger. 'The twins are under three, are they not?'

'You are very well informed.'

'Jago keeps me up-to-date with all that goes on, and if he leaves anything out my wife more than compensates.'

The Magistrate rumbled his great laugh, which was so addictive that John found himself laughing alongside.

'But Rose is at school and loves it so much. It would be cruel to take her away.'

The Magistrate poured himself another glass of punch and offered one to John, who accepted.

'Well, it seems to me that you must do the least cruel thing.'

'Which is?'

'To take the children with you. The boys hardly know who you are – or so I've been told – and by the time that you return from such an excursion would regard you as a complete stranger. As for Rose, her love for you is so important to her that to break the bond would be ruthless. They have schools in Boston, don't they? Or are the Colonies breeding a race of savages? So there's your answer, my dear fellow. Take your talents to the Americas.'

John sipped from his glass. 'Thank you, Sir. Do you know, I would not have even considered such an action had my father been alive. But now . . .'

He did not finish what he was about to say and it was the blind man who spoke.

'Here's to your great adventure, my friend. May the Colonies bring you well-earned success.'

'I'll drink to that.'

'God bless you, John.'

And John Rawlings was so surprised to be addressed by his first name that he could merely answer, 'That is only the second time you have done that, Sir.'

'What?'

'Called me John.'

The Magistrate bellowed a laugh. 'Well, damme, so it is, Mr Rawlings. So it is.'

So it had come at last. The moment of departure. John felt at that second that he didn't want to go, that he would change his mind at the last minute and stay with his friends on the quayside. For they were all there: Samuel, extremely weighty; Serafina, extremely thin; Joe Jago, looking raffish; Jacquetta and Gideon, looking in love; Nicholas Dawkins and Olivia, she with another baby on the way; and last but very far from least there was Robin Hazell, now on the threshold of manhood, and young Fred, scarcely an inch taller.

John had made the household arrangements some weeks earlier. He had written to Josiah Hallowell and told him that he would be obliged if he could find lodging for six people, three adults and three children. Hannah had jumped at the chance of going to the Colonies, while Irish Tom had wept when John had given him notice and declared that he would rather work as a hand on the ship than be separated from everything he held dear. Number 2, Nassau Street, had now become the residence of Gideon and his wife, while the shop at Shug Lane would become Gideon's domain, along with the two apprentices.

'But it's not as if I'm going for ever,' said John as he hugged Samuel closely.

'I should damned well say you're not,' replied his oldest companion, applying a large handkerchief.

Joe Jago, man of mystery and dear friend, gave John a low bow and said, 'It's been a pleasure working with you, my good Sir.'

Serafina, the former Masked Lady and the greatest gambler in London, threw her elegant racehorse frame into John's arms and cried openly.

Gideon grinned farewell and his wife wept. Nicholas buried his face in his wife's shoulder, while little Fred and Robin bowed in unison as John and his party mounted the gangplank. A fiddler started to play and everyone was shouting out 'Goodbye' as the elegant cutter, *Breath of the Sea*, slipped its moorings.

John's eyes were full of tears as Rose said in her politest voice, 'May I walk round and see the ship, Papa?'

'Yes, but be very careful. I don't want you falling overboard.'

'I promise to be good.'

John was weeping like a child and it was only the steadying arm of Tom that stopped him swimming to shore.

'Hang on, John. 'Tis a great adventure we're going to have.'

'I'm a fool,' the Apothecary answered, wiping his eyes.

Rose came running back, bubbling with fun. 'Oh, Papa, I've met such a nice man. He bowed to me and I gave him my best curtsey.'

'You little witch. What pranks are you playing talking to strange men.'

'But Papa, I know you're really going to like him. He told me his name.'

'And what is it, sweetheart?'

'It's Julian Wychwood. He said he was going to the Americas to find his mother's fortune.'

John turned to Tom and they stared at one another before they both started to laugh.

'Well, well,' said John Rawlings, 'this is going to be a very strange adventure indeed.'

Historical Note

Old readers of the John Rawlings series will know that he actually lived and dwelt in eighteenth-century London, serving as an Apothecary. The adventures which I have given him have, of course, been works of fiction. I have had one or two enquiries from readers who believed that I have abandoned John Rawlings in favour of Nick Lawrence, an inoffensive vicar in a village in sleepy Sussex. This is most definitely not the case and John will continue as long as I do, I promise. But Nick and his fellow villagers are quite charming in their way and I suggest that you might be interested in dipping into one of their adventures by way of a change.

Samuel Foote, the actor with the wooden leg, actually lived a very full and vibrant life. Those interested in finding out more could not do better than read a truly delightful book, *Mr Foote's Other Leg* by Ian Kelly, published by Picador.

I found the young men working as archivists in Bristol most delightful and friendly and, through them I came across a little snippet which I thought I would pass on to you.

'3rd September, 1721, St Michael on the Mount Church, marriage of Commodore and Venus, two negroes.'

The slave trade was unspeakably vile, but it had its upside as well. Sometimes the negroes adapted and became family friends and pets, even respected businessmen and professionals. In other cases they were treated worse than dogs. A microcosm of everyday life, perhaps.

I hope you enjoy this book and that you will contact me via my website www.derynlake.com if you like it.